71 DAYS TO SAVE THE WORLD

AN ALTERNATE VIEW

ROBERT PINS

authorHOUSE®

AuthorHouse™ UK
1663 Liberty Drive
Bloomington, IN 47403 USA
www.authorhouse.co.uk
Phone: 0800.197.4150

Photographer: Charlotte Fox
Title of image: Point 2 of 4 - Winter on Sea - 09/04/2013

© Charlotte Fox

Website: https://charlottefoxphotography.com

Published by AuthorHouse 03/29/2017

ISBN: 978-1-5246-7843-2 (sc)
ISBN: 978-1-5246-7844-9 (hc)
ISBN: 978-1-5246-7846-3 (e)

Library of Congress Control Number: 2017903230

Print information available on the last page.

This book is printed on acid-free paper.

Re: Mustelids

Neville

That's weasels to you.

What part of "no negotiation" until Article 50 has been triggered do you not understand? Weasel MP's think they can debate the process and agree on a plan of action,' terms of agreement' in the UK parliament. It is akin to agreeing the terms we should offer to Adolf Hitler before offering them to him. "Nein", brokers no argument and no discussion. Your elected wankers appear to be suffering from the delusion that they can make a difference to 27 other sovereign states positions of negotiation before the Article has been triggered when, and this has been stated right from the dawn of the new age, NO negotiations will take place until said event. MP's are spectators not participants. While on the subject, why are our MP's now desperately wanting to get involved in our government after decades of abrogating responsibility and an effective inability to govern within the UK as they have surrendered wave after wave of sovereign powers to the failed EU experiment? Their very actions and cloying attempts to frustrate the clear will of the people proves beyond any doubt that they do not understand any part of the process other than how to secure their own positions for their own personal gain. Our MP's are fond of promoting badger culls as a cure for virulent disease in cattle. As we all know, badgers are the largest British member of the weasel family. Time to commission a cull of badger brethren, especially the ermine wearing ones. My negotiating position is quite clear. Trigger Article 50 and tell them to spin on it. The balance of trade is wholly in our favour and they suffer £3 for our £2. Match any tariff imposed on the UK with a reciprocal one of the same size. Hive off the 50% surplus and pay back the surcharge to all UK exporters. The analogy I am fond of spouting is that of Formula 1 during the rain. The UK has elected to leave the slow wet track and has decided to put dry tyres on. We may have one or two slow laps and then our speed will pick up and suddenly every other team will realise that they are on the wrong tyres and want to join us. You Remain'ers keep expecting us to skid off the track and end up beached in the gravel track. Well, it ain't gonna happen.

Debate is the opium of the masses. I am not a drug addict.

This ought to keep you going for ten minutes, I'm offski to the Golf Club for fireworks. I might take notes about Guy Fawkes and his plans for the Houses of Parliament, 100 Tonnes of high explosive would save all the refurbishment costs as an added bonus.

How dare you quote the sovereign rule of law as your saviour when you and yours are busy surrendering the same powers to those superwankers over the water? Arseholes, dipshit, utter, utter, utter wankers, if only they could find their own sexual organs without instruction from Brussels. Utterly beneath contempt. Viva the revolution. I see Hollande has reached a new 4% approval rating, it's in the papers so must be true. Second most important man within the EU supporting nations, god help us.

Byeeee for now.

R
XXX

Sent from my IPad

Re: Mustelids

N

Well, well, well, well, well. Is any place so impenetrable that an ass laden with gold cannot enter? Let's ask Trump shall we?

Will this change your outlook on Brexit? Worms turning, half a world away. There must have been a shortage of soap in the northern hemisphere.

Tee hee.

R
XXX

Sent from my iPad

Re: Day 71 November 11th Friday

N

The end of the world is nigh. Interruptions of its orbital spinning have been registered. The world is an immensely more dangerous place (in 70 days, anyway) and the most overriding reaction that I have felt is humour. I keep laughing out loud at Trump, president, leader of the greatest nation on Earth and the gullibility of the American electorate. It was close, too close to call for many hours, a real nail biter but eventually reality crept in and Hillary Clinton won the majority of the popular vote but lost the war. Trump, president, wow. The feeling of emancipation, the release of worry, the hours of agonising over front and back, left or right, simply evaporated as I realised that it doesn't matter what I do, however shit it looks, however ridiculous, however much it appears to be a vain attempt to retain my former glory it doesn't matter. Not one jot, a single iota, I am content in the knowledge that however much a twat, an arse, a figure of jest I portray outwardly, I will be accepted by virtually half the people. I have placed my order, after months of self-loathing, indecision, dithering, procrastination and downright angst I have finally done it. I have ordered a delivery from a knob-thatcher, a peruke, a finest creation from a perruquier. I have ordered a postiche. If Trump can look like a complete arse in the entire eyes of the world, then I can cope with the local residents of BPINS.

Knowing how you spend your working time in court, with your thatched knob (yes, how amazing, it really is in the dictionary) I know that this has never been an issue for you. You have always been blessed with a harder exterior, a more carefree attitude to how you are perceived by others, whereas I have always been a shrinking violet, too embarrassed and too shy to make my presence felt in this world. Well, no more, Trump has shown me the way and as an added bonus I have gone for the waterproofed, thermal, non-iron, fire proofed (bonfire night was near and you can never be too careful) fully irradiated, sustainably produced natural fibre version that even has go faster stripes on it. From the computer screen mock up I think it makes me look like a badger, renowned for their serious considered outlook on life (just ask Mr Toad) although I had to persuade Jan that it didn't have a more than passing resemblance to a beaver.

Thank you Trump, thank you from the heart of my bottom. I am content, I can face nuclear Armageddon with a full head of hair.

Sorry, just had to break off to read an incoming email. My knob-thatcher has confirmed my order for delivery for the first week in Feb 2017. Oh fuck, oh fuck, oh fuck, fuck, fuck, that's over 80 days, it's past the 20th of January. What to do if he destroys the world in those two weeks? It took God six days to construct it and demolition is normally quicker. Oh bollocks, I'll have no finger nails left. I could ask Jan to knit me one. Oh shit, the worry is already getting to me, I can already hear cries of "Geronimo". It's right on the edge of my hearing, a bare whisper that I can only detect in the dead of night. My head hits the pillow and there it is, "Geronimo" and I know, I just know that in the morning my pillow will be ever so slightly more hirsute while my head is ever so slightly more glabrous.

I can't cope with politics, the uncertainty, the idea that people might vote incorrectly and choose the wrong arsehole.

Did I ever tell you about what happens in the first hours of life after conception? I'm sure I did but I'll give you a refresher. The fertilised mammalian egg divides into two, then four, eight, sixteen etc. until the ball of cells reaches a critical mass. The ball is in fact more like a pancake with an inside and an outside and then something wonderful happens. It folds over on itself to form a tube. Now we still have an outside that was always on the outside, an inside that was always on the inside but in addition we now have an inside that used to be on the outside. These regions form the three basic epithelia that form the human body. The outside that was on the outside forms your skin. The inside that was on the inside forms all your internal organs. Now for the clever bit, the inside that used to be on the outside forms your alimentary canal. My usual punchline is "The next time someone tells you, you are talking out your arse, you can agree with them".

What has brought this to the fore? A commentator describing Trump's election success said "The voters that felt they were excluded and on the outside are now on the inside". Which, by my reckoning, and by a wonderful coincidence, means that the Trump supporters now form the alimentary canal. This may well be fortuitous given the immense amount of shit they are going to have to put up with.

What is it they say? Oh yes, every cloud has a silver lining, well maybe not this lining. Hey Ho, only another 70 days to the end of the world, at least we get another Christmas. The coldest week of the year is statistically around the 13-20th of February so we won't have to suffer that either.

Or, just maybe, it's a possibility that we should at least consider, maybe el unfollically challenged one will make a success of his presidency and relaunch a new and invigorated America onto the world stage. An America that reverses the trend towards globalisation that rewards the investors at the expense of the now redundant factory workers. An America that protects Americans over the squalid working conditions endured in Bangladesh or Mexico. An America that shields the fruits of its labours from the Third World on their dollar a day wages. An American that kills strangers because they don't want to kill the ones that they love. An America that builds a wall along its southern boundary and actually upholds the rule of law, a subject that I know is so dear to you. An America that roots out and expels 11 million illegal immigrants and seeks to control the passage of Muslims.

Wow, seems like a shit place to live.

Have you heard about the Canadian immigration website, it keeps stalling due, it's thought, to the excessive increase in visitors. I am reminded of a comment from a Canadian comedienne on Have I Got News For You. Please don't come to Canada, she implored before reference to both the upcoming Brexit vote and the acceptance of Trump as the Republican Party candidate. "We'll have to build a wall to keep Americans out" "Mind, Americans aren't very fit, so it won't need to be very high, perhaps a kerb will do".

Democracy at work, that most cherished of institutions beloved by the free world has weaved its magic and given the wrong answer, again. Where do they get these arsehole voters from? Don't they recognise a good thing when they have it? I'm so disgusted with the neo-unsilent majority that I may never vote again until the next election. What to do, Canada appears to be off limits, Europe may soon be off limits, the smell of the great unwashed is assailing my nostrils and spoiling the taste of my muesli? I am bereft, thatched-knobless, stranded without a leader, peering down the silo barrels of thermonuclear destruction, without a hope left in the world. Why, what is driving my depression? I have a fear, an irrational fear I know, but it's still real. After 40 years of parsley I might not like the new herb seasoning. What if it's coriander, I don't like coriander. Oh fuck, what about tarragon. My life will never be the same when they change the seasoning. Because, and this is both the irrational and the important bit, whatever Trump, May, Boris, Hollande do, by the time it filters down through all the levels of corruption of government and emerges out the alimentary canal, the initial unpalatable bolus of garnish smells and looks like every other bolus of garnish lovingly prepared by our Great Brain chefs. Maybe the key to my salvation lies in another path, I should eschew the realm of politics and tread a more spiritual one, I should find a faith, a belief, a tenet to hang my worried brow upon. I should find *Turdus* and worship at the stone anvil until the life-force ebbs from my pathetic human form and I become secure for eternity within a mud lined nest. If only I can put up with the incessant 'tap, tap, tap' of unbelieving snails yielding their soft innards up to the sacrifice.

Have I finally cracked, have I loosed my grip on reality?

"Calm down, calm down" I hear you say, we survived Reagan and George Dubya Bush, there is hope for humanity yet.

But that is the fundamental problem, for the one thing humanity has none of, it is hope. It cannot recognise it nor understand the need for it, it is as invisible as the joint in Trump's hair.

Starting to rave a bit now, so better have a rest.

Trump, it really, really makes me laugh.

R
XXX

Sent from my iPad

Re: Day 70 November 12th Saturday

Dearest N

One of the most amusing things about yesterday was the complete ignorance of the event in the British press. It wasn't called until around 8.00AM long after the editions had been distributed. Today saw the first two dozen pages of the Daily Mail devoted to the result with in depth analysis of what went wrong and what went wrongerer. It does occur to me that the journalists had worked overtime producing the background stories for el presidential elect given that one of the versions had to be discarded. Hillary Clinton, failure, soon to be retired and to go down in history as the most reviled woman in American political history. Too harsh? She lost to Trump. Soon to be the most reviled man in American political history. It must hurt to finish second behind that.

Today's TV media is immersing itself in the transitional details of the new administration with intense speculation over Trump's first moves in the White house. Debate and counter debate is rife but through it all there appears to me to be an overriding sense of denial. He can't possibly build a wall against Mexico. He can't possibly walk away from the Paris climate change accord. He can't possibly renege on free trade agreements. He can't possibly impose 35% and 45% import tariffs against Mexico and China. He can't possibly honour any of his pre-election pledges.

Or maybe he can, maybe he will, maybe he should. Maybe he meant it. For while all the political commentators are perfecting their ostrich defence mechanism with one breath, with the other breath they label him as the most powerful man in the world. And the funny thing about being the most powerful man in the world is, the job comes with power. The power to make change.

I have written to you before about the dangers of hydrogenated vegetable oils and the fact that they were banned in Denmark in 2004 with a 40% reduction in heart attack deaths within two years. While our gutless political masters have elected for a 'voluntary arrangement' whereby our food manufacturers can continue to poison/kill us while they 'get their house in order'.

Imagine, a politician of Trump's calibre, a gun toting shoot from the hip kind of guy who might just have the wherewithal to impose a ban on such products and save thousands of lives from a premature end.

What strikes me is the parallel with Brexit, not the protest vote, the denial of the mandate, the denial of the intent. A majority voted for Trump and Brexit in the belief that they would get what they voted for. The media seems to have some form of brain damage, at best a form of inertia, at worst an all pervading tumour that blinds them to the reality of the new political order.

To plot any successful coup against the ruling party one of the first essentials is to trap or cease the present incumbent. Obama and Cameron have both been trapped and removed from the equation. Given that the coup is normally led by the army it is reasonable to assume that they are on-board to support the new regime. Ours was a very different coup, a bloodless one with the army confined to barracks while the only lead ammunition expended was the lead in pencils describing X's on ballot forms. The next step as laid down in my Observers Book of Coup's is to seize control of media outlets to ensure that the citizenry are exposed to the correct message. Here we have failed miserably, the media have been left in place fighting a rear-guard action as they make a disorderly withdrawal. In the best traditions of a fighting rear guard, volunteer snipers have been deployed to sporadically attack and undermine the morale of the advancing new order. Of course the other possibility is that they 'should get with the programme' and support their fellow tribe members as they in turn would have expected them to fall in line with themselves if the result had been different. The Remain debate is sterile, Clinton's likewise. They are both dead parrots, they are not resting. They are extinct, they just haven't stopped breathing yet.

On a more serious note I must apologise for my earlier error in nomenclature. I am not, as previously stated, thatched-knobless, I am in fact thatchless-knobbed. I hope you can see the distinction, I don't want you to think that I am in search of a merkin either and it is perhaps for that reason that the earlier term has fallen into disuse.

Now, having sorted that misunderstanding out, I wonder if you could impart some of your solicitor advocate knowledge to me. In your professional capacity you are several years ahead of me (ahead, did you get that?) in the thatched-knob stakes. I wonder if you could offer homing and care advice for my soon to be delivered natural fibre beastie? What would your views be on the five year extended warranty option for moth damage? How much space do they need for relaxation overnight? Should I use a 'pet safe' shampoo or one suitable for babies? Do I need to worry about shrinkage and can I tumble dry it? How much exercise is enough and where do you book yours in to while on holiday? Do you use Broughton Vets or should I seek out a more exotic familiar practice?

You might laugh at my obvious ignorance of these matters but my purchase represents a significant investment for me and I want to offer it the very best of environments in return for what I hope to be many years of service. While I normally try and resist it with pets, there is likely to be a very close bond between us and I may even have certain 'stirrings' for it, if you get my drift? Do you have a name for yours? I thought about Katie, from **K**nob **T**hatch but wondered whether tongues would wag over the obvious female connotations?

Oh, I'm in such a dither, my obvious lack of confidence is there for all to see what with worrying about how Katie and I will get along together with the imminent end of the world in 68 days. Am I worrying too much? It's enough to make your hair fall out.

At least if the world ends on the 21st of January I won't need to worry about my new found relationship with Katie. Thinking about it, I should just concentrate on one issue at a time, no need to think past the 22nd after all.

Should I take all my pension out and spend it? I won't get a tax bill until the end of January 2018 which won't exist so no worries there. Oh bugger, if I took all my pension drawdown I could build and furnish my own nuclear bunker and furnish it with food reserves for many years. But then I'd still be alive on the 31st of January 2018 with a tax bill to pay. Why can't Armageddon be simpler? Of course, if I didn't fit a letter box …

What am I saying, of course it would have to be hermetically sealed with nothing entering or leaving, not even air, so no need to worry about tax bills.

I'm calming down now, I can see the path.

Sorry, just had my architect on the telephone, still haven't got planning through at Mum's house, that's two years now. They seem to have dropped the zebra crossing and now want a 'landscape statement' design for visual aesthetics. Sounds like another waste of time and money if you ask me.

Oh fuck, how am I going to get planning and building control through on my bunker before the end of 2018? The whole thing is getting utterly out of hand. What we need is a new corruption free government with a 'can do' attitude that will look out for its own citizens before others. If we didn't subsidise the Jimmies so much with our taxes we'd have our own BPINS bunker in Maureen's paddock by now. Now there's an idea. If I pumped out my Pop 20 I'd have my own underground bunker. I know it's not very deep and wouldn't survive a near hit but at least it gives me a chance. Can Jan and I use your toilet facilities after, say the 19th of January? Gives us a bit of time to acclimatise and fit bedding and the satellite dish.

I'd ask you to join us, but, to be honest, I don't think you'd fit through the single round egress/ingress point. Oh wow, wow, wow, wow, have I just gone full circle or what? Think about it, close your eyes and visualise it. I know it's made of plastic and it's in the ground but with its single round entrance point it's so very near to my proposed design for the Temple of *Parus*. Even the ventilation pipe could be seen as a perch. Genius or what, absolute fucking genius. Not only have I hedged my bets by leaving my pension intact, I have saved our lives by utilising an existing structure where I only need change of use from the council and not full planning permission, and I have found God in *Parus*.

Oh bollocks, bollocks, bollocks. I have a peanut allergy and I don't like coconut. I couldn't even eat it if my life depended on it. How to persuade any survivors making offerings to the Great God *Parus* to bring muesli and milk in the morning, prawn salad at lunchtime and meat and two veg at dinner time? And to avoid any cross contamination with peanuts?

I can begin to understand why Jesus took the easy option and had himself nailed to a cross. What a selfish bastard.

I think I need to do a bit more analysis. Please let me have your thoughts on Katie's care so I can at least be prepared for that at least. Sorry to put this burden on you, but what else are friends for?

R
XXX

Sent from my iPad

Re: Day 69 November 13th Sunday

Dearest N

I must apologise, I was forgetting that you were absent when I had the discussion with Abigail. You may remember that Abi called me down to the Pop 40 sewage treatment plant to discuss the blockage problem. We decided that one option was to carefully lower a volunteer into the primary settlement tank so that they could properly inspect and release the apparent blockage in the pipe between tanks one and two. Community minded as I am, I have to say that I baulked at volunteering to stand nipple deep in the communities effluent. I suggested to Abigail that she would be ideal given her slight build and the ease at which she would be able to enter. I even offered her the use of my old angling waders, after all they would come up higher on her than they do on me. She volunteered you on the grounds that she might not have the physical bulk to dislodge the blockage. It was at that point that I decided that you might struggle to fit through the access, even with a bit of persuasion. So you see, I hadn't just flippantly decided that you were too big to fit in my ad hoc nuclear bunker/pop 20 treatment plant, I had considered it carefully.

Now when I said persuasion, I meant easing your body through the access with tyre levers with a liberal coating of grease (animal fat, it's safer for the environment and mineral grease would interfere with the bacterial culture in the second tank) or failing that a few blows with a pickaxe handle. It should be relatively safe as long as I keep the grease off my hands and retain my grip. Abigail was getting quite enthusiastic at this stage, well, at least I thought she was. When I realised that you almost certainly wouldn't be able to get out again I understood just what true enthusiasm looked like. I hadn't realised what a strong sense of humour your wife had until I heard that laugh. I thought she hadn't heard me properly when I said you wouldn't be able to get out especially as she had this far away dreamy look in her eyes. I thought she was daydreaming and hadn't realised what I had said. Of course, not being in the communal scheme I assume this option was discussed at your monthly management meeting before resolving to have Cammock and Willcox pump and jet it out.

N, see, I hadn't casually dismissed your BMI when considering your entry requirements for my bunker, I had put some real thought into it. Sorry if I offended you, I'd hate to fall out over something so trivial. If you are really concerned about Trump and the end of the world I am prepared to try. The scars of my shoulder arthroscopy have healed but I still have difficulty in lifting both arms overhead but I am prepared to try the pickaxe option if you like, it's the least a true friend could do.

Coming back to the earlier issue of the blockage, sealing the hole with your greased body may have done the trick on its own. Each downward movement would have increased the air pressure in the chamber and may well have provided the impetus to release the blockage, particularly with shock loading from a well-placed blow. I'm quite sure it would have succeeded and would have saved you the expense with Cammock and Willcox. Have you had the bill yet, just out of curiosity?

On a serious note, have you made any thought about legacy, I realise it's all a bit pointless with the end of the world just 68 days away. It seems rather sobering to be considering the end of the civilised world so calmly. In a perverse sort of way I actually think that this statement is incorrect. For in a truly civilised world Mutually Assured Destruction would not be on the agenda. A few microseconds of searing heat and ensuing blast may in fact do more to achieve civilisation than all the religion, education and science has achieved since the advent of agriculture. Just a shame that there will be few people left to witness if. Oh well, what goes around, comes around.

Back to the legacy issue. I have to say I'm really struggling to think of something worthwhile. It's a bit late to scratch a bit of graffiti on one of the Egyptian pyramids and if all the prophecies come true I don't fancy being hounded through eternity by some irate Demi-God or other. Everything just seems so ephemeral and insignificant. What was the point of it all?

I don't suppose we could implore Trump to leave a legacy beyond scorch marks and piles of radioactive ash. Have you any thoughts on the subject? I had considered assassination but then the problem could be exacerbated while they try to fix the blame rather than the problem. Then of course the problems could multiply and at the outset, ignoring the practical difficulties of achieving the ambition, is the additional problem of just who to target? Without Trump to counterbalance Putin or Putin to counterbalance Trump the world might just end up a more dangerous place. I still think on balance that we just have 68 days left. Damn the electorate, why do they continually and persistently get it wrong? You'd have thought by now with all the extremes of advertising that we are subjected to, no bombarded with, that we'd have developed a filter to remove all the extraneous bollocks before it settled on a brain cell. We should have hides as thick as elephants, impervious to all but high velocity rifle bullets. It does strike me that there is a bit of a parallel here, with elephants. They are being poached to extinction, their lives sacrificed to satisfy the need for what, exactly, a trinket on the shelf, an ornament. But where and why does the demand originate? Essentially it originates from the ego of man, the satisfaction of an urge as substantial as a butterflies wing beat and just as capable of generating a storm as powerful as any hurricane. Although in our case, and in just 68 days' time, the storm will be borne not of a butterflies wing beat but wholly of the ego of man. Is this truly that which separates us from the lesser beast, the sense of self, the ego? An ego that knows no bounds, no limit or control, an ego that demands the end of the Earth in return for? But we need not worry about Trump, for even if he shrinks from his promised path and I live to see my Katie others will take his place as the Earth dies the death of a trillion cuts, inexorably creeping to the chasm and the certainty of oblivion. And there we have perhaps the greatest contradiction, the monstrous perversion of intent, for as we strive so earnestly for life our greatest product is death. But death awaits us all, it suffers no prisoners, it takes no hostages, it underscores all activity on our planet and will remain for eternity. Death ignores ego, the 'self' has no privilege as self has no purpose. Was this the expulsion from the Garden of Eden? The knowledge of self, the creation of ego, the special dispensation card, the 'get out of jail, free' card that pervades our actions and intent. Borne of our DNA, we represent the implacable codes that drive the machines in the Matrix and Terminator. It is ego that strives to control and dominate the world, it is ego that has the power to destroy without a first thought. It is ego that drives the extracurricular, the force multipliers, the temples to God, the drive to GDP, the race to death. That then will be our legacy, a scratch-mark on a cliff face that says "I was here". Once the libraries and other great repositories of knowledge have been erased in the warm glow of our home made suns that is all that shall remain. Who is to say that our scratch-mark will not be discovered in 40,000 years by our successors to be viewed in quizzical wonderment as we have done before in prehistoric caves decorated with painted hands and beasts of the range? Expressions of ego from our ancestors as they strove to leave their own legacy on the history of this home. A legacy of their egos that we embellish with our egos to elevate to a higher plain in search of meaning, a tint of culture, a hint of understanding beyond the common beast, a justification of our self's. In simple terms, 'business as usual' or if you'd rather, 'here be princesses'.

Neville, I'm surprised at you forgetting about my plans for the Temple of Turdus and Parus. I thought you'd agreed to become one of my first converts. I'd had half a mind to offer you a promotion as one of the founder members. Anyhoo, I searched out my previous correspondence with you on the subject and have reproduced it below:

When at school studying for my A level Biology I resolved to study song thrushes and their anvils. These birds collect snails and carry them to selected stones which are used by the birds to break the snail's shells making the interior accessible for consumption. I often heard the tap, tap, tap of these birds as they beat their food on the anvil. As a project it had a lot going for it, not least of which was the ability to bunk off school and wander around the countryside legitimately. You can see, even then, how I was showing such promise at making my work commitments bend to my true needs, and all with the consent of my tutor. During General Studies I elected to study the provision of playground equipment in the local parks. I seemed to concentrate my attention on Queens Park "because it was the one nearest to my school and I only had limited free periods or G S lessons to devote to research" and the fact that it adjoined my girlfriends college and facilitated extended lunches with her may have had a bearing on it.

Unfortunately for me, I struggled to find thrush anvils when I needed them and after a couple of weeks the weather had turned and I was still in need of a project so reluctantly settled for a different avenue. I realised today how amateurish my attempts at satisfying two needs at once were. What I should have done is looked anew at the thrush anvils and should have tweaked the perception slightly. With hindsight I could probably have received a grant even at pre-university stage. My plan was to look for patterns in colour, size, location and frequency of use of these stones and I now realise all I had to do was alter the nomenclature. If I had but realised that the thrushes were in fact sacrificing the souls of the unbelieving molluscs on the altar of the great thrush God Turdus, I would have been on a winner. It's taken nearly 40 years so what has led to this epiphany. The article in the Daily Mail replete with photograph of a chimpanzee wielding a rock in an agitated manner before 'smashing said rock into the shrine of similarly sized stones placed so carefully at the side of a tree. You must forgive me, for some reason I could not muster the will to read the article so cannot in all honesty say that this was simply an expression of amplified aggression often documented in chimps who will beat their feet on tree buttresses or bash the equivalent of dustbin lids to generate noise to exaggerate their physical presence when they feel the need to assert themselves. Perhaps if the journalists had read a book other than the bible, say a Terry Pratchett one, Soul Music, which describes itself as a "story about sex and drugs and Music With Rocks In" the gist of the article might have been a little different. Instead of which I was greeted with the strap line "Do chimpanzees believe in God?" It could have been "Elvis has returned, as a Chimp". I despair at the quality of our journalists, but you knew that anyway.

Sorry, I must apologise, I normally give the Latin for native species, Turdus philomelos, derived from the Greek origin of 'loving' 'song' and Turdus that every school kid knows, means thrush. (Or something similar). (Only a few school kids got as far as the American robin, your search engine awaits).

Back to my school days and it was obvious I was showing real promise for public life, the only real issue was that nobody liked me. (Surprise?) (It was mutual). I have illustrated how easy it was to corrupt a common need to suit a personal one. In later years I could easily have used my skills to obtain a top of the range Range Rover or Jaguar say, to ensure that the charity I represent didn't come across as a cheap, struggling enterprise unworthy of support. After all, you couldn't possibly turn up to some posh money raising function in a Vauxhall Astra and anything less than a Saville Row suit, could you? It would be wholly inappropriate for your charity to provide you with a clothing allowance, that would smack of corruption, so much cleaner to take a salary commensurate with your responsibilities. And, as an added bonus, salary gets locked in for future years so no need to fight that battle again. And, you never know who you might bump into if you dine at the finest restaurants and holiday in exclusive resorts. It's just win, win, win, it's brilliant for everybody.

Of course I needn't have taken such a mercenary view and gone into charity work, I could have spurned such petty tasks and concentrated instead on higher orders. If I'd done the legwork I could have voiced the needs of Turdidae and become High Priest, the conduit of inter species communication with the added bonus of their pan- Eurasian distribution. As the original illustrator of their previously ignored worship I would have commanded the respect of other human believers and ensured my unassailable position as 'vicar to the God Turdus'. With just a little extra work I could have spread the message on behalf of the *Paradae*, after all these delightful little beasties entertain so many householders with their acrobatic antics. With hindsight it becomes obvious that they have tried so desperately to attract the attention of the human species with their bright colours and cheerful disposition and we had failed to make the connection. How to design the temple of worship, you need to command respect after all? The stone altar would have to be the starting point for thrushes and as they line their nests with mud it would be reasonable to accept the use of stone structures reinforced with mortar and a choir to celebrate their singing abilities would also be required. Architecture for the *Paradae* is a bit more problematical as the tendency to use wooden structures yields a credibility issue. How to design a wooden structure with a single round ingress/egress point without it looking like a tit box? Perhaps the real skill is to embrace it, after all many human supporters happily supply such boxes for the tits in their garden, why not accept a community point of worship on a grander scale? A large section of society already makes offerings of peanuts, suet and half coconuts without recognising the true calling that provokes them to do so. A little education produced on my behalf ought to see the tithes rolling in for the first temples, on my behalf. I can already see the first schism on the horizon as many believe the garden robin to be a thrush whereas modern science is leaning towards them being flycatchers. They also favour the use of old kettles and half open fronted boxes which would conflict greatly with stone built temples. Mind, it's only a problem if you don't plan for it. The trick is retain control and don't let anybody else hijack your position of pre-eminence. Mine is a divine right after all.

Ring any bells or have you been to bed since then?

R
XXX

Sent from my iPad

Re: Day 68 November 14th Monday

Dearest N

While legacy seems to be a non-starter I think we owe it to humanity to leave a warning. It would be such a shame if we recovered our civilisation over the millennia for us to suffer the same fate again in the next cycle. I've given it some thought and decided that we need to post a warning underground in either a tunnel or better still a natural cave. My thoughts are that tunnels are likely to be occupied by people and while they may or may not survive, the occupants may deface any messages that we append. No, I think it would be better to go the natural route, at least caves have been shown to survive the test of time. I think we need to penetrate a reasonable distance underground and into the more inaccessible places for fear of defacement by others. I think we need to recruit the hobbit like qualities of Abigail to penetrate into these deeper recesses. If you or even I could enter then it just leaves them wide open to abuse. Maybe we should risk some cryptic clues nearer to the entrance lest our real efforts lie unseen and unheeded for it would be a real shame if our warning was ignored.

This practical side is relatively straightforward and I have begun to research potential sites on the Internet. My biggest problem, and some help from you could well be beneficial, is what to write. Straight away that illustrates the problem because we have no way of knowing what language or culture will remain. I think we have to come up with something in pictorial form, something akin to a stained glass window which can be interpreted against the written word in some alien language. No, scratch that, the key to unlock would not exist. We need something simpler, the most basic of pictograms.

How about a representation of the wildlife that will probably disappear and some pictures of people. A bit crude I know but if we drew lots of animals, the noticeable big ones, you know, like mega-fauna, rhinos, bison, red deer, bog elk, elephants, tigers, that type of thing then our eventual followers might just interpret the disappearance of these animals as a consequence of Man. Hold on, here's an idea, as a consequence of the hand of Man.

Human hands are quite unique, even when compared with other great apes so what would be clearer that hand prints or stencilled hand shapes on the rock. That way our successors could tie in the absence of mega-fauna with the activities of man. Maybe that's what the ancient humans were trying to tell us at the end of the last ice age as they hunted the mega-fauna to extinction, "don't make the same mistake as us". Oh wow, we've been down this route before. Oh bollocks, it didn't work for them, why should it work for us?

Back to square one. It's beginning to have an air of inevitability about it, isn't it?

Please let me have your thoughts, you are well educated and should be able to offer some valuable input.

Oh why did the Americans have to go down the 'democracy route', why not a dictatorship like Stalin? Only joking, what I meant to say was a democracy like Russia's where there is only really one candidate and you don't get nasty surprises dropped into your lap. If only because it isn't a surprise.

Why did it have to come down to Clinton or Trump? Think about all of the potential Great Brains that could have stood for election instead. Millions of Americans and it comes down to a choice between Trumpton, it beggars belief. Why, out of all the intellects and potential champions of a new world order did we end up with a choice between two alpha males intent on competing on the stage of Miss Universe? "What would you do if you became Miss Universe?" Oh, I'd like to end world hunger and bring peace to everybody".

To be fair Trump might well achieve it. In 67 days most of us will be at peace, eternally, and by definition, there won't be much hunger either. A solution of sorts, I suppose.

Separately I see the media is still in denial about Trump and his intentions and even the EU has called a special meeting to discuss Trumps election victory. I see our man Boris has told his EU counterparts to end the "whinge-o-rama" over the result. On the one hand you'd think that the EU Great Brains would be getting used to electoral surprises but on the other hand that would require a tiny modicum of imagination or even sense so I can see the problem there. How is it that commentator after commentator is feigning either disgust or disbelief over the result and that applies equally to Brexit as well? Have they got two brain cells to rub together? Imagine the furore if two teams entered the football pitch to play until a result was called after extra time, golden goal and even penalties, only for the winning team to be discounted because they'd won.

I spotted this on Teletext.

For the first time dementia has overtaken heart disease as the biggest killer. The reasons explained for this situation are based around the rising age of the population. Devastating as this condition is, and its deserving of its attention it begs a slightly different question for me. In passing, the comment was issued that deaths from heart disease had reduced. Just suppose that the reduction in heart disease was as a direct consequence of the reduction in consumption of HVO's as defined in Denmark.

This saving of premature deaths has slipped into the UK consciousness unannounced and without explanation. Not much chance of establishing cause and effect and no suggestion of fixing the blame. But there is a wider issue here, namely, you gotta die from something. Moving the goalposts springs to mind. The paradox. Let's save lives from heart disease and then complain when they die of 'old age' instead. As paradox's go, it won't be around for long, just over two months.

Then out of the corner of my eye I spotted something else on the BBC's Teletext. An NHS employee hit the 'send to all' button and sent an email to the NHS, all 840,000 of them. Then employees opted to complain, by sending it back to all 840,000 of them. Needless to say the entire communication system went into failure. It's nice to know that in the event of a real life affecting emergency that the mass transmit communication device will stall in the dissemination of vital information to the healthcare profession. Good job nobody's life depends on it.

Have you given any thought as to your own nuclear bunker provision? By the way, I'd appreciate a bit of secrecy over my own plans for my sewage treatment plant, I wouldn't want to find others trying to 'squat' if you get my drift. I haven't even told Jan of my plans yet. I could see people getting a bit desperate near the 20th. By then it really will be every ape for itself. You can't attempt the same with the Pop 40 without the rest of the community finding out and there really is no way that they can all fit in it. It really is a terrible dilemma isn't it. You are torn between helping others and looking after yourself. But if you help others there is no way that you can survive. I think the emergency services have a standard methodology for similar circumstances, namely never risk your own life in the pursuit of somebody else's. Brutal and desperately unfair I know, but being dead doesn't help anyone else either.

I'll give some thought to your situation and come back to you.

R
XXX

Sent from my iPad

Re: Day 67 November 15th Tuesday

Dearest N

I've been scoping out Magna Park and the Asda warehouses, it strikes me that with over one million square feet of storage in each of the three buildings there ought to be a reasonable repository of provisions for years to come. Always assuming of course that they survive the blasts. They are within easy walking distance and I think the biggest threat will be interference from other survivors. I don't think there will be too much in the way of community spirit in the aftermath and competition will move to the fore. In itself I don't think the competition element will be any different to normal societal rules it's just that the stakes may be a bit more urgent and interactions significantly less polite. I wonder if you should stock up on shot gun ammunition for me, I don't think I can have too much. I can't imagine that we'll be the only survivors gravitating towards Magna Park. It's a shame the local residents were so anti with the planning. Another ten million square feet of mixed storage could have come in really handy and each extra building may have sheltered its neighbour increasing the chances of survival.

Am I overreacting? Does Trump truly herald the end of the world? We only have his election soundbites to go on. When he becomes the President for real he might be that preoccupied with grabbing pussy that the 'day job' slips into the hands of his team. There is so much debate about who might or might not be in the crew. I've had a stab at it, I've gone for "Hugh, Hugh, Parsley McChew, Dogbreath, Dribble, Tug" as my starting six. I have a bit of a dilemma though, it's a bit of a paradox so let me explain. If Trump is preoccupied with his new found babe-magnetism, who steps into the breech. We know Trump is eminently qualified to be President otherwise half the US electorate wouldn't have voted for him. So if he keeps his eye on his balls, who steps in to run the show. By definition, any lesser mortal, Hugh, for example, isn't qualified because he didn't pass the test of winning an election. In that scenario then, we have an obviously unqualified individual stepping up to the plate to bat on the behalf of the most powerful country in the world. And because they aren't properly qualified they might try blagging it to our obvious detriment. Conversely, if Hugh, Hugh et al are capable of running the show without Trump's hand on the tiller what was the point of the fashion parade and subsequent election? I can't quite get my head around it yet. Some further thought is needed. I can't get past the herb seasoning argument of the Great Brain chefs.

I have an idea. If Hugh, Hugh, Parsley McChew, Dogbreath, Dribble, Tug are going to end up running the show why didn't they stand for election as Team President? At least then the American electorate could have made a rational balanced judgement as to who they wanted to represent them. Otherwise it would be like voting for Britain's Got Talent before you'd seen the acts. (If it shortened the TV season I'd vote for it). It strikes me that what we've actually done is voted for Simon Cowell. In the interests of impartiality I should point out that other talent shows exist on ITV. Only, they don't, it's Simon or nothing. Hmmm, not much democracy there.

This of course spills over into the Brexit vote. We were asked the question as to whether or not we wished to stay in or leave the EU. The Great Brains determined the question, presented it to the electorate and then presented the arguments for either answer. The electorate voted, the results were counted and the result declared. Democracy in action.

Except that now the result is queried. The *Mustelids* are seeking to vary and query the previously agreed terms because they got the wrong answer or rather the right answer, just not the one they wanted. So now they want to query the result in the law courts or demand the right to vote on progress or have the right of veto if the negotiations go badly. By 'going badly' you can assume that this means 'actually happening', Brexit that is, as their major activity seems to be attempting to frustrate the will of the people. Tell me again why we had the opportunity to vote. Tell me again if we were voting to stay in or leave the EU. Tell me what the issue is.

The broader argument revolves around the term abrogation, the legal surrendering of rights to another party. All the Remain MP's have been successfully surrendering our nation's sovereign rights to Europe for decades and now, all of a sudden, the right to surrender more rights is precious. As an old house material buyer friend used to say to me, "it don't stack up".

Although, I think I have an answer to the Scottish question. Why would the majority of Scots want to remain in Europe while a near majority wanted independence from Britain? Either you want independence or you don't, it doesn't make sense. But, there has to be a but, just suppose that the hard core support for the Scottish National Party wants independence from Britain AND Europe. The SNP then becomes the Scottish Independence Party. How then does reconciling the hard core vote for independence with the SNP's desperate attempts to remain in Europe work? I smell a dilemma, an impossible conundrum which is readily answered by one simple solution. The SNP representing the majority of Scots wanting to remain in Europe cannot be the SIP representing the near majority of Scots wanting independence, but that doesn't stop them trying. The two groups are mutually exclusive. Yet it is the Scots wanting independence that are the hard-core of the SNP's support base. What a tangled web I weave, it's enough to question the entire notion of democracy. You have to question the leadership N, but as you know from previous correspondence, we have no leaders, only followers with a head start. How then does Nicola Sturgess lead the herd to independence while simultaneously leading it to continued subjugation by Europe? Her task is to see which way the herd is moving and to position herself in front of it before shouting "follow me chaps, I know the way", although in this instance it should more accurately be "follow me chaps, I know the ways". It's enough to suggest Nicola for a Nobel Prize for practical use of quantum physics having cracked being in two places and travelling in two directions at once.

Is it any wonder I'm in need of a knob-thatch? Tell me N, do you ever suffer from heat exhaustion while in court? I imagine that the deep thinking process generates heat. I wonder if I was a bit rash going for the thermal option. Thank you for your advice about mothballs by the way. I'd forgotten that naphthalene also repels spiders and you know how Jan hates them. They could come in really handy, I might kit out the bunker with some, I can always utilise them on Katie if the world survives to my delivery date, here's hoping.

R
XXX

Sent from my IPad

Re: Day 66 November 16th Wednesday

Dearest N

Sorry to have wasted your time. You are absolutely correct. The thermal option will certainly come into its own during the nuclear winter. I wonder just how many degrees cooler it will be. At least there's one good thing to come out of it all, the end of the Global Warming debate, it's had been doing my head in lately until Trump declared it wasn't real. At last, someone with an honest approach that can cut through all the bullshit. It's such a shame that as he's solved one long term problem he's creating such a short term one instead. In a strange way it's a bit of a relief really. What's the point of worrying when it's so far from our control? It's all been way above my 'pay-grade' and yet it hasn't stopped me worrying about it. Now that oblivion is staring us straight in the face I find I can concentrate on the things that matter.

I've thought about having a bit of a community bunfight, a bit like the summer faith barbecues we have. It would be nice to have one last get together before the end. We can't really have a barbecue in January and I can't think of an excuse to call one. "Hi Chaps, please come to my end of the world bash" doesn't really bode well for the evenings mood does it? Then of course the questions start "What are you doing", "Where are you sheltering", "What weapons have you got"? And you can't give them a straight answer because you don't want to show your hand for fear of being targeted. I've never really been comfortable lying either, I've always felt such an amateur compared with the Great Brains. We could tie it in with New Year's Eve but then I don't think I can handle that, what with everyone looking to the future, a new beginning and all that.

I haven't decided on whether to buy Christmas presents this year or not. On the one hand it all seems a bit pointless, but on the other I can max out my credit cards without worrying. Having said that though, I've had to apply for some others so that I can order tinned food and bottled water, I don't think you can have too much credit.

By the way, I hope you realise that I was joking about the pickaxe handle. I had tried to explain what a maul was to Abigail but she just kept giggling. You probably know that it's basically a great big rubber hammer used by kerb layers to tap the kerbs into place in the dry mix concrete. I reasoned that because it's heavier it wouldn't take so many hits and the rubber would cushion the impact a bit and was therefore the most humane option.

I spoke to the Planning Department today, can you effing believe it, they want full plans and £360 plus VAT just for change of fucking use. I've half a mind to just do it without telling them. What's the worst they can do, fucking jobsworths? You'd think, just once, that they'd actually relax the rules wouldn't you? Something's might actually be improved by a thermonuclear device. I might come up with a list.

I've been Googling for sump pumps on Amazon so I can pump my 'bunker' out. I've already got a pressure washer for the final rinse. Anyway, I'd put my selection in the basket when I thought, hang on, hire it, you'll only get to use it once because there won't be any electricity afterwards. So I've booked a three inch petrol pump instead from Lutterworth Tool Hire for delivery on the 18th of January. That should give me enough time provided we can use your facilities a day earlier than planned. I had said the 19th but one day won't matter will it? Give us another chance to chat as well.

R
XXX

Sent from my iPad

Re: Day 65 November 17th Thursday

Dearest N

I've been Christmas shopping today but I have to say my hearts not really been in it. What do you buy the people you love that have everything when they don't know they're about to lose it? The shops are still packed full with goodies though, you'd never imagine that the end of the world is near, to all extents and purposes, its 'business as usual'. Even M&S are still banging on about Plan A "because there is no Plan B". Well, I beg to differ, there is a Plan C. It's nearly enough to make you depressed.

I must say I'd feel happier if I knew which route for personal safety you were adopting. Time is moving on and your options are getting more and more limited. You need a plan, a viable plan, you won't be able to muddle through this one I'm afraid. What strikes me the most is the utter stupidity of my previous life and all the things I used to worry about. Have I got enough money in the pension, can I get my kids into the right school, are my clothes stylish enough? All seems like inconsequential bullshit now doesn't it.

Caught a bit of the news yesterday. Apparently NATO Secretary General Jens Stoltenberg has warned President-elect Trump that "going it alone" is not an option for Europe or the United States. I must say that that page is missing from my copy of "How to Make Friends and Influence People", you know the page that leads with "You don't want to do it like that. You want to do it like this instead". Perhaps it was edited out after the first edition?

It strikes me that Trump doesn't behave in the correct manner. It's like he's working off his own agenda. He'll never make a Great Brain with an attitude like that. How he persuaded millions of Americans to vote against Hillary Clinton I can fully understand. What I can't quite get a handle on is how he managed to get them to vote for him instead. It appears to me that the only reason he won was because he persuaded enough people to say "no" to Hillary. Then the flip side kicked in and having decided "no" to Hillary this left only one automatic option which was "yes" to him. He left the electorate with the 'no thought option'. Americans are programmed to vote and vote they did, but how many voted 'for' and how many voted 'against'? The problem with this route as I perceive it is that you end up with the least worst option rather that the best one. Way too clever for me to work out, I'm obviously not Great Brains material.

R
XXX

Sent from my iPad

Re: Day 64 November 18th Friday

Dearest N

I think Trump's beginning to soften his line a bit. Some comment about only deporting or locking up 3 million illegal immigrants, ones with criminal records, gang members, that type of thing. Something strikes me as peculiar, perhaps your years of working for the CPS can yield some insight. You'll have to forgive my stupidity, I'm sure there is a simple explanation I've missed. What is the difference between 'criminal' and 'illegal'? If you lay in wait at the US border with the intent of entering America you would be planning an illegal act. Once you have entered America without legal consent then surely at that point you have committed an illegal act and have become a criminal. As far as I can see, an illegal act is a criminal act, therefore an illegal immigrant is a criminal immigrant and by definition has a criminal record as soon as their presence is detected by the judiciary. How then can you differentiate between 3 million deportable illegal immigrants and the other 9 million non-deportable illegal immigrants? I thought the point of the election pledge to deport illegal immigrants was to deport illegal immigrants. On the face of it, 12 million illegal immigrants represents 12 million jobs taken from legal Americans and that could also include 12 million voters. But 12 million unemployed Americans could have partners that vote and could therefore represent 24 million voters.

It seems to me that he's trying to deport the criminal criminals while leaving the criminals alone (for now).

But of course not all of the illegal immigrants will have legal jobs given that many will be excluded from law-abiding employment. This leaves them with 'making a living' by indulging in other illegal activities, let's call it a 'life of crime'. So another reason for removing them from general circulation is to reduce the background level of crime. Crime which can impact on the electorate again and can influence more than a potential 24 million voters.

It makes perfect sense to me and I can see why both Trump would promote it and the electorate would vote for it. So having positioned yourself in front of the herd to attract the herd's attention so that you can lead, why do you then change direction? Trump is a herd follower with a head start but the instant he changes direction he ceases to be a follower and loses his lead.

Unless of course Trump is corrupt and only followed the herd until such time as he had realised his ambitions whereupon his real agenda can be allowed to surface. What does that leave for the herd? Has the herd taken its decision and subsequently switched off by deferring decision making to other herd members? If enough herd makers defer, who is then leading the herd? I am reminded of a starling flock where the starlings hide from predators by hiding among themselves. The benefit to each bird is protection whereas the protection to the flock is non-existent. The same number of birds will die each day.

What of the detractors, the commentators and media pundits, the opposition politicians and elder statesmen? These are the herd followers that have yet to establish a head start or who have lost the head start they once held.

But what if Trump is not in fact corrupt, it is the system implementers that are corrupt and they frustrate his ambitions by corrupting the intent and direction because they have their own agendas to achieve? Alternatively, they corrupt because they don't understand the question or don't understand the answer so simply provide a corrupt product. And the beauty of this form of corruption is, they don't even know its corrupted (Shades of the blind leading the blind leading the blind.) because if you don't understand the question or the answer then you don't understand the corruption either.

Where then to hang your hat, what is real and what isn't? Trump, the saviour of the American nation, or Trump the corrupter or corrupted or the victim of corruption?

I think I need my bunker.

Incidentally, I've realised something else about the sewage treatment plants, both the communal one and mine. Because we were worried about the high water table and the possibility of them floating up out of the ground, we encased them in concrete, remember. I am absolutely sure that they would survive all but a near hit. I think you and I ought to meet up and have a serious discussion about utilising the Pop 40 unit. Why don't you call an extraordinary management meeting for the 17th of January and announce that the Pop 40 is broken and the other residents need to 'cross their legs' or something while we get it fixed. That way you and I can pump and jet it out without raising any suspicions. I'll think of a technical excuse for the problem, they all trust my advice on them so they won't suspect anything. I think we can expose the top and unbolt the chamber with the inspection opening. This should give you enough room for access, we just have to think how to seal it afterwards. Hang on. If you went in first, I could bolt it down. The hardest thing is keeping the other residents at arm's length, you know how community spirited they are, cups of tea and biscuits everywhere. Exiting shouldn't be a problem, pop Abigail through first and she can undo the bolts to let you out.

I think we have the very real makings of a plan.

R
XXX

Sent from my iPad

Re: Day 63 November 19th Saturday

Dearest N

I am still struggling to get my head around Trump. It's the corruption bit. Did they vote for him because they believed him? Did they vote for him because what they heard was corrupted by themselves to fit their own personal expectations? What did 'build a wall mean'? Is it a physical barriers between two states or a metaphysical barrier of bureaucracy to deter legitimate migrants? Is it a mental wall designed to harden the attitude of Americans to get them in the right frame of mind to accept tighter border control? This same attitude could see suspected illegals being reported to the police whereas before your average American let it slip by. Equally the police now need to be primed to respond with vigour where before they prioritised their activities in other equally important areas of legitimate concern.

In Britain, post-Brexit, incidents of xenophobia have risen to the fore with statistically insignificant reports of heightened race/hate crime directed toward foreigners filling the media. I could argue that the expectation was created by the prospect of freedom from Europe and its diktats and the herd obliged. While some felt that the climate was now right to vent their frustration out on foreigners, others felt it right to identify and report it as the story was there to find because they expected to find it. (I do accept that at least one murder attributed to race hate has been identified, terrible as it is if the victim was no stranger to you, it is still statistically insignificant, no pogrom's here yet at least). The 'message' is corrupted. Vote to leave Europe and regain control of our borders. Or was it vote to leave Europe and regain control over the neighbours in your street? Or was it vote to leave Europe and save tax money so as to spend it at home on our needs? Or how about, vote to leave Europe and hope to see your wages rise to pre-European influx levels? What was the message apart from all things to all people and if that is the case how is any of that message corrupt when it is all things to all people? "Yes, but you see, I did vote to leave Europe so that I could persecute Eastern Europeans in the streets" is valid but so is "I voted to leave Europe so that my kids could go to school in a classroom that isn't full of Polish children ruining my child's education because of the language barrier" is equally valid. In a simple sense it is impossible to describe the message as corrupt or corrupted because there is no correct interpretation. What we are left with is measurement of the interpretation and this is unequivocally corrupted by the act of measurement. The media take it upon themselves to measure and report the findings that they expect to find, indeed that they have sought out in expectation, secure in the knowledge that their august analysis will reach the intended target audience. And in this and every other audience the target is their wallet.

In America illegal immigrants fill the voids that Americans deign to fill, cheap farm workers, cleaners, child minders or cut price labour in cut price factories undercutting local legitimate firms who in turn are undercut by cut price factories south of the border. Middle class Americans benefit with cheaper cleaners and childcare and cheaper fruit and veg on their plates and cheaper meals on plates washed more cheaply. Whom is robbing whom? Deport all the illegal immigrants and pay higher wages to Americans to do the same jobs and lose money out of your own wallet in the process. Shut down the illegal using cut price factories that undercut your legitimate wage paying factories and you still have the issue of cheap goods imported across the border. Now we need to build a wall, a wall of import tariff to protect American factories from 'Third World labour rates, a wall that will drive the cost of consumer goods up to American wage standards.

American factory activity could explode back into pre-globalisation levels not enjoyed for decades. Taking Mexico in isolation the reverse will hold true. Mexican factories will lose their competitive edge secured through low labour rates and either have to export elsewhere or suffer mass unemployment which coincidentally triggers an increased desire to enter the United States for employment and a better life. Then you need to build a wall, to protect the original wall.

Given the financial strength of the Mexican Drug Cartels that is reaped primarily from the US and Canada to the north you need to build a wall. But a wall against drugs already exists so a truer term might be a permeable membrane that allows the passage of goods and people across it and that includes illegal immigrants and illegal drugs.

Build the wall then and raise the tariffs and create widespread unemployment and financial hardship south of the border. Drive the Mexicans to poverty and the desperation to find a living and don't be surprised when they turn to the movement of drugs and the illegal ingress of migrant's north in pursuit of a better life.

But doing nothing is not an option either.

And what if Trump had not won and his pledges of wall building had not been made? Back to 'business as usual' with casual acceptance of millions of illegal immigrants and casual acceptance of cheaper childcare and greater cash in the pocket for millions of Americans. Those with jobs that pay for childcare anyway, and less cash in the pockets for those at the fringes of American society, too dumb to earn a proper living, too expensive to offer cheap jobs too.

R
XXX

Sent from my iPad

Re: Day 62 November 20th Sunday

Dearest N

Who would have thought that we'd be having these sorts of discussions now, when we were at school together all those years ago? If only life had turned out as simple as Maths with Mr Wallace. Yeah, I know, simple for me, just thought I'd remind you of that. Bet you're glad I've got your back now though, aren't you? The primary settlement tank is 2.5 m deep and 1.4 m wide by 3.6 m long on the Pop 40. By my reckoning this is around 40cm of concrete surround to all sides including the top and a further 40cm of loose fill over as well. Both sites are relatively level so any blast should just pass over and I'll have to risk that my walnut tree is either blown away completely or away from my exit point. My Pop 20 tank is slightly shorter at 3.3 m otherwise it's all the same. I've ordered some 'test plugs' to seal the infill pipes, we don't want any 'shit to enter the fan' when the 'shit enters the fan', do we?

I've given up with the wankers at the planning department, not least because I don't want them writing to the neighbours for comment. Comment, you might as well say complaint. "It's so unfair, why should he have a nuclear bunker when I can't have one". "Dear Sir, I wish to object in the strongest possible terms to the loss of visual amenity when this construction blocks my view". (It's in the fucking ground, dipshit). I bet you can guess whose door they'll be knocking on the 20th.

We have another problem and as I know how you like your bible I thought I'd frame it in biblical terms. If I said "Noah, Dove and was there a Raven in there somewhere"? We need some way of determining when it's safe to surface. Can you give it some thought at your end?

Scrub that, turns out you can download an App for IPhone for £4.99. Have you or Abigail got one, I'm with Samsung? Seems that in the rush for life we have covered all the bases for death as well. We need some solar panel battery chargers and can rig up some DC lighting. All we need is a grant from the government which we'll never have to pay back and we'll be quid's in. At last, a positive use for government. It had to happen eventually.

Turns out Hugh and Hugh is actually 'Reince Preibus and Stephen Bannon. The knives are already out. And surprise, surprise, racist attacks are rife in the new America. What was it they voted for again?

R
XXX

Sent from my IPad

Re: Day 61 November 21ˢᵗ Monday

Dearest N

Day 60, how the time has ticked away. Strangely I don't feel any great sense of urgency although I suppose there's plenty of time for it to creep in. I've been thinking about what Trump said earlier in the week "You don't need to be afraid of my presidency". WTF?

How can you pledge radical policies and actions that impose on millions of voters without it introducing real change? Unless of course, you had your fingers crossed while making the pledges. Change, such a simple word, guaranteed to drive fear into the hearts and minds of the herd. In its simplest form then, the absence of fear = no change. Would that be 'business as usual' by any chance? My personal version would be 'bullshit as usual'. Well worth the fight for the White House, not.

I've tried to open an account at Makro, I used to have one years ago and to be honest I wasn't sure if they still traded or not. I got it through the company and we used it for the Beaver and Cub Scout groups. Bulk discount prices on beans and sausages helped stretch the budget. Failing that there's always the supermarkets. If push came to shove we could trawl around all the local Asdalavista's buying a bit here and a bit there. We don't want to spark any panic buying do we? I remember when there was only one whereas I know of seven within about 15 miles range. That doesn't sound very far but it covers over 700 square miles so we shouldn't raise any suspicions. If we were really pushed, there's always Tesco. I'd go to Waitrose but I've always felt out of place. I've never managed the smug facial expression and don't intend to start now. Having said that though, I do feel a certain superiority over less able people who haven't worked it out yet. I want to shout at them to warn them, "You're all walking towards a precipice in the clouds". I know it will all fall on deaf ears so I bite my tongue instead. My biggest fear is that realisation of Trump's true ambitions will surface nearer the date and while it will all be too late for them, I don't want them interfering with us.

That reminds me, how's the shotgun ammunition order doing?

I saw the other day that Europe has vowed to strengthen its defences, whatever that means, probably another 200 troops to Estonia. That'll show Putin, won't it? Reminds me a bit about the German push into Holland dragging the British and French north before they cut through the Ardennes and snook in behind them. At least in Estonia the troops are only hemmed in by Russia to the east and south in Kaliningrad with the Baltic Sea behind them. No, I can't see any drawbacks there.

R
XXX

Sent from my iPad

Re: Day 60 November 22nd Tuesday

Dearest N.

Thing is with Trump, if you voted for change, then you should be fearful that you won't get any. "No need to fear my presidency"? How can that work?

I'm worried about Katie, I thought I'd got it sorted but the numbers worry me. I've been looking at the numbers for Trump's win and it makes for uncomfortable reading. Trump won with 60 million votes while Clinton got 61 million. I don't care about the overall minority vote winner being declared the winner. That the Yank's system, not my worry. My problem is the 231 million eligible voters in total. Trump won with only 26% of the total electorate.

I thought, if Trump can win an election looking like a complete arse, I can look like a complete arse as well. Half of Americans accepted Trump, I could live with that. I could walk down the street sporting Katie knowing that half the people approved. Now I've taken the plunge and spent the money only to discover that only 26% approved of el unfollically one. That's only one in four! Three out of four people could be sniggering behind my back. Just when I thought I'd got my confidence back. I'm distraught. What should I do old friend? Please help me.

R
XXX

Sent from my iPad

Re: Day 59 November 23rd Wednesday

Dearest N

Thank you old friend, I knew you'd have the answer. Three out of four might take the piss, but, and I think you're probably spot on, what's it matter when 99.8% of them are probably dead. I knew you'd see it clearly and set my mind straight.

I seem to remember talk of nuclear radiation from my youth in films and books about radioactive iodine settling in the thyroid gland. The first thing troops and survivors were offered were some form of iodine tablets to stuff the thyroid with 'clean iodine' to stop the radioactive iodine settling there. I don't know whether the idea still holds or not but I'll see what I can get from the chemist. I'd also read somewhere about vitamins protecting against cancers, something to do with anti-oxidants and free radicals cancelling each other out. For once the vitamin industry might actually serve a purpose other than flavouring your urine. I don't suppose we'll get much access to fresh fruit and veg in the short to medium term so I thought we should invest in multivitamins by the box load. I've sent Jan to Holland and Barrett to have a gander. She just thinks I'm turning into a hypochondriac. The penny sale might come into its own for once. We probably need to stock up with paracetamol as well, the 32 tablets maximum per customer is a real pain. There they are trying to stop people committing suicide while they ignore the obese, smoking, boozing idiot's hell bent on their own slow-motion suicides. Just as long as they don't go the fast track root everything's hunky dory. Pathetic or what, "no, no, no, you can't buy 200 paracetamol tablets, you could kill yourself" when so many elect to do themselves in anyway with barely a comment. I wish I had a brain cell.

Jan and I are at the O2 for the end of year tennis championships for the next couple of days. Might as well go, not much else happening to take your mind off what's over the horizon. I suppose I could call it the end of the world tennis championships. I bet the audience spends more time looking at their smart phones than the tennis. They did last year. The funny thing is, the smart phones are smarter than the owners. All those 'court in the background' selfies will count for nought in such a few short days. Knowing what is actually happening makes the whole life experience seem so ephemeral and inconsequential, almost as though nothing is real. When I think about all the things I used to lust after, I realise now how inconsequential my life was. At least now we get to concentrate on what matters, food, shelter and security. In a perverse way I am quite looking forward to the new adventure. You can't get much realer than the need for day to day survival. We only have to concentrate on the basics, everything else is just extracurricular. I'll have a look through my flower books when I get home. I know they used to make flour out of silverweed roots, *Potentilla anserina*, for example. We'll need to hit the ground running with knowledge. It's quite funny really, the cleverer we've got the less we know. If we had a time machine and could slip back a couple of thousand years most of the issues facing us would be second nature to us. All the information we could ever need to survive is behind us buried in the archive. The language keeps changing and it slips tantalisingly out of reach.

Time to pack for tomorrow, thanks again with help with the arse thing.

R
XXX

Sent from my iPad

Re: Day 58 November 24th Thursday

Dearest N

Just a short note today, what with the tennis and all.

I keep wondering if there is a way. You know, to avert it all. Does it have to happen? What can you do, 'disgusted of Tunbridge Wells' won't hack it. Why is there no mechanism to prevent it all? Eighteen months the Americans buggered around sifting out the talent until they'd reached the very bottom of the barrel. How is that possible? But when I think about it and go back to the beginning, they started with dross and finished with abject detritus. How has politics arrived at such a sorry state of affairs? How does a process designed to find the greatest brains, the greatest leaders, fail so abjectly? Imagine what you'd come up with if you tried to do it badly? Only, we don't need to imagine. How can the system be so corrupt? So unfit for purpose. The only ray of light is the fact that we won't have to live with it for much longer.

Commentators try and put a brave face on it by saying some banal trite along the lines of "checks and balances" as though that has any relevance.

I am reminded of a 'Comic Strip Presents' feature from ages ago. I think it used to air on Channel 4 and featured Adrian Edmundson, Dawn French and the gang of Alternative Comedian's in the different programmes. The opening credits for the series featured a 'comic strip' of an atomic bomb being dropped onto Britain. In one of the episodes a group of soldiers were travelling across the countryside trying to find safety. They had all been blinded by the flash and had come to rest in a group when one asked "Any more of that lager left"? He was passed a 'tin' and removed the ring pull before offering it up to his lips. The 'tin' was a hand grenade. How can the most powerful nation on Earth, champion of democracy, leader of the free world, engineer a system of control on a par with blinded soldiers in search of a drink?

R
XXX

Sent from my iPad

Re: Day 57 November 25th Friday

Dearest N

Concentrated on the tennis today. Decided there was no point in watching the herd and its antics between points. A thought struck me, it took me right back to my first days at infant school. Of course, mine was a much betterer school than the one you and Jan started at as five year olds. Shame you didn't start at a properer school with me until you were eleven. Anyway, I'm digressing, I suppose it had to happen eventually. I think, with the end of the world near I'm going through a slow motion slide show of my life. No flashes for me, at least as long as the ad hoc bunkers function, anyway. Can you remember early school assemblies where you sat, cross legged on the floor, praying? Then little George would say "Miss, miss, Edward hadn't got his eyes closed during prayers". I remember Edward being told off once, but usually the teachers just smiled. Of course I now realise that for George to know that Edward hadn't got his eyes closed, George had to have had his open as well. I used to squint through eye slits to spy on my neighbours. Point is, I don't want you thinking that I spend all my time watching other people not watching the tennis. That would be pot and kettle calling time wouldn't it? I don't squint through eye slits either.

When our family used to caravan around Europe in the summer holidays back in the seventies my dad fitted a periscope device to his car. It was strapped/suctioned on to the top of the windscreen and gave him a better view over the car roof and through the caravan windows while towing. We'd often stop on the way into a campsite and have German's examining the device, even sitting in the driving seat at my Dad's insistence. There are a couple of 110mm diameter access openings on the treatment plants. If we get some small bits of mirror and use some 63 mm diameter rainwater downpipes I think I can make us each a periscope so that we can have a look around while still safely ensconced underground. I will get us another bung for the bottom of the pipe on the inside and a straight bar to use to push the existing top seal off from the inside. That way it looks perfectly normal from above until you activate it. Thereafter you can seal it from the inside until such time as it is safe to surface. We can also push the iPhone

Geiger counter app through on a stick to check radiation levels as well. Tell the neighbours that the solar panels battery chargers are for a new battery backup for the treatment plant in case the power fails. If I tell them it's a new Environment Agency requirement they'll believe me. They believed all the other bollocks spouted by the EA so one more lie won't be noticed. And at least my lie will actually provide some benefit. We'll need to anchor the panels down really well and hope they survive.

Still thinking about the real task in hand. In the gaps between the matches, thank you.

R
XXX

Sent from my iPad

Re: Day 56 November 26th Saturday

Dearest N

Back from the tennis. Quite enjoyed it thanks, in spite of everything. I've had to zone out of the media while away. I'll try and catch up on all the erudite bullshit and get filled in with the 'facts'. Funny thing is, I bet today's facts are different from Monday's facts. In fact I think that's part of the problem, a lack of truth. Every truth is spun, corrupted, invented or downright lied about and all in the interest of securing an audience. An audience of likeminded individuals who agree broadly with the content. Because if you don't agree, you don't buy that paper, watch that TV channel, skim that internet website. It makes me realise just how easy it was for Joseph Goebbels to spin his webs of truth. They were only lies to 'unbelievers' and they didn't listen to his speeches or read his newspaper articles. Good old Joe only ever spake the truth.

R

XXX

Sent from my iPad

Re: Day 55 November 27ᵗʰ Sunday

Dearest N

I've cracked it. I've been dropping casual hints to my three young adults but they've all been falling on deaf ears. I can't show my true hand for fear of them ignoring me, at best or sectioning me at worst. By my reckoning most of the northern hemisphere will be gone. Israel will take out the Middle East while Pakistan and India will polish off the subcontinent. This leaves Africa and South America relatively intact while Australia and New Zealand will probably take a pasting as staunch allies. I've booked my three and their partners on what the brochures call 'a holiday of a lifetime'. How apt, I thought. I've put them on safari in the Kalahari for three weeks starting on the 17ᵗʰ of January. Not only have I kept them hopefully out of harm's way, I have also linked them in with the Bushmen who have all the skills needed for 'living off the land'. I had a Plan B, Papua New Guinea but I've heard that they had some peculiar eating habits in years gone by. I've hopefully secured their present and future. It's cost me nearly £15,000 but that's what credit cards, are for, right. "Sorry, did my cheque get lost in the bomb blast". "I'll send you another one when I can find a post-box".

It's like taking candy from a baby as well as being quite liberating. Thirty seven years I've been paying my mortgages and I still have another seven and a half years to go. I've never missed a payment in all that time and what will I end up with in the final analysis? Shades of the Great Fire of London," that's my land, there, under those ashes, next to that pile of ashes. I can prove it, I have this pile of ashes that used to be deeds". I bet I still get a council tax bill. No, I bet I get fined for littering the streets and leaving my pile of melted plastic out on the wrong day. Fucking jobsworths. I bet most of them never did a full day's work in their lives. I think I'll add this to my list of the benefits of nuclear Armageddon, no more jobsworths.

My kids may never forgive me for not saving their partners parents, but hey, it's every ape for himself. At least none of ours have had kids of their own yet. It's hard but we'll have to abandon our parents. They are all getting on into their twilight years and to be honest, if the shock doesn't kill them, I think the shock probably will. That's a point, do you think we could get the money back from the undertakers from the pre-paid funeral plans. Here, can you cremate these ashes please? How much? Bollocks to that. I'm beginning to struggle with credit now so the refund would come in handy.

I've thought about cashing my pension in, but what can I do with it? Buy a new car, take out health insurance, buy enough food for the next thirty years? I live in hope, actually, if I live, I hope, fingers crossed.

I'm beginning to get relaxed about it. I've ordered some so called 'heritage seeds' which are supposed to breed true. There's a genetic seed bank in a frozen tunnel up north somewhere but I don't know what number bus to catch to get there so these will have to do. Also I've invested in some top quality stainless steel kitchen knives and pots and pans, simple technology but could be worth their weight in gold. I've bought them through a club book on credit, am I getting good at this or what? I've doubled the numbers up for your three so no need for you to worry. Any luck with the archery sets? Good idea of yours for when the shotgun cartridges run out.

It's almost fun planning for the end of the world. I realise now that our civilisation has been working towards the end of the world for eons, I bet we're the first to actually plan for it.

Bye for now, trying to bone up on the media.

R
XXX

Sent from my iPad

Re: Day 54 November 28th Monday

Dearest N

I've been thinking about the available space in the 'bunkers'. Everything has to enter through the top round manhole access and there isn't much room internally. I've thought about making a frame to bolt together when inside the tank. I can use tongued and grooved board to deck the frame when in situ to make a sleeping platform and even a dining/lounge area by removing some of the boards. We need to make your bed two deep, perhaps you on the bottom and Abigail and Edward above would be the safest. I think we should be able to get some inflatable camping mattresses as well. If we store the food and water underneath I think we can get by. There won't be enough room for Abi's sewing machine and it will all be a bit caravan-like but it's infinitely better than nothing.

I have given some thought to the toilet facilities, it ought to be possible to rig something up to connect to the units outflow pipe but they'll be no washing facilities as such. Perhaps we should stock up on baby wipes? If we lay plastic sheeting over the top of the unit and lay it to a fall we could drain any rainwater into the last 110 mm pipe and it will flush any effluent away down the exit pipe. We can drag off some of the loose stone cover and re-lay over the polythene to stop it blowing away. All a bit crude but it's better than nothing. Don't forget to pack plenty of haemorrhoid cream, old friend. Abigail often tells me how you suffer greatly. Having said that though, any rainwater is likely to be full of radioactive dust to begin with so when you squat over the 110 mm pipe you could be receiving a dose of radiotherapy. Fingers crossed, it might cure your 'grapes of wrath'

I'm beginning to get up to speed with Trump and the media.

He's announcing various appointments of people I've never heard of and probably never will. All the experts are scraping the barrel of knowledge to discover something disparaging or other. "Ooer, he attended a KKK meeting or made a racist/sexist/misogynistic comment and is eminently unsuitable for a lead role in Trump's administration". Forgive me for being cynical, but I'd have thought that thoughts/comments of that nature would have been an essential part of Trump's pre-qualification process. Notwithstanding the simple fact that these elements were placed front and centre of Trump's entire election campaign and the electorate placed their confidence in him. It strikes me that Trump's success illustrates the disconnect between the 'official' carefully cultured facade of loving tolerance and the reality on the ground. The simple fact remains that virtually all people harbour these thoughts and ideas and simply suppress them when in public and reproduce them in private. We are family group/tribe members first, it is what makes our species what it is. It is underwritten by our basal instincts and provides an evolutionary advantage to each individual in the race for life. Deny if you can and while you are at it deny that jealousy, resentment and spite exist.

I wonder if that's the key to Trump's success. Appeal to the base, primal instincts and let the DNA take over. After 18 months of in depth analysis and electioneering the result was coloured by appealing to the lowest common denominator, the gut feeling, instinct. An illustration of the difference between what Man can do and will do. The failure of intellect over nature. Is their hope for humanity? Nearly half the electorate failed to cast a vote, nearly three quarters didn't vote for Trump although this is invalidated by the fact that a quarter voted for Hillary. What did the half see that failed to vote, what drove them to indifference, was it indifference to the result or indifference to the process? Is it as simple as failing to recognise either candidate or the process as relevant to their own tribe or family? Welcome to the Disunited States of America. But they never existed anyway. Racism against Chinese, Red Indians, Hispanic's, non-Christians. Slavery against Blacks followed for decades after with the segregation of apartheid. Has Trump opened old scars or simply exposed wounds that never healed? If you examine the social development of America it charters a continuous subjugation of people's by successive waves of migration and development. Each new wave brings vigour and drive to the nation and suppresses all before it. We are currently seeing the growth of Southern European's overrunning the previous Northern European's with predictions of a Hispanic majority in the not too distant future as the demographics of birth rate take hold. How curious that Trump seeks to recruit the northern whites over the southern whites via the ballot box. I can't remember the indigenous people being invited to vote in previous ages. Where in Europe would you draw the line of acceptability I wonder? North of the Alps and Pyrenees? I am reminded of a trip I made from Cuenca in the centre of Spain to Pau in southern France. Driving for hours in full sun and temperatures in the 30's through Spain I saw the temperatures drop to the mid 20's as I climbed into the Pyrenees before reaching the 5,000 metre long tunnel under the border. This tunnel north of Jaca glides downhill gently into France before emerging into what was that day a different world. It was 15 degrees C and raining, all in a little over three miles.

On another occasion I stayed in Puigcerda, a town on the Spanish border with France where the border passes through the conurbation. I stopped for coffee and asked for "Cafe con leche, grande, pro favour" to be met with a stony silence. "Cafe au lait, sil vous plait" elicited the desired response just yards across the border.

Nearer to home I've stumbled across a bit more as well.

I see the Maltese Prime Minister has warned Britain that the EU is deadly serious about tying 'Freedom of Movement' to access to the 'Single Market'. That's the beauty of the EU, what with Malta about to hold the presidency by rotation. According to https://www.worldometers.com Malta's population is 420,000 people. An Internet website suggests that Manchester has a current population of 430,000 people. I don't think I need to say any more on the subject. But I will. WTF? Can he smell the summit dinner already? Has he got his EU President handbook for behaviour learnt off by rote? This is a tail hair wagging the front end of a dog.

I've just see a Belgian minister giving a sound bite on the Turkey issue. The EU parliament has held a non-binding vote to suspend all talks with Turkey over joining the EU. Turkey's president has threatened to reopen its borders to the EU for thousands of migrants to enter in retaliation. The EU is concerned that Turkey is no longer a democracy after the actions taken as a result of the failed coup. So what has the Belgian chappie offered? "We should not be discussing membership with a country that is no longer a democracy". To me this seems a little perverse, given the EU's reaction to the democratically held 'Brexit' referendum. Sorry, it just flashed up on the BBC news channel and I can't be arsed to sit through another hour waiting for his name to reappear. Most of the other soundbites since the referendum seem to revolve around how the EU can punish Britain for being democratic.

R
XXX

Sent from my iPad

Re: Day 53 November 29th Tuesday

Dearest N

I've been thinking about Mexico, as you do, and Trump. Jan thinks the Mexican Drug Cartels might assassinate Trump but I think that they'll encourage him as much as possible. Let's just suppose that the combovered one follows through on all his election pledges and builds his wall and imposes the import duty for starters. Factories across Mexico close down shedding jobs and the prosperity that they provide disappears. Increasing poverty leaves Mexicans with two growing opportunities, illegal immigration and the drug cartels. Either way these options increase the pressure on the wall for the illegal transit of goods or people. The transit of people funds the border mafia (AKA drugs cartels) who increase their revenue. The desire of poor Mexicans to earn a living drives them into the hands of the cartels with a reduction in 'recruitment costs' and cost benefits. If the wall works and the drug flow north is reduced then the price of drugs that succeed will increase in value and not impact on the earning capabilities of the cartels. In the meanwhile the cartels increase in strength while the official Mexican government is left weaker by rising unemployment and increasing poverty. A weaker government is less able to combat the corruption of the cartels and at the extreme Mexico could become a failed state. It is not inconceivable that Mexico could join the ranks of Afghanistan, Libya and Iraq where the legitimate governments have been removed by external forces leaving a vacuum. In Afghanistan vast tracts of the country are outside the jurisdiction of any official government and are controlled by the Taliban who in turn operate the drug production fiefdoms providing income to the local residents as they export death far and wide. How would we define a state as of having failed? A failure to provide law and order, a failure to protect its citizens, a failure to provide socioeconomic stability. In a sense there is the potential for history to repeat itself. When American introduced prohibition in 1920 they created the environment for the illegal manufacture and distribution of alcohol together with all of its associated criminal activities. They created an environment for an alternative culture, a counter culture to the rule of government. Through his actions Trump has the potential to do the same.

But while converting Mexico into a failed state is at one extreme, all of his actions and policies have a capacity for creating counter cultures. Equally, for Trump or even Clinton, doing nothing is not an option. Nothing, is not something a government can do, indeed I would suggest that 'doing' is what a government does. Governments thrive on change, the change of administration, the injection of fresh ideas or simply the polar change between opposing political ideologies. Governments are like a sailing ship tacking into a headwind, swerving left and right as they move forward, less generously the term is yawing or oscillating.

One of the counter cultures produced as a consequence of Trump's rhetoric is that of heightened racism with increasing reports of attacks on ethnic groups. But equally, the media is looking for precisely that, the counter culture to justify the medias own rhetoric. Instead of calling them the media it would be fairer to call them commentators and commentators seek out the 'action'. When watching sport the crowd is often partisan and react differently to the same event played out in front of them. Will it be a brilliant save or a stupid shot? But if we went political then on balance the commentators will be either for or against and the voters will either agree or disagree with the sentiments expressed.

It isn't only Trump that has created this environment for comment, our own Brexit has seen similar reactions and for that matter if Hillary had won the polarisation of commentary would have yielded the alternative response.

The impotence of the media has been adequately illustrated with the near lead story on the BBC 'news' of VP elect Pence having been booed by the audience and then addressed by a scripted actor making a political statement on behalf of the diverse people of America. "What, really, somebody holding a different view in public to the VP elect? Well I never, I must go to the foot of my stairs and book the air time. This will knock Syria off the headline slot". This event tells you infinitely more about the BBC than it will ever tell you about Pence or Trump's administration.

I must point out that in the later editions, and in the interests of fairness, the BBC did acknowledge the respect granted to Pence by the actor for having the respect to stop and listen to the comments. (But only after they had expressed the tweeted condemnation of the event by Trump first.)

On a more serious note I have been arguing with Jan about tinned food supplies. I have suggested we go on a 'wilderness holiday' without power, stuck up a hillside in a tent for two weeks. I still can't tell her what's really happening. Even then all I got was "I don't like camping and I'm not sleeping in a tent", so I had to end up searching for a trendy yurt with a secure lock on it, "I don't feel safe in a tent" before she'd even engage in the discussion. We're only hypothetically going to fucking Yorkshire, it's not as though there's any tigers there to be frightened of. She doesn't like rice pudding and wants beans amongst other things. Firstly, how can we warm them up without fuel and secondly who wants to be sealed in an underground chamber with a baked bean consumer. Thirty six years we've been married but I can honestly say, I don't think I could love her that much. They might be high in fibre and protein but as far as I'm concerned there's only one thing they are super at. She's even found some curried beans for fuck's sake. I've ordered and stripped down some activated charcoal filters for extractor hoods and mackled up some makeshift filters for the ventilation system but they can only work so far.

Anyway, I've tried my best to accommodate her and while I won't put any beans in the bunker I will stock up the old underground water tank that served the old Hall with them. The brick tank is thirteen feet deep and runs under one of the old outbuildings. I can't seal it and it fills with rainwater over several months. I will pump it out with my 20mm sump pump which will hold it for a while as it gradually fills up again. I'll raise some planks up on stacks of concrete blocks to form a raised floor to store the medium term food reserves which should keep them dry for long enough. It does occur to me that this could serve as a slightly more practical shelter in the longer term than the treatment tank/bunker. I had better fit a door to it as well with a secure lock. We don't want to emerge from below ground to find our reserves all ransacked or the shelter occupied. I did buy a couple of old fashioned ornamental cast iron water pumps donkey's years ago for use as a garden feature. They are supposed to work and I can 'plumb' one in and get it working so that we can drain the water in the longer term without electric pumps. The whole tank is around 12 feet wide by nearly 20 feet long and could accommodate us all, provided we survive. We used to drink the water straight out of the old house wells before I had the borehole sunk. I can rig the second pump up to the house well for drinking water into the future. The old Victorian infrastructure may well come to our rescue yet. (Well, did you get it? Well, oh never mind). As an added thought, there is a spring quite near the entrance to the back lane from the highway which is probably the same water source as the wells provide. If all else fails we will be able to collect water from there.

R
XXX

Sent from my iPad

Re: Day 52 November 30th Wednesday

Dearest N

I will have to save Jan's cats, she still calls them kittens even though they are 18 months old. There's no way I can accommodate them in the bunker with us so I've come up with another idea. I'll take a trip up to Travis Perkins and buy some lead sheet. I have used it for soakers and flashing on roofs before, indeed my plumber once complimented me on my workmanship. (I think he thought I'd used a different plumber). Anyway, I will construct an oversized pet carrier encased in lead sheet and bury it in the ground. I will put a ventilation system on it and can stock it up with dried food and water for a couple of weeks. We used to make slatted floors for cowsheds out of concrete. The dung was scraped by remote machine or simply trodden through the slats by the cows into a deep chamber underneath the cowshed. They used to store six months of slurry under the building, enough for a whole Scottish winter. Anyway, I will slat the floor so that the cats dung and wee falls through and keeps them relatively clean. My problem is working out how to open the box automatically. We might be underground for a couple of months while we wait for radiation levels to reduce a bit but I can't leave the cats for that long. I've just had an idea; I could bury a rope encased in a plastic water pipe that can join the two 'bunkers' together and release the door mechanism remotely. My biggest trouble will be in leaving it as late as possible. If I release them too soon they could die from radiation whereas if I leave them too long they could starve or dehydrate. It's a real conundrum that I haven't worked out yet.

Do you want me to make another one for your cats?

It does make me wonder what will happen to all the native animals. Will they all become extinct or will enough survive to breed? Plants should have it relatively easy given that most have an insurance policy with inert seeds. Some can survive for many years and still germinate when the conditions are right. I think on balance that there are enough geographic features in the countries topography for enough areas to be shielded from the blasts for plants and animals to survive. People will, for that matter, it's just that it will be kind of random and much of our infrastructure will have gone.

I think that it may actually benefit the fauna and flora in the near term what with the reduction in human pressures. I suppose that we could view it all as a 'fresh start' for Planet Earth. It's strange really when you think about it. All the conservation bodies, all the nature reserves, all the policies to protect animals are all designed to do just one thing. To protect them from us. And if 'us' is no longer part of the equation it gives the planet a chance to reset. All these years you've been buying peanuts for the tits in your garden and what you should have been doing was funding nuclear armament. But of course you have been funding nuclear armament through your taxes. But not to worry, you've also been funding the destruction of the world with all your monetary purchases and, coupled with advances in science and technology that have accelerated the process, the earth is in sore need of a reset. How ironic, all the conservation in the world and what we really needed was the UK Atomic Agency and its various international counterparts.

I wonder, is there is a Nobel Prize for Conservation? Who would have thought it, a Nobel Prize for Trump? Just a shame he won't be able to collect it with his other commitments of being dead. Stockholm probably won't exist anyway and I don't think Oslo will be volunteering a 'Peace Prize' somehow.

R
XXX

Sent from my iPad

Re: Day 51 December 1st Thursday

Dearest N

What was I saying, El Trumpo will be whisked away to some secure bunker of his own. I bet they won't even have to pump the shit out, although I think in this case they'll end up pumping the shit in if you get my drift. I bet he won't get beans for tea either. Secure in his bunker does he realise that the view from Trump tower will have disappeared, as well as the tower, as well as his Presidency, but, on the positive side, if he makes a trip to Scotland, it will be ever so easy to get a 'hole in one'. No, scratch that, he won't be able to get out of the sand trap.

It begs the question, why? Egotistical, maniacal, stupid and downright daft. Yep, I think that sums up Trump. But it also sums up every other candidate, president, prime minister, chancellor, king, queen, you name it. They are all failed individuals with monstrous egos, essential qualifications for the highest echelons of leadership worldwide. Why then is he so ridiculed by the media? How can they ignore these essential characteristics in all candidates yet focus so intently on Trump's apparent failings? The Mail on Sunday peppers its commentaries with innocent expressions such as "spooky truth", "henchmen" and "The Fright House". Bloody hell, if he spent more time stroking his pussy instead of chasing it he would make for a brilliant Bond villain.

It's nice to see they have retained perspective, when in fact we know they wouldn't recognise it if it grabbed them by the bollocks. Strange that they are so remote from their own bollocks when they so eloquently spout it.

I remember taking my kids to Disneyland, Paris and queuing for hours for mere minutes of rides when we alighted on the Ghost Train/Haunted House. It had been ignored by all and sundry and we walked straight into the lift and down onto the ride. Having emerged we walked back round to the entrance and repeated the experience. We never got the third ride, our activity had been spotted and we emerged to a queue hundreds deep. To my family it was 'spooky' and a 'Fright House' and I suppose the staff could have been described as 'henchmen'. I think we can now guess what the journalist is getting confused with.

I see Teresa May hasn't fallen out with too many of her own henchmen yet. David Cameron was always condemned for his reliance on members of the Bullingdon Club. Osbourne, Boris, now they were proper henchmen straight out of the top drawer. They'd never have any hesitation in 'henching'.

Spooky is used in North America to indicate something that is 'easily frightened' or 'nervous' whereas over here it's something 'sinister or ghostly' in a way that causes fear or unease.

Should the end of the world spark fear and unease. Curiously, if the end of the world was apparent to 'those in the know' they would suppress all knowledge of it for fear of causing 'fear and unease'. So we have a peculiar situation whereby an Extinction Level Event (ELE) would be suppressed from the public realm. Yet the press are suggesting that a Trump presidency heralds the end of the world and have thereby placed an ELE into the public realm. I believe the press Neville, that's why I have gone to such lengths to protect our lives. Actually I don't believe the press, surprise, I think what we have here is a double bluff. Declare that the world is going to end, then deny it, because it is.

And while we are at it we had better look at strong, fit men having well developed muscles, the sort of people you'd want at your side in the event of a brawl. Yep, that sounds like Parsley MeChew, Dogbreath, Dribble and Tug, brawny political advisers to complete your inner circle of henchmen. If all diplomacy fails you can always beat Putin up. Excepting of course that with his shirtless posing on horseback and history of martial arts, Putin is the real henchman.

Is Trump getting organised to retire at the end of his short tenure as President? Safely ensconced with his family in the most secure bunker imaginable as the world is destroyed around him he must realise that that's not conducive to a good footfall in the hotel business. I have it, Trump's hotel business is failing and he's going for a massive loss to end all losses. This time he can't offset it against any taxes due so why not finish your career as the richest man in the world as well as President for life by removing all others, rich men and political opponents alike. His ego will allow him to be President of the 0.2% of the population left alive. He will still be the richest most powerful man on Earth and that's all that matters. If you think I'm being unreasonable, take a look at Bashar al Assad, is he the richest most powerful man in Syria (left alive)?

I see he's settled his Trump University claims for $25 million. I think the claim is up to 6,000 students have all been misled. The idea was that you could enrol in Trump University for $35,000 ish and learn the secrets of Trump's success in the real estate industry. Forgive me for vibrating one of my brain cells, but, if 6,000 people know something it's hardly a secret is it? And, sorry, another one of my brain cells wants to contribute as well, when 6,000 people are all pursuing the same idea, it loses all commercial advantage. You succeed by ploughing your own furrow, not by following somebody else's. Who exactly was deluding who, here? Imagine being in prison in America, not one of our hotels over here, and being offered the secret way to escape for a price. In 'Porridge' the currency was always tobacco but my guess is that the criminal fraternity has moved on to higher dependencies now. You pay your dues and secret yourself at the due time and place to find that you are not alone. In fact there are another 5,999 inmates queuing at the point of escape. On the one hand you quite rightly feel that you have been duped but on the other, the man with the secret plan now has all the currency and all the power and is untouchable. Not much of a fraternity either, is it?

I've been trying to work out how much water to store in the bunkers. The EA talk about 200-120 litres per person per day. We can't cook, bathe or even flush the toilet so these figures are way over the top. In the past when my house well ran dry I would bring in bottled water from work to basically fill the kettle with. I still had water for bathing and toilet flushing but I never thought it was clean enough to drink. I used to collect ten litres every couple of days and that covered the weekend as well when we were all at home. I think if we allow three litres per day per person that ought to do it and would leave enough for teeth brushing. The next problem is how long do we stay underground? We can't stay down for six months or anything like it so I think on balance we should aim for about 6 weeks. We could always emerge for short periods to begin with to replenish stocks from the midterm store in the old water tank. Well, Edward and Abigail can, you'll be bolted in. I think the biggest problem will be radioactive dust on the ground and in water. Hopefully the groundwater wells contain 'old' water that's been in the ground for a long time and should be free of radioactivity for some time. Let's go for 40 days at 3L each which is 360L for you and 240l for me. I have another three wells in the garden and I have thought of stocking up on propane gas bottles. I can suspend them on ropes into each well to protect them from damage. All the wells are 4 m deep and 1.2 m in diameter so we can fit a good number into each well. We have to buy the bottle as well as the gas so they will be about £140 each. Can you do it on your credit card, I'm maxed out at the moment? I have a Bullfinch boiler that we use for boiling the Christmas puddings. It's what roofers use for boiling buckets of pitch but it will be ideal for heating water and cooking with. I will store it in the old water tank with the food but daren't store the gas there for fear of losing it all.

R
XXX

Sent from my iPad

Re: Day 50 December 2nd Friday

Dearest N

I spotted a note on BBC Teletext about Obama threatening to weigh in on Trump after leaving office. Usually outgoing presidents hold their tongues over their successor's actions. Obama's worried that Trump may disturb key American values

How does that work then? Eight years Obama's had to cement core American values in the hearts, minds and crosses of the voting public. Unfortunately for him he must have been using defective cement, probably cheap Mexican stuff without quality control. FDR succeeded in winning four presidential elections and after his tenure the constitution was changed to prevent any future president from serving more than two terms. Obama's had his turn, time to bow out and retire to the golf course. How can Trump succeed at the ballot without appealing to a majority of like-minded voters? (A Majority? Well if YOU can't be bothered to vote …). "What we have here is a failure to communicate" as the bemused local sheriff said in one of the Bond films with Roger 'eyebrows' Moore. Alternatively what we have here is a failure to recognise an alternative, a counter culture, a different perspective, a herd with a different set of needs, let me call it a pro forma. A standard methodology based in what exactly? Obama has failed, his legacy is failure, his ideas, his ideals, his ambitions are all at risk of being dismantled and replaced by the new broom. But the broom didn't sweep them away, the voters that failed to engage in them did. Don't shoot the messenger Barack, it's your fault, you had 8 years after all and you failed, get over it.

Have I mentioned Brexit lately? A subject so close to your heart Neville, I know. They had 40 years to bind and blind us to the virtues of their project. After 40 years that's not only defective cement, that's defective sand, aggregate, reinforcement, engineering and architectural design failure. In fact, a monumental fuck up. Yet still our Great Brain's strive to frustrate the will of the herd.

Zac Goldsmith has lost his Richmond Park seat to the Liberal Democrats. You will remember that he resigned in protest at the government preference for Heathrow's third runway. Now we have the future mapped out for us N, the Lib Dems will ride in, lance in hand on a white horse, and save us from Brexit. So says Tim Farron, leader of the party. Seems we are back to a two party political scenario again. Let's ignore the maths and the geographical variations between London and the Shires. Will anybody else bother to ask where the other 315 other Lib Dem MP's needed for a majority are? Why does the word puerile spring to mind?

Meanwhile, shock horror, El Trumpo has spoken directly with the president of Taiwan-breaking with US policy set in 1979 when formal relations were cut. China sees Taiwan as a breakaway province, and has threatened to take the island by force if necessary. It's beginning to look as though I made the right decision in sending my kids off the Southern Africa rather than PNG. Looks like he won't be content with only one superpower at a time.

R
XXX

Sent from my iPad

Re: Day 49 December 3rd Saturday

Dearest N

I have looked out some of my old biology school textbooks and have calculated the airflow requirements for the bunkers and determined that passive ventilation isn't enough. I've ordered some fans and ducting for car dashboards that will fit inside the vent pipes. They run on a 12v DC current so the solar battery chargers we have ordered for the mobile phone/Geiger counter device can double up. It's a fine balance we need to strike between having enough air and allowing too much radioactive dust in. Hopefully the filters will do their work. I think it might be an idea to reverse the flow every now and again so as to blow any dust off of the filters. We should take the car batteries off of our cars and run them at night with recharging during the day. I just hope there's enough sunlight to make them work what with all the dust in the atmosphere. It makes me think about all the Global Warming bollocks and CO2. I'm struggling to do the calculation for 2/3 people in a controlled environment so how can you do it for the planet with so many variables? Except of course, you can't do it for the planet simply because there are too many variables. Hasn't stopped them trying though, has it? If you think about how our Great Brain *Mustelids* weasel their way out of every problem and issue without providing a solution you realise that the whole road map to a 'save the world resolution' was just a PR exercise designed to cement their own positions at the top table while they preside over plausible deniability. "You can't blame us, we followed the best scientific advice available". "Our nation performed, it's all the rest". "Sorry, I've retired now, have you read my memoirs, heard one of my speaking engagements"? And we let them. Anything you want to impose, low energy light bulbs, insulated houses and fridges, better MPG, wind turbines, solar farms, carbon taxes, you name it, we'll wear it. It all makes sense, it's all plausible, except, and this is the one thing that would actually make a difference, as long as we don't have to modify our behaviour. One three word mantra, "Business as Usual". "Bollocks as Usual" more like. Sorry N, am I overusing 'bollocks'? What are my alternatives? Bullshit, Katanga (as in don't step in it), Lies, Delusions, Excuses, Nonsense, Useless, whatever, they all represent 'Failure'. There was a joke about a politician touring Africa giving speeches to numerous local crowds who kept responding by chanting "Katanga". The politician felt reassured by this positive response until he visited a cattle farm and was walking across the bull pen when his guide said "Be careful, don't step in the Katanga". I must apologise to the residents of Lubumbashi, capital of the former province of Katanga in the Democratic Republic of the Congo between 1966 and 2015 prior to it being split into four smaller provinces. I think, on balance I will stick with 'Bollocks', but please remember to insert some venom into the pronunciation.

Is it too late to expect some leadership from our Great Brains? Can the world be saved from the ego of Man? Where is the mechanism, where is the control, where is the override switch that disables our genetic programming, the stop button, the hope for Planet Earth? Does anybody else recognise a tiny smidgeon of ego in El Trumpo or is it just me? But it was there in Clinton as well, in spades. In fact it's an essential requisite, a prequalification for the post of Great Brain. "You don't want to do it like that. You want to do it like this instead". Where is the answer? It doesn't exist, it has never existed, it will never exist, it is without the wit of Man. Your church N, teaches you the meaning of hope and then transports it to another plane, reachable only through death. Death is something we are experts at, we are the masters of the world and we know not what we do. We exert all of the control without a single grain of it, control, entering our consciousness.

Come the 21st of January what will mourn the end of the age of humans?

Day 71 confirmed our dilemma, Trumpton was the choice, Trump won Clinton didn't, we all lost. But Day 71 wasn't D Day minus 71, it was D Day minus 60,000 years of modern humans leading up to Day 71. Trump is a product of the American political system built over 230 years of independence, founded on 700 years of Magna Carta, resting on a couple of thousand years of Greek Democracy, underscored with 56,000 years of modern human nature. We are what we deserve to be, it's no one's fault, it's all our fault.

Getting tired now N.

Catch up tomorrow.

R
XXX

Sent from my iPad

Re: Day 48 December 4th Sunday

Dearest N

Is it time you went on a diet, old friend? Nothing personal, it's just that I can't balance my calculated calorific intake for you, Abigail and Edward with the available storage space. Unless I start going down the Kendal Mint Cake route I just can't accommodate all of your family's requirements in the space available. I can't reduce the water and the living area is already cramped with the double decker bed. I'm concerned about a lack of air circulation as well. We don't want any dead areas for obvious reasons. Sorry to say it but it's quite ironic really, if you weren't so big I'd have more space for your food. I need a real commitment from you, a solemn pledge to observe your calorific allowance without you pinching Abigail's or Edward's. That wouldn't be fair, taking more than your allowance would it? It makes me think about the wider world. If all the fat Americans only ate what they needed instead of what they do eat, would there be any need for starvation in the world? A rhetorical question really, because if the American's didn't eat it they wouldn't grow it would they?

Starvation on the face of it is caused by a shortage of food, whereas it's actually caused by a failure to distribute it fairly. But then how can you define fair? We don't produce food to feed people, we produce food to produce money and we produce money to excess to feed our egos. So we grub out that half mile of hedge, drain the lower field, poison competitors be it plant or beastie, in the pursuit of a better life. For many, life is measured by being alive at the end of the day with a full belly and warm with shelter. Whereas many of us just take it for granted that this will be. What matters, what really matters is the size of our TV screens, the horsepower under our boots, the size of our pensions, the model number of our telephones. Well not for much longer, matey. We are all about to get a lesson in life and many will fail to enrol. And one of the first lessons will be; money has no value. All the money in the world's banks will not bring anything back to life, put food on the plate (there will be no tables) or secure warmth or security. Value will be held in steel pots and pans, knives and cloth and indeed, if the clocks could be turned back, all the monetary value of Manhattan would be exchanged in return for food and shelter in the most unequal barter for centuries. What goes around, comes around. I could prove a point, if I felt the need, the soon to be most powerful man in the world is a billionaire. The previous losing candidate is also a billionaire. How they must identify with the poor, the working man, the single parent. ... And yet, these are some of the very people who have been recruited to secure the position of El Presidente. The very idea is bizarre. Ah, sorry N, which idea? The idea that money has a value? The idea that our lives have any value? The idea that El Trumpo gives a shit? The idea that the human race has any salient thought processes? Face it, we haven't got a fucking clue. Hopefully, old friend, we may find out but only because it will be too late.

In the meantime talk to your doctor about a suitable calorific intake please and let me know.

I stumbled across a pejorative term 'famous for being famous' used to describe a celebrity who has achieved fame for no apparent reason as opposed to celebrities who are celebrated for having actually done something. As ever this provoked a thought process in particular just what is it that qualifies as an achievement? It is estimated that the greatest proponent of the 'FFBF' brigade is Kim Kardashian with an estimated earnings last year of $50 million. In itself, earning $50 million a year for being famous is an achievement and tends to invalidate the earlier pejorative term. Who or what determines the respect due to the celebrity's and whether they are deserving of our approval or derision? Katie Price and Paris Hilton are other examples and I have to say I can't think of any others. What a sheltered life I live, N. But as luck would have it, I don't need a longer list. If my calculations are correct then being a successful sports star is sufficient to qualify as a real bona fide celebrity. Freddie Flintoff, David Beckham are two examples that spring to mind. Consequently they cast a shadow on the planet beyond their performances on the green stuff. There is a boxer out there, Tyson Fury who held a number of the World Heavyweight titles before relinquishing them. He made various comments about paedophiles, homosexuals and abortion and rounded off with anti-Jewish sentiments all of which brought much comment and indignation from the media and targeted group representatives. Tyson Fury is a boxer, or was, and was used to standing in a ring and receiving blows to the head. I'm not trying to apologise or justify his comments here, what I am trying to establish is how, standing in a boxing ring trading blows has any bearing on his views of society? If he was a professor of sociology or history or economics then I could understand the idea that his views had any relevance to the rest of society. By entering a boxing ring and becoming World Heavyweight Champion suddenly the media has appended celebrity status to him and has sought to publicise his views before subsequently attacking them. I realise that I have committed Hari Kari here N, because I have dared to write to you expressing my views without being either a professor or other learned person whose views might be worth considering. (Then again, you've got so far you might as well see where it ends). And then again, again, the university professors are all a product of the pro forma, blinded to it and immersed in it.

We'll ignore this particular faux pas and I'll continue with my argument. You wouldn't invite Tyson to appear on Question Time because he was a popular British boxing champion. Nor would you want to buy his clothes or smell like him or drive the same car as him and any other of the myriad of potential promotional activities he could engage in through his new found fame/infamy. Yet the world is full of celebrity endorsements whereby the singular ambition appears to me to be that by buying said celebrity endorsed product some of the fairy dust might just fall on you as well.

What value has celebrity got?

But, N, as ever, I'm not talking about celebrities, I am thinking beyond them. Having realised that the media for all its intent and portentousness is for entertainment purposes only then I have and you should be considering where celebrity starts and finishes. Celebrities seek out the public eye, the red carpet pimping, the sound bites, the long lens photo's snatched at the beach, the endorsements and the freebies forced upon them by promoters anxious to have their wares associated with their lifestyles. We hear tales of 'multiple tens of thousands dollar goodie bags' doled out to guests at the after Oscar night parties in Hollywood to bribe them into attendance. And the question you should be asking is what have they achieved to warrant this attention? Are they not all FFBF? I grew up with comics relating the stories of valour and bravery of our fighting men from the great armed conflicts, Douglas Bader, lost his lower legs but continued to fight to defend his home, VC after VC and how they fought for us. Real people and real heroes who slipped back to the obscurity of normal life without prostituting themselves to some advertisers needs.

Now for the leap across the chasm N, I've made it as narrow as possible. How do you differentiate between the celebrity pimping themselves on the catwalk vying for the public's attention from the politician pimping themselves on the lawns of the Palace of Westminster, the QT studio on tour, the interview rooms of Newsnight, the editorial columns of newspapers, the carefully created photo shoots on the industrial shop floor, adorned in safety hats, goggles and Hi-Viz jackets that have never seen a seconds work?

And then, get this, the media ask this question: "How has a man best known for a reality TV series, with no previous political experience, become President of the United States of America?

That's a real poser, that one N, I might need to think on that for a nanosecond or two, I'm getting old, you know.

It was Jeremy Corbyn's latest missives that set me to thinking N, he's effectively famous for being leader of the Labour Party, a party that is out of government and riven with ideological divisions and that quite literally leaves him as being 'Famous for being famous'.

Whatever next, David Beckham for Premier? (No, I think he's overqualified).

R
XXX

Sent from my IPad

Re: Day 47 December 5th Monday

Dearest N

I've given some more thought to money. Money is the source of all our misfortune. How can you barter the labour of man against the labour of ICBM scientists? That's a long while since I've heard or even used that term, Intercontinental Ballistic Missile. Not so long ago they were at the forefront of people's minds before the screen-wipe of Global Warming relegated them to a forgotten memory. We seem to only have the capacity to deal with one threat at a time, each new one erasing those that went before.

I could suggest that the one threat that has existed near permanently for our species has been other members of our species. It is they that threaten to occupy our territory, steal our breeding partners, steal our food and shelter. For we are the experts at adaptation and exploitation of resource and eventually it is human pressure that yields the ultimate obstacle, other people. If there is one thing our history teaches us, it is that all other obstacles are overcome and subjugated to our will. Dangerous animals, eliminate them, too much forest, clear it, pests eating our food, kill them, disease controlling our population, learn to overcome it. But all the while we strive to outcompete our fellow humans and it is this beyond anything else that will guarantee the end of the world. That is why Americans can and will be fat while others starve because they have no care beyond their own appetite satisfaction.

I see El Trumpo has softened his criminal pursuit of Clinton, well, abandoned it to be correct. Probably realised that his own behaviour may be subject to similar scrutiny in the future. What am I saying? There won't be any future. He'll certainly leave a monumental legacy, if only a flat dusty one.

It's strange, but I am actually looking forward to the end of the world. It will be a big adventure. And for a change, the supply chain will be shortened. What do I mean by that N, any ideas?

We work to survive, to pay our bills, to put food on the table, to pay our taxes and it is all remote and intangible. Not for much longer. And, no more taxes, yippee! We'll get to eat, shelter and survive based on our efforts and won't be supporting anyone else. To live or die by your own hand, terrifying or invigorating?

I wrote yesterday that "We are all about to get a lesson in life and many will fail to enrol." I realise that was a major error on my part because most will "Get a lesson in death". But that isn't correct either because 'lesson' can be defined as "a period of learning or teaching". Hardly applicable, can you imagine the university lecture theatre; "What is that blinding lig". Perhaps you can teach me something N, should I put a 'speech mark' at the end of an unfinished speech? Or how about the House of Great Brain's; "I move a motion to censu". Yes, I think that might just work, I can see our MP's moving a motion, fuck all else though. Because when it actually comes down to it, what do they do, what have they ever done? I hope a MP survives and we get to meet one, we could invite one to dinner, they'd enjoy that. We can pick a hilltop, something with a view, not a mirador, I have in mind more of a summit.

What lessons have we ever learnt N? How to destroy the world.

Just before, bastard timing as ever, El Trumpo became world destroyer elect, I had my attic offices painted. And to think I was worried about how long the white gloss paint would stay white? I chanced upon my daughters school report for 2003/4 while at the High School. (Probably all the cannabis the teachers smoke?) I've only just opened it and my eyes settled on the page entitled **Citizenship,** which was a compulsory part of the curriculum in those days. It introduced students to a range of important issues. It's that important that they got to keep track of their citizenship education in their own personal folder.

Citizens: becoming thereof.

1. Legal, human rights, responsibilities, an introduction to the criminal justice system and how they impact on young people.
2. The diversity of religious, ethnic, regional and national identities within the UK. How this calls for mutual respect and understanding.
3. The public services offered by local and central government, who pays for it and how to contribute.
4. The lies to children guide to parliamentary and other government forms.
5. A guide to voting and its importance.
6. The work of voluntary groups locally and nationally in the community.
7. Fair conflict resolution.
8. Media and the significance that they hold over society.
9. The global community with all its implications and sub-divisions into the E U, Commonwealth and the UN.

N, I am stunned, speechless.

The root of the pro forma. Learn to comply, to observe, to become a model citizen, to surrender to the herd, to enrol in the human bait ball. Fail to question, to consider and above all fail to THINK, for we have done the thinking for you. Welcome to the matrix, you will not feel a thing while we upload the program. Just as importantly, you will not feel a thing afterwards either.

1. Now I know why we have no prisons and have no need for locks.
2. Now I know why the Scots want independence and 'race-hate' has disappeared from our streets.
3. Corrupt. The alimentary canal between the Great Brain's and the bait ball.
4. Isn't it time for dinner yet?

5. Where do they get these stupid, ignorant, unwashed voters from that do not and cannot understand the most basic of ideas and keep voting incorrectly?
6. Oh God.
7. At last, the end of conflict.
8. Oh, for fuck's sake.
9. The world is safe in our stewardship, we can relax N, it was all a bad dream.

I didn't stay speechless for long, sorry.

I cannot express how utterly bereft I am. Karl Marx had it, he wrote in 1843;

"To call on them to give up their illusions of their condition is to call on them to give up a condition that requires illusions".

Trump, bring it on.

Please.

But not before the 20th, still got some planning to do.

R
XXX

Sent from my iPad

Re: Day 46 December 6th Tuesday

Dearest N

Sorry about yesterday's wobbler, I care, that is my problem, underneath this figure of Adonis I have a heart and a brain. I think about what could be, if only. I think about all the bullshit initiatives that serve only one function, to provide for the initiators. None of them fail in their aspirations, it's just that their aspirations are not contained within the mission statement, they are contained in their pay packets, their egos, their awards, their national recognitions and if they are really, really lucky, their blue plaques. The entire process is stultifying to the extreme. And we pander to it and accept it and the same old, same old grinds on to its inevitable conclusion.

Just a short note today N. I still can't quite get my head around yesterday's discovery. We have a chance, a chance to create our own vision of life on Earth free of all the abject bollocks. How long will it be before something else creeps over the horizon?

Corbyn has declared that he will impose conditions on Britain's exit from Europe and will demand continued access to the single market. WTF? All political mandates must be secondary to the referendum vote. Our political master wannabes search and leave no rock unturned in the pursuit of any angle of weaselling.

"'Labour will seek to amend any bill on the Article 50 process to withdraw from the EU" J Corbyn has said. The Labour leader commented to say that this was to ensure Britain maintained access to Europe's markets, workers' rights and environmental protection measures. But his party would respect the EU referendum result". It strikes me as wonderful how the Great Brains, although not so Great in this case, can cherry pick the will of the people and the will of the EU. If we ever leave the EU I may still go on holiday there and I plan to use my European road atlas so that I can continue to find my way around. I do not need to be in Europe to consult the atlas or indeed to plan my route. Adherence to the EU workers' rights need no relation to the Article 50 resolution unless of course the plan is to prevent and frustrate Article 50 from being triggered. And of course all the waffle emanating from Europe is that we cannot cherry pick the good and leave the bad. Figures out this week suggest that a third of a million people entered Britain in the year to June. They need 100,000 houses eventually although they are content to live in 50,000 to begin with. If my reckoning is correct that means that we have been ripping up our green and pleasant land that has been protected by the planners for decades so that we can surrender it on a whim to foreign invasion. You only have to take a drive in the area to pass a multiplicity of building sites under relatively recent construction. My eldest, as you know, is a Chartered Landscape Architect and he has seen the relaxing of the rules as government has declared open season on residential land use. I can't understand why we have been protecting it for so long from the British so that we can gift it to others. We still get Great Brains making the case for immigration on the basis of a labour shortage, this in spite of the fact that we have 1.5 million unemployed. If our unemployed are unfit or unable or unwilling to work why do we call them unemployed and not pets that we house, care and nurture on a non-profit making whim?

I have just realised something about the papers N, there are some items packed full of truths that you can rely on into the future. I refer of course to what Jan refers to as the Horriblescopes. The authors are so adept at reading the signs and predicting the future that it leaves me with a few questions;

1) Who trains who, are the journo's trained by the 'scopers or are the scopers fully trained journo's?

2) How does one get employed by the media? What qualifications are required to justify employment in such an important section of the paper?

3) Has anyone ever bothered to compare future predictions with actual predictions? Not as complex as I make out, most tell you what to do today, tomorrow, next week or next month. Say you were told to grasp a new employment possibility with both hands next week, what does it say you should do today when it is next week?

Now, no doubt you will be laughing and saying I'm taking these things too literally and that they are provided solely for entertainment. Well, there's the rub N, because that then becomes the definition for all the other content of the paper. You shouldn't take what the papers say too literally because they are only provided for entertainment purposes. So you can take your lead articles, editorials and investigative items and be entertained by them but whatever you do, do not believe them as they are for entertainment purposes only. The entire media industry then is simply a toy, a game provided for entertainment only.

I begin to see the light and understand the role of the media in society. What a shame I cannot travel back in time to my daughter's school report time and share the secret with the teachers. What annoys me is I knew it then, I just hadn't framed it into words. I wonder if this is what Pink Floyd meant when they sang about another brick in the wall?

R
XXX

Sent from my iPad

Re: Day 45 December 7th Wednesday

Dearest N

Thank you for your attempts to bring me round old friend, depression is not the way forward under the present circumstances. I'm feeling better actually, really looking forward to a fresh start, a new paradigm. Good news about your diet, I can really work with those figures. No cheating though. I know it's tempting to cheat yourself, not that cheating does anyone any good mind, but you'll be cheating the ones that you love. If I asked you a different question; do I leave Abigail or Edward outside? Point made, I will say no more on the subject. Is now a good time to tell you I can get a bloody good price on Kendall Mint Cake? Joking.

I've ordered some File Cup Spark Lighters and loads of spare flints for the gas bottles. One of the big gas bottles does all my hob cooking for around 18 months so the 16 bottles I have ordered could last us nearly 20 years. A bit longer than a box of matches and you have to worry about them getting damp. What was it the adverts used to say, something about "Now you're cooking with gas". These things only cost a couple of quid each but could be worth their weight in gold. Who would have thought it, our lives could depend on rubbing two sticks together. A bit nearer the date I think I will bury a selection of tools, saws, hammers, that type of thing. They should really come in handy. Oh, and a spade. I'd better not bury that though, could be self-defeating. See, I'm getting my spirit back.

I've been thinking some more about Trump. It's so unfair that billions must die for the vanity of one man. I've thought about the assassination route again, but I don't really just want to kill him. I want him to suffer first, non-lethal shots that miss his vital organs. Three shots to the head should be safe. But it doesn't matter. It makes no difference except in time and numbers. Billions must die for the ego of one man and the Earth with it versus the alternative path whereby the Earth must die for the egos of billions. Hmmm, what a choice. In the olden days, before we were born, entire wars could be resolved by the actions of two champions. Now it could break down to the actions of two egos. Except of course, no self-respecting champion would enter the rink of death without being. What? Why, self-respecting of course. My champion's better than your champion. Neither of the champions expected to die either, for each was better than the other. We have learnt so very, very little haven't we? We have adapted beyond our abilities. What was it they used to say at Christmas, "What do you buy the woman that has everything and doesn't know how to use it"? How about "What do you buy Man who has everything and doesn't know how to use it"? And it's not even Christmas. Sorry, N, I have cocked up again, because we do know how to use it, we just haven't learnt why we shouldn't. And we never will. Just suppose we unilaterally disarmed and dismantled all of our nuclear arsenal. History proves that this would be seen as weakness, a weakness that can be exploited and before you know it, we'd need nuclear weapons again, just for defence, you understand. We cannot uninvent that that we have invented. But that's not true either is it, because we can forget or we can fail to remember? We have forgotten how to live, to feel the wind in our faces, the soil beneath our feet, the purpose of life and have replaced it with our credit cards and air-conditioned cars and 50 year work ethic and the school farms that rear our young and prepare them for the life that will deny them of life. You and I differ N in our beliefs and tenets and I know you may be asking "What would Jesus do"? You might as well ask "What would David Beckham do"? I have an answer though N, it's "What will I do".

Trumpton is a symptom of our malaise, a product of our corrupt political systems that blinds and binds us to our pro forma's in equal measure. But I am wrong to single out politicians in isolation for they are simply a product of our corrupt society that has adapted way past the point to which it has evolved. We simply do not have the mechanism to exist in our billions, it is beyond our core, our code, our program, our DNA. We simply create crafted lies of command and control as we subjugate, politely, and impolitely our fellow man. We are all born to die and die we shall, how about living first? That's what excites me N, the chance to live, to start afresh without the corruption.

R
XXX

Sent from my iPad

Re: Day 44 December 8th Thursday

Dearest N

Now that we've resolved the space issue in your bunker I suppose it's only fair to ask if Abigail or Edward have any special requests. I know you haven't told them of the plan yet for fear of the neighbours finding out but you could turn it into a bit of a game. "If you were stuck on a tropical island without electricity what would you most want to have with you"? I think you get the idea. An ocean going boat, satellite telephone with battery backup or winning lottery ticket are not on the option list. It will be a long 40 days underground with little light and minimal space to move around. In fact too much moving around might compromise the oxygen supply. There's room for a Monopoly Board and nearly enough time to play one game. Actually, the tropical island game could prove very useful. If you opened it up to a debate it could provide a multiplicity of ideas and answers that get them and us in the right frame of mind. I am bound to have missed something and we won't be able to pop out and get one. If you play devil's advocate, (I know, you'd prefer to play God's advocate, you can still wear your knob-thatch though) it can educate them in the upcoming demands. On your desert island everything is limited, space, food, water, shelter and security from storms and even circling sharks. You will all have to live within your means and jealously guard the islands resources. You can't eat all the coconuts in one go or fell all the trees for firewood because there won't be anymore. What you plunder today is gone forever. You need to operate in a healthy way conducive to your own lives but also conducive to the health of the island, because if the island dies, so do you. At least on the island you have no worries about oxygen although I think our biggest problem chez bunker will be too much carbon dioxide. We really are stuck between a rock and a hard place in this respect. It's such a fine balance between allowing enough air in while keeping enough radiation out. Do you want to die today or die tomorrow is about the crux of it? At least El Presidente will resolve these questions for so many. No, that isn't true, because our species is already making those decisions all the time now, the only thing we are arguing about is scale. "Would you like to buy these cigarettes for the pleasure of now in exchange for ten years of your life"? Or how about "Would you like to buy this diseasel car for ease of transport in exchange for the premature deaths of others due to pollution"? These are all rhetorical questions because we already know the answers. Yes, yes and yes. I know I haven't asked a third question, but you're the one with the knob-thatch, you can ask your own. And if that doesn't crystallise your mind, nothing will. But that is the failure of our species, nothing ever penetrates the bait ball and nothing ever crystallises our minds, we are not an accident waiting to happen, we are the accident happening.

How did we ever arrive at this position? It was all done with the consent of the people, just like Trump was given the keys to the White House with the consent of the people. But we know not what it is we give consent to. There is no way of determining what we have actually consented to. So how have we consented to it? Yet it rolls on, relentless, apocalyptic, *Homo non-sapiens*, the greatest intellect that never existed, the most organised disorganised species to grace our planet.

Tuesday's Daily Mail led with the story floated by Mark Carney, Governor of the Bank of England no less who is predicting the demise of fully half of all the current jobs that are done in the UK. We'll have robots to thank for the change in the work ethic with "the middle classes particularly hard hit". Some professions could disappear entirely such as accountants that can all be replaced by computers. I have to say N, I am hard pressed to think of a more boring occupation that being a computer. I almost feel sorry for them, stuck in an office crunching numbers all day with just the occasional defragging and backing up to fire the old electrodes. Truly hell on Earth. Much better to be an accountant. Carney points to the historical delays between the advent of new practices (Agricultural machinery and farm labour for example) and the delay in new employment soaking up the slack. Forgive me, but have we not been suffering from such a delay as we exported all of our manufacturing jobs abroad in the name of Globalisation. While Carney is painting a picture, I think it is only a very small part. Fifty % unemployment equals 50% less tax which equates to 50% less schools, hospitals, pensions, transport investment, nuclear weapons and their delivery systems to name a very few. Nannies, hairdressers and carers are supposedly immune from the process and will retain their jobs, so that's all right then. But what will our new found unemployed find to do to distract themselves, look after their own kids perhaps or care for elderly relative's maybe? And as for the hairdressers, they've just lost half their customers who cannot afford to have their ears lowered. The rest of us on average are currently devoting 40% of our earnings in tax. But if only half the people are working we need to work for 80% of our time to pay tax and this doesn't include the increase in unemployment benefit that will be required. I think it perfectly reasonable to work one day a week for myself and the rest of my time for others, so no problems there. The real stupidity of the report is the simple fact that all UK businesses investing in the new robots are automatically reducing the number of customers they have to a quarter. "Brilliant, look how much more efficient we are, what a shame we've lost half our customers to unemployment and the other half are taxed out of the market". "Yes, but you see, if we are at the forefront of the process we can slash OUR labour costs and become more competitive, stealing a march on our opposition". You only have to consider the short term benefits of opening on Sundays when you were among the first with the long term disadvantages of longer opening hours to sell in 7 days what you used to sell in 6 before everybody else opened on Sundays. Neville, I seem to think I've written this before somewhere, something to do with short term gain while ignoring the long term consequences. It'll come to me no doubt. Amazing to think that the Luddites had a base in Hinckley.

But this borders on a much broader topic, namely the myth of employment and the blind pursuit of GDP. If our Great Brains doubled the tax per capita to compensate for the receipts shortfall then the system would break. I think the job interview discussion would go something along the lines of "Bollocks to that, I ain't working 32 hours a week for everybody else". Let me throw a suggestion into the pot, as an aside really, something to make you think. If medical doctors only earned half as much, we could employ twice as many. If nurses only earned half as much, we could employ twice as many. If teachers only earned half as much, we could employ twice as many. As an added bonus their jobs would also be reduced thereby reducing the stress and discomfort of their extreme workloads. If the jobs were easier they wouldn't demand such high wages. Twice as many professionals earning half as much equals no change. I will ignore the personal benefits of the extra time that they could spend away from their previously intense work stations. It's obvious to anyone with a brain cell that they'd all get terribly bored with nothing to do and would simply waste their lives. The only ones they will ever get so we don't want that to happen do we? But of course if they only earned half as much they wouldn't be able to afford to buy houses would they. But then, if nobody was buying any houses nobody would be selling them either so their values would drop. Of course it is perfectly reasonable to assume that house prices don't in fact go up in line with wage growth and there is no way on this Earth that house prices would go down if wages fell, no way on Earth. I think, just on the periphery of my mind that I can see a bubble bursting. What then is the justification for working a 40 hour week? An idea has just floated across my mind, we have forty year mortgages because twenty five just isn't enough. As a basic calculation we work a nice round 40 hours for 50 weeks or 2,000 hours a year ish. Your mortgage demands twenty five years of 2,000 hours of toil equivalent to 50,000 hours to satisfy your housing needs. I know, it's only a proportion of your hours but bear with me. A forty year mortgage equates to 80,000 years. Why not a fast track solution to this thorny issue? It's so simple really, I don't know why someone else hasn't thought of it. Why not work 64 hours for twenty five years instead?

The Babylonians appear to take the blame for the origin of the seven day week which has pretty much been adopted around the civilised world. Why not eight or six? How many days will occupy our week after the 20[Th] N? Will it have any relevance or significance beyond the smoke palls? I'm in danger of mentioning circadian rhythms N, the posh name that we all know as our body clock. The one that settles so comfortably into the 24 hour clock, or not, if you happen to be an insomniac. The one that freewheels easily in one direction but not the other. Ever wondered why it's so easy to go one way when the clocks change, but not the other? But which way, I'll let you figure it out. Just a thought N, make sure your watches and back up watches are all working in the bunker. If you rely on your sense of timing you might get a nasty surprise. Forty days underground might turn into 18 or 60, the only way you'll find out is to do it. And if you get it wrong and eat all your food in 18 days you'll either be forced to evacuate prematurely or discover that you are trapped underground unable to leave via the exit. The films all feature disabling electromagnetic pulses N, should we be worried? Some old fashioned wind up clocks might not go amiss.

So who do we blame for the 40 hour week? I realise that this will be met with some bewilderment in France N, "Who is this imbecile, what is he talking about", try it with a French accent N, for best effect. Variously described as the sick man of Europe for productivity and work ethic and yet they enjoy a higher life expectancy than we do. Sick man, indeed. Henry Ford appears to have his nose in the equation somewhere, or was it the labour unions? There is one word that settles the argument and the origin N and that word is arbitrary. A scratch in the sand, a pair of sticks hammered in the ground to mark the passage of time. An axis for the rotating Bait Ball. It isn't real. Once upon a time it was "Have I got enough food to eat today" O'clock?

Your mission N, best read while humming the 'Mission Impossible' theme tune, should you choose to accept it, is to stay underground for 40 days and nights without eating all the food, quite literally, on pain of death. This message will not self-destruct in 30 seconds and will be repeated as I bolt you underground on the 20th. I might even slip a copy into your Monopoly set for Abigail to find, or somewhere else, time will tell.

Just when I thought I would never laugh again N, something comes along, a gift, out of the blue to put a smile back on my face. It was close, the list had got some real contenders on it and yet the judges saw the light. Am I referring to the weasels debating the legal formalities for Brexit? All eleven Supreme Court judges in one room, the highest counsels in the land delivering their stern assessments and legal arguments, four days of sitting. I have to say I am amazed, shocked even, that such a gathering of immense intellect in such a confined space has not produced a disturbance, a ripple if you will, something akin to a chain reaction, in the reality of time and space. All eleven, all eleven, my god, can we afford the lunch costs? What nearly broke a rib or two was the announcement that one Donald J Trump has been selected as Person of the Year by Time Magazine. Not only, but also, he's knocked Clinton and Putin into the also rans. Not content to be a billionaire, not content to be a Reality TV star, not content to be President Elect of the United States of America, he's only gone and become Person of the Year. I have it now N, the second coming. All those waiting in vain for Christ to be reborn have missed his birth on the 14th of June 1946 and have allowed him to develop unhindered and slowly (Trump's a slow developer) until he burst onto the world scene on November the eighth, the New Messiah. Hallelujah.

And then I saw this Neville:

Pope Francis has issued a statement to the media decrying 'media disinformation' and has called it as of being "probably the greatest damage that the media can do". This is to be taken in context with the "fake news" crisis across the online media surfacing after the US elections. Search engines and social media platforms are failing to control the spread of fabricated stories. Apparently the pope himself has been accused of 'endorsing' Trump.

Neville, I have torn some intercostal muscles, genuinely, they are torn. My GP says that it's the worst she's ever seem without an underlying injury. I have to rest for two weeks. Timing is so unfortunate and I will have to load up with painkillers and woman up to it. It was late, nearly midnight and just before going to bed I dipped a toe into the BBC Teletext pages when I spotted this. How I laughed, tears streaming down my face, my jaw aching and then I got this searing pain in my chest. I genuinely thought I had broken ribs. I was up most of the night and managed to get in the doctors first thing.

Where do I begin?

A story about media disinformation appearing in the media. Is it true or made up?

A story about media disinformation appearing in the media which is full of disinformation.

A story about disinformation in the media when we know that it's real because it's in the media. If it wasn't real it wouldn't be in the media would it? And the only way we can disavow the media consumers of their disinformation is to feature it in the media.

A story in the media about disinformation from the most trustworthy source on the planet, the pope.

Forgive me Neville for reminding you that I don't believe in fairies, however much I try I just cannot see my way to turn my brain off.

By my definition N, the most trustworthy source on the planet, the pope, is the greatest source of disinformation on the same planet and currently resides at the head of a lineage of thousands of years of similar delusional disinformation. This isn't pot calling the kettle black time, this is way, way beyond that. This is worse than Tony Bliar complaining that he's been misrepresented in the media when he employed a whole team to misrepresent to the media. The media do not know what the truth is. There is no truth so how can you misrepresent it? "Disinformation", doesn't he mean lie?

We have a hard wired convention that dictates that there are official truths with no foundation in fact. So it is that we accept that tigers are being saved from extinction, all the efforts to halt global warming will succeed, all the treaty signatories will abide by their commitments and Santa will deliver necessities to half the world's kids. Charities serve their recipients, all employees work constantly and conscientiously for the task in hand and not their own reward and every effort is made to reduce waste. Oh, and there's no such thing as a jobsworth and hanging peanuts up in your back garden helps birds and the police will protect us from crime and all the criminals stay locked up.

Of course the media cannot challenge the veracity of the pope, it is taboo for exposing such doubt will alienate a proportion of your followers/readers. Then again the pope has exactly the same problem, for if a section of his followers believe that he supports Trump, then he risks alienating them as well. What a choice, select the leader of a bunch of people who believe any old lie you issue or believe Trump. I nearly said, it beggars belief. What I should have said is 'it exhausts the means of' because the earlier statement is what the pope does, he exhausts the means of belief, belief being very much his orbit. Whatever next; *Santa has issued a statement attacking his detractors and accusing them of undermining his position. Santa has warned that in this heretical climate it is becoming very difficult to recruit and keep Elves and that Christmas may be compromised unless those sections of the media withdraw their accusations. BBC Teletext November 31ˢᵗ.*

It's a good job I spotted it when I did N, all reference to the pope had gone by 9.00 the next morning. Had the day shift turned up to see which keys the drunk office cat had randomly trodden on? It strikes me that they ought to give the cat a proper job, something it can really get its teeth into, highway engineer perhaps?

R
XXX

Sent from my iPad

Re: Day 43 December 9th Friday

Dearest N.

I still have two small treatment plants for the two bungalow conversions which have never been used, they have only ever been filled with water during the construction phase. They are way too small to accommodate anyone but I am thinking of pumping them both out and using them as storage bunkers. We can get hold of some of those vacuum seal plastic bags advertised on the Sky channels before the world wakes up to store clothes in. Who would have thought that a TV advert would ever come in useful? You put your clothes in, hook up your vacuum cleaner hose and suck. It compresses them down to minimal space and keeps them dry and clean until opened. Because they are not in use I can pump these out, wash them down and set them up way before the 20th. We could fill one with clothes and bedding and the other with food for a strategic longer term store. Actually, for safeties sake we should go 50:50 to spread the risk, but as they are side by side if one goes the other is likely to follow. This might present a problem for you if you start spiriting Abigail's underwear away again, I don't really think she accepted the alibi I provided for you last time. On balance it's probably safer if you just bought new and then she won't find out and the same goes for Edward and for that matter your own clothes. If you order over the Internet you could collect from one of the local 'pickup' points and they need never know. Play your cards right and you can get it all on credit so no money worries there. Don't forget to make allowances for your newer sylphlike figure. Don't forget shoes and boots, real heavy-duty wouldn't go amiss.

I see our Chancellor has volunteered another few billion pounds for science and innovation. Just what we need to accelerate the rate at which we destroy the world. I call science, education and technology 'force multipliers'. Such a quaint term coined by our military which basically breaks down to "How can we get our one soldier to kill more than one of theirs? Strange how they always dress it up as 'progress' and as of being of benefit to mankind and the world. It seems that the more we learn about our world the faster we increase our efforts to destroy it. I have a suspicion that these skills will take a back seat after the 20th and we'll have to rely on our wits instead. Given what we know do you think I can ask for a refund on my taxes? All these announced road bottleneck improvements are going to be redundant in such a short time, still if nothing else it proves our governments sincerity in reducing CO_2, NOX and noise pollution by discouraging the use of cars. Did Trump make any pledges about reducing CO_2 production, I can't remember? What is it they say "Out of the mouths of babes"? It should be rewritten to "Out of the mouths of ego maniacs". How do you separate the obvious wisdom emanating from Trump from the obvious wisdom emanating from Clinton? How does the electorate differentiate between the diametrically opposed truths? I don't think "You can fool most of the people some of the time" provides an answer either. There has to be a flaw, a failure in the cognitive process, a blindness to reason almost. Do we have a stupid gene? A stupid gene could explain the bait ball, but, the same stupid gene must have provided an evolutionary advantage otherwise it would have long since been bred out of the species. Is it a new mutation that has yet to meet its nadir and therefore cruises along within our DNA awaiting its 'fitness' test? I think its fitness test is nigh, well, 42 days nigh.

We went to Compton Verney museum and art gallery this afternoon for a flying visit. It's the last week before the winter shut down and our daughter wanted us to visit before she finishes. They have an exhibition of Picasso sketches and other artworks which I found quite informative. There was one particular piece which struck a chord and introduced a level of understanding to my otherwise impervious mind. A picture of a woman's head but produced in such a way that the profile and portrait were positioned around the vertical axis of the nose ish. I got it, I really got it. Now I just have to work out the later women with three tits and I might begin to get a fuller understanding and appreciation. Ours will be a different world after we emerge N, hopefully no three titted women due to nuclear radiation. Although, don't ask me where I read it, but about 40 years ago, I learnt that one in eighteen men had a vestige of a third nipple. Was it Scaramanga that had a third nipple in 'The Man with the Golden Gun'? Good job it was a work of fiction N, Bond might have saved the world from the wrong megalomaniac. Jan told me years ago that one of her high school friends had to have her third nipple treated to stop it growing. I don't know why I'm worried about extra boobs, our lives have been blighted for long enough by complete tits. Although, wouldn't it be funny if our lives were saved by people supplying offerings to our temples of Parus.

Actually, at the risk of digressing, I went to Compton in the summer and a new addition to the folk art exhibit was pointed out to me. It was a wooden T in a frame designed to spin on its vertical axis. You wrapped a string around it and gave it a pull to start it spinning. The top of the T was a short length of 2 inch square timber set at 45 degrees as if to shed water. Glued onto these angled pieces were lots of small mirrored glass squares. All they could suggest was that it was thought to be a lark decoy but nobody knew how. While holidaying in the Algarve about 30 years ago I was out wandering around an old dune system, camera in hand looking for butterflies, lizards and flowers when my eye was taken by a glistening reflection on the ground. On closer inspection I had discovered a thin spring loaded wire trap that was baited with a flying ant impaled on a spike. The ant was still alive and wriggled its wings trying to escape and the movement produced the glistening image that had caught my eye. Soon after the 'great white hunter' appeared with a number of dead songbirds slung around his waist, proof positive of the effectiveness of his trapping methods. On the one hand if we get bored with squirrel and rabbit we could turn our hand to spuggies. I explained to my daughter how the folk art decoy would work, the spinning mirrors would replicate the effect of breeding ants emerging from the colony and would bring small birds, larks would have been a generic, down within range of the hunters. Problem solved, except that she wouldn't accept my explanation on the grounds that it wasn't documented and wouldn't offer it to the museum staff by way of explanation either. Even though I had seen it with my own eyes. I will stock up with mouse and rat traps N, we may need to guard our food stores going into the future and the mouse traps can double up for spuggies. Compton has its own version of the truth, documented and with provenance from another authority. Yet the art exhibitions are full of art, art designed to stimulate the imagination and vibrate a few brain cells, to defy documentation and evoke emotion in the eye of the beholder. I smell a paradox.

What will pass for art after the 20th? Will we have the capacity for it or will we spend all of our time struggling to survive? Is art an expression of spare capacity, life beyond the act of simply living? Does art represent the human spirit or just the expression of extracurricular capacity? But art is present in all we do, the art of staying alive, the style we adopt beyond the basic function, is not the human spirit present in every endeavour? Folk art is so described because it was produced by and for the common man, no academy educations but a basic style embodied in the minds of men. But basic is the wrong term to use, for it's not basic but elaborate within the confines of ability and time spent away from earning a life. True art, the art beloved of museums and palace walls is extracurricular and crosses the boundary from need to indulgence. Folk art is the keeping of beasts of the field while 'true art' is the keeping of pets, provided for pleasure and not profit. How strange then that 'true art' commands the stratospheric wallets, to be bartered and invested in, in equal measure. Not just pets but of the rarest pedigree, the finest bloodlines, aloof and beyond the common man, the emperor's new wardrobe. A perversion of the original intent perhaps, where art has failed to stir the heart but stirs the consumer greed instead. The great irony will be the total eradication of monetary value from these treasures. Countless items secured in vaults screened from the vision of the common man will doubtless survive, secure behind high security doors and walls beyond the technological reach of the New Stone Age Man, to sit, without dust, lost to us all. As unreadable as a rope full of knots from some South American culture until they themselves revert to the dust from whence they came. But many are already lost, buried to appear sporadically in the auction catalogues before once more disappearing, a mere catalogue entry with price attached. The price becomes the prize, the corruption of the value to the human soul, the collection of price tickets rather than the goods themselves. How corrupt we are. But why single out art for its corrupt perversion, look around N and find it everywhere. Doctors striking to improve their pay packets while rationing care to patients, people will die because of it, is this why they swear the 'hypocritic' oath? Hospital Trust Chief Executives loading their remuneration packages while presiding over the lottery of life giving resource. Patients playing fast and free with life's little pleasures of smoking, drinking and eating to excess while demanding their share. My beloved highway engineers reaping the career long benefits of pointless initiative after pointless initiative while achieving SFA. Ambulance chasing lawyers desperately seeking to achieve the highest possible recompense for themselves over the needs of their victims. There is one ray of light though Neville, the Environment Agency, for without their foresight and aptitude we'd have nowhere to shelter from the imminent conflagration borne of these corruptions. Every one represents a cut N, in the death of a trillion cuts that our planet is enduring, each one drawing the life blood from our future, squandering our past and present, the chain reaction that destroys us. A chain reaction that we pursue with all the vigour and ingenuity our species can provide.

I think we can make room for some felt tip pens and paper in the bunkers N, it will give us something to do while waiting for the corruption to settle. Was it Turner whose sunsets were coloured by dust from some distant volcanic eruption? Ours will be coloured from the eruptions from a distant chain reaction of corruption, a meltdown that will make Chernobyl look like an indoor firework. An inevitable chain reaction, centuries in the making, for we have no off switch.

R
XXX

Sent from my iPad

Re: Day 42 December 10th Saturday

Dearest N

I am so sorry to hear of you getting 'burned' studying the ladies underwear section while at work. You should have been more careful, thirteen year old boss's daughters are particularly impressionable especially when it's "Take your son or daughter to work day". I don't think I can offer any form of alibi this time either, my friend. How embarrassing, but just remember that the smiles will soon be wiped from their faces. They won't be laughing when they've been vaporised. You've only got another 41 days of being a pervert to endure.

I have to say that I'm tempted to throw caution to the wind. All my life I've abided by all the rules, I don't speed, I don't even park on double yellows, I pay my taxes (well, mostly), I sent my kids to school, I have done everything expected of me and for what? To stand at the back of the queue for health care, to wait two years for a planning application to be processed, to pay the salaries and pensions of all the useless jobsworths. Life has never been fair has it, we always end up carrying the burden of idle gits and self-inflicted wastrels and for what? Don't get me wrong, the ill and less able need our help, it's the self-inflicted idlers that piss me off. It's been hard going through life with someone else's hand in your pocket.

Is that El Trumpo's allure do you think? Promise change to the disaffected, the shat on, the strugglers that suffer all the injustices as they've watched their coal mines shut down to save the planet or factories moved over the horizon to provide for others, strangers, that they do not care for. "We have to provide for generations unborn. They will not forgive us" doesn't really cut it when your own generation and your own new-born that you can't provide for suffer here and now. America for America was the rallying call, "Yes we can" was the reply before evaporating to "Well, we tried" eight years later. But America for Americans doesn't work does it, for they are still strangers to each other, be it black, Hispanic, Indian, Asian, Caucasian or simply from another street or town or state or church or age group or educational standard or 'brung up' or dragged up or polite or rude or clean or drunk or migrants, legal or not. Trump then is all things to all (26%) people whereas Clinton only managed it for some (27%). Stand in any old meadow and count the ant hills, each representing a nest, each fighting for territory and resource and the right to life and then look for the parliament, search for the leader, the common cause. They are all ants. They have no leader beyond their own queen. They squabble and fight to protect their own, they do not understand cooperation beyond their scent control. This is the model for *Homo sapiens*, not Congress or the Senate or El Presidente, they are aberrations, alien concepts shoehorned in to the mix in the belief that it works.

How can you fix such a system? Thereby lies the crux of the problem, what system? An immense pyramid of advantage elevating Trumpton to the apex (bet there's a dinner) borne on the backs of every subordinate who subordinate every subordinate until you reach the base and there is no one left to pass the problem onto. These are the true disaffected, the alimentary canal, the conduit for every subjugators shit, ably recruited to heave another level, another echelon of advantage takers. How dare he offer them hope? For the truth of the matter is, the only possible explanation is, his ego blinds him from the damage he does and he believes his own bullshit. What's that Sting song lyric, "I'm an egomaniac in New York"? But you can't blame Trump, it could just as easily have been Clinton and that's why I refer to Trumpton, to cover both bases. That is why the world will end on the 20th of January 2017 N, the journalists have got it right and we will be ready.

Well fancy this Neville, it seems that Trump is looking to appoint a third Goldman Sachs executive to his administration. This would be the same Goldman Sachs bank that he slagged off during campaigning while accusing Clinton of becoming the "bank's puppet" if she won.

Despite vilifying the Wall Street bank while campaigning, he is tipped to pick Steven Mnuchin - the incoming Treasury Secretary - and Steve Bannon - the new senior White House adviser is likely to be joined by Goldman president Gary Cohn to lead the White House National Economic Council.

Oh, Lordy, Lordy. Of course he didn't say that if he won he would be the bank's puppet as well, so no lies told there.

And then, get this, Russia 'intervened to promote Trump'. Both the Washington Post and the New York Times have run stories about Russia acting covertly to boost Trump's chances in the election. Trump's team dismissed these intelligence service led reports saying "These are the same people that said Saddam Hussein had weapons of mass destruction"

Firstly, Saddam Hussein did have weapons of mass destruction, his actions promoted and controlled the destruction of much of Iraq's infrastructure, the only thing he didn't have was his own finger on the trigger. He provoked others, George Bush Junior pressed the button and the mass destruction began under the chirpily entitled 'shock and awe' onslaught rained down from the skies. What Hussein possessed was weapons of mass delusion, ably supported and abetted by those that exploit weapons of mass delusion, those that also have control over real weapons of mass destruction.

Secondly, it would be a terrible thing if Russia was proved to have influenced the outcome of the American election. Interference by one sovereign state over the internal affairs of another sovereign state is unwarranted. It didn't stop Obama from dipping his oar into the Remains' camps water though, did it? What was he said, something along the lines of "Trade agreements and backs of queues", "Britain should remain in the EU", I seem to remember.

Thirdly, evidence once again of the rear-guard sniper activity of journalists, don't they know the people have spoken? The king is dead, long live the king.

Fourthly, although it doesn't matter, where would you like Trump to draw his team from, the local kindergarten?

Fifthly, thank you for that vote of confidence issued to all employees of the US security services.

Sixthly, can you believe it, Trump slagging off Goldman Sachs during the election campaign only for him to kiss and make up after the result was known. He's got no other form of doing this has he?

Seventhly, what do you expect, hand on heart, what did anyone really expect from Trumpton? Why wonder that half the American people couldn't be bothered to vote.

Eighthly, I better get this sorted out quick, I'm running out of numberly's, how do you change any of it? Whatever you attempt will simply be frustrated by the system of governance I will call the Bait Ball.

R
XXX

Sent from my iPad

Re: Day 41 December 11th Sunday

Dearest N

What, a full disciplinary just for looking at scantily clad models in a catalogue? Fucking jobsworths or what? Hang on though, think about it, it could work to our advantage. See if you can get suspended, a bit of garden leave wouldn't go amiss with all the work we need to do? And when all is said and done, who gives a shit about your employment record post apocalypse?

We have a problem N and I can't see a way round it yet. Jan doesn't know anything, she just thinks I'm building her new chicken sheds in the bottom garages and doesn't want to spoil my surprise for her birthday. Obviously Abigail and Edward are in the dark as well. How do we force Edward and Abigail underground while I bolt you in on top of them? I have the same problem with Jan. I can't get past the Rohypnol idea at the moment. Ketamine can also be used as a date rape drug and I think that's used as a horse sedative. In your CPS capacity you must have come across many purveyors of drugs. Failing that, your active membership of the Conservative Party must have put you in league with some sources. We won't have long to slip into the bunkers and can't allow any argument or dissent, I need to have you hidden from the rest of the neighbours promptly for fear of it turning nasty. Of course after the blasts it won't be an issue and they will both thank you for it. I simply cannot think of an alternative. "Hey, Jan, just pop into the sewage treatment plant while I screw the lid on from the inside" just isn't going to work. They don't even drink enough alcohol to incapacitate them. Why is it so complicated saving people's lives?

We could come clean and just tell them but we have no way of knowing how they will react. I bet Edward will want his girlfriend and she'll want her sister and they'll want their parents and Abigail will want hers and, and, and. We have to be brutal N, it really will be every ape for itself and the way I see it, if they haven't the foresight to see what's happening, it's not my problem. It can't be my problem because there just isn't a solution.

This has to be one pyramid where we are at the apex and everything else is subjugated to our whim.

We could try to reason with them, to explain, to find an alternative route to the apocalypse facing us but there simply is no answer. How can we motivate enough Americans to protest and demonstrate and demand real change from their political elite? Been there, done that, still got the Trumpton. Eighteen months of inane bullshit pledging bollocks they call the election process and look what it threw up, in the red corner, egomaniac number 1 and in the blue corner, egomaniac number 2. Oh, and for good measure, it's a round ring, there are no corners. By my reckoning 18 months is 550 days and we only have 40 left and no multimillion dollar budget or campaign team or credence with the American public. Face it we haven't got a prayer. I thought I'd throw prayer in just for you N. What I wanted to say was "We haven't got a magic wand". There simply is no mechanism in existence to change the status quo, where's Canute when you need him? "Yes but you see, the system we have has evolved and grown to its present structure over centuries of refinement by trial and error to ensure the smooth transition of power between the various elites that understand and respect the values of the various elites". "Well of course we listen to the demands and needs of the little people, we are a democracy after all and, just occasionally we have NASA train its least powerful orbiting telescope onto the earth's surface so that we may observe the needs of the people".

How can you convince the American electorate to ditch the new incumbent waiting for his term to start when 26% voted for him and 27% voted against? A quarter of all voters felt that egomaniac number 1 was suitable for the job while another quarter felt that egomaniac number 2 was suitable. Half of the American voters voted for an egomaniac while the other half couldn't be bothered to contribute.

While Trumpton promises to destroy the world we hear about the checks and balances that buffer the president's actions. Sorry N, I've never really been sure, is it checks or cheques? And for that matter, is it bank balances?

Ok, I understand, you think I'm going overboard.

The UN will save us, the International Community will charge in on a white horse and resolve the situation for us. Mention this in Aleppo and realise that in spite of everything they have endured they can still raise a laugh, in your face. Mention this to an elephant and advise that the International Community has resolved to ensure their continued survival and realise that, in spite of their size, your comment will fall on deaf ears. Mention this to Fijian's and advise that the International Community has taken steps to ensure the continuation of their island home and realise that they haven't cancelled their swimming lessons. How many years has the Syrian civil war raged, have elephants been poached inexorably toward extinction, has the solution to Global Warming been appended to the 'Out' tray?

But we don't even need to travel overseas N, we have our own home grown talents to contend with. Schools that educate our children in the matrix, for longer and longer, with higher and higher exam grades and lower and lower skill bases. A Health Service where health and service are an accidental by-product of the employment factory. Even Highway Engineers that have launched 22 initiatives in 40 years to control our speed in residential areas where each new effort testifies to the failure of the previous one(s). Still they command my taxes, my sweat, my life and for what, so that they can earn a living off my back. There is always a way N, I understand that, it's just that the way always leads to more of the same, immersion in the Bait Ball and the continued destruction of the planet. Just to remind you, lest you forget, it's the only one we have.

But in 40 days the tense will change to had and then the new challenge begins if we are resolute in our aims. Our continued survival will form the merest pinprick on this earth and that is how it should be.

R
XXX

Sent from my iPad

Re: Day 40 December 12th Monday

Dearest N.

Oh N. Why didn't you tell me Abigail was claustrophobic before? I begin to understand her hysterical giggling when I suggested she go into the Pop 40 to unblock it. We really must pursue the Rohypnol route. When's your next Local Conservative Party meeting? If you struggle there then one of us will have to get close to some of the local Labour MP's although I think Keith Vaz might be off limits, once bitten and all that. (It was in the papers so it must be true). Actually, there's an idea, we could pose as rent men and expect to be offered drugs. Or we could trawl the web for rent boys and see what they can supply. We need advice on dosage and timing as well. We can't carry them down to the Pop 40 from your house, we just need them compliant but still active. You'll definitely need that Monopoly Board to keep her subdued when she's fully aware.

Actually, on balance I think it would be better if you posed as the rent man, you'd be much more plausible than me old friend. Nothing personal, but I think there's much more chance of mind altering drugs being needed if you were there.

I never realised just how much of a good friend you'd turn out to be N. Strange isn't it, you were always the teacher's pet at school and then, apart from that one school reunion in '91 no contact until you moved in to our little community in '98. What a surprise we both had when you came to introduce yourself. BFF's.

I see Trump's calling for unity "One nation together". Jeez, is there no start to the man's talent. You spend 18 months creating a seismic divide in the people and then you ask for unity, WTF? "Hello, my name is Donald, I just thought I'd pop round to admire your garden. The neighbour on the other side told me how much work you put in to it. You don't mind me parking my tank on your lawn do you"?

I always used to refer to our little community as Battesby Parva (Independent Nation State) stuck out as we are from the main village. We really will be able to make a Unilateral Declaration of Independence, but, here's the thing, there'll be nobody left to make the declaration to. Takes all the fun out of it doesn't it. We could erect a sign, 'Population 5'. Then again, it really would be unilateral.

Isn't it amazing how need drives invention? Every problem that hove's into sight can be sorted in a direct lineal fashion. No need to go round the houses, through committees of supposed experts, putting to the vote and all the political shenanigans that poses as decision making in our world. I am tempted to ask how it is that we do so well but I already have the answer to that. We don't, do well, that is. Face it we are crap at it. Imagine our soon to be enforced scenario N. Trapped in our underground spaceship isolated from the greater world as self-contained as possible with only filtered air and solar power trickling through from outside. (And effluent trickling down the sewer pipe). We have to get it right or we die. We won't get any second chances. We can't nip out to the shops to restock or fetch something we've forgotten. I usually say "What" in reply to this statement "This is it" but that's usually in response to the old Coke advert bollocks. Well N, "This is it" and no turning back. But haven't we been here before? Actually we are there now we just choose to ignore it with all the defence strategy of ostriches and I'm not talking El Trumpo. I could list all the species driven to extinction by our hand and all the species threatened by our activity currently and add in all the habitats at risk of elimination and degradation and then ask "What second chance have they had or are having"? But I don't think my computer has got enough memory to list them. The world is crying out for a reset and I won't say a new beginning, just an end to the old start would do. But it's alright because we have the Great Brain's and the NGO's preserving our futures while simultaneously accelerating the process of destruction. They dig a hole in one resource to fill a hole in another. Eventually all we will be left with is holes and nothing else. At least Trump's activities will be honest without the bullshit. There will still be plenty of holes though, well, craters anyway.

It seems Clinton's feeling left out by the 'fake news epidemic' and has called for urgent action to stop the proliferation of untruths. Apparently they threaten America's democracy and can have 'real world' consequences.

I wonder, would she recognise the 'real world' if it bit her? Her principal fake news story seems to have been 'pizzagate'.

Well that's good then, at least I know I can trust what Trump says, he hasn't been implicated at all. What flavour pizza was it Neville, Katanga? And when she says 'past year' doesn't she mean past 18 months? But that excludes the career spans of all the Great Brains so that can't be right either.

R
XXX

Sent from my iPad

Re: Day 39 December 13th Tuesday

Dearest N.

Forty days underground is a very long time, I think we'll all be going stir crazy before the end. We can't exercise much for fear of burning up the oxygen. I think that we could best occupy ourselves with learning. We need to be able to recognise plants and some of their properties. I am already quite good at recognition, my hobby of photographing had to come in useful eventually but it's the 'lore' that we need. *Saponaria officinalis* for example is known as Soapwort and used to be used for cleaning clothes. I know of some growing in a roadside ditch near Cadeby on the road to Market Bosworth. That really is going to be the problem. There is so little variety in the local flora that we'll really struggle to find anything unusual. Modern farming practices leave so little at the fringes and even without the heavy hand of human intervention, nothing can recover from a base of zero. When out and about with my camera you can travel miles and see nothing of any interest. Then you drop on a nature reserve and the variety increases instantly. The nearest reserve I am aware of is Narborough Bog which is still seven miles away as the crow flies. It's within walking distance but that's all you can say about it. There's another one at Croft at about the same range. Even if we had all the old knowledge, we still have to find the plants. It shouldn't stop us trying though. We might even be able to source medicinal drugs so the effort has to be worthwhile. I think a trip to the local libraries might be on the cards. Funny isn't it, we've spent so long putting everything on Google and it's all going to disappear. We might have a problem, I don't know if you can remove reference books these days or not? At the very least we can scope out the titles and then Amazon them.

I think the agricultural fields will have an impact on plant life for a long time to come. They have such high fertility that without regular maintenance they will simply clog up with rank vegetation which will limit the variety of species still further. Don't forget that most of the commoner weeds are so called arable weeds and only germinate on freshly disturbed ground. If the warehouses at Magna Park survive we'll have no issues for our lifetimes but we must pass the knowledge on. Not exactly "The Book of Eli" is it, but I know which one conveys the advantage.

R
XXX

Sent from my iPad

Re: Day 38 December 14th Wednesday

Dearest N.

Everything alright at your end? You've been unusually quiet, you haven't responded to a single text. You probably know by now, but Abigail was on the 'phone late last night wondering where you were. I have to admit I was a bit 'rabbit in the headlight' with my responses not knowing if you needed an alibi or not. She just said that you'd popped out for a bit and would be back later and still hadn't returned at midnight. I think I calmed her down a bit with some reassurance but feigned ignorance and blamed it on having just been woken up. I said you'd probably had one drink too many and we all know how your mobile battery keeps draining unexpectedly and not to worry.

Anyway, I have some news on Ketamine. I spoke with Virginia at Ashby Saddlery and Livery and she can let us have some K. It's all highly irregular but she knows me from old and has even advised me on dosage levels for the kid's old pony. To think that Rupert used to ride her. He could probably pick her up and carry her now. She must be 31 years old and I just lied a bit about the need to calm her down when the farrier came. She's got a bit of arthritis in her joints and doesn't like her legs being lifted. I could lie for England. I've spent my life being honest and truthful and people trust me. Something useful at last for being the 'good guy'.

We've been Christmas shopping again. Feeling a bit more like it, I suppose. It always takes me two to three visits to get my head around the whole Christmas shopping business. "Have they got this, do they want that"? Is the constant refrain. My view is quite straightforward, if you don't know them well enough to know the answer, why are you buying for them anyway? That puts me firmly in a majority of one, so no change there then. I've never bought for my family since whenever. We decided as kids not to buy each other presents and the rule still holds, even birthdays. I tried to be a bit devious, steering Jan towards the 'practical' clothing range that I've ordered for her. "I'm not wearing that, what do you think I am, a farmer's wife"? How to break it to her gently that I've ordered ten of everything and it's sealed in the Pop 6? Sartorial elegance will be the least of hers or my worries. They won't last forever, even elastic perishes after a while simply with age. It can be completely unworn but still knackered. I've selected easy wash, non-iron and whenever possible gone with the ones with drawstrings. We shan't need to worry about low temperature eco-wash soon N either. We can't broach the subject with Abigail yet, but her knowledge as a textiles teacher may well come in handy. Then again I don't suppose she's had much experience of weaving crushed nettle stems together. I'll let you try the first pair of nettle fibre underpants N, it's important that you feel part of the programme. No, I insist.

The worst thing I hate about the whole shopping trip is walking through the perfume departments in the different stores. The assault on the senses is quite profound. I used to take a deep breath and try and walk through without breathing in the past. Getting too old for it now though. I think a nosegay or two might not go amiss after 40 days with little more than a spit wash and a daily baby wipe ration. If you'd rather N, we could use the alternative name for a nosegay, a tussie-mussie. Strange how a necessity becomes a luxury which then becomes a necessity after it's no longer a necessity. You're the one with the solicitor training N, I'll let you work that one out.

(Ok then, you needed perfume to disguise the smell of unwashed bodies, then with the advent of soap and bathrooms you no longer needed the disguise, then you needed the disguise presumably to persuade bees to try and pollinate with you and couldn't possibly live without it making it a necessity for everyday living even though it's been superseded by soap and water and is no longer a necessity. Do you think I could have been a solicitor N, have I got the sharpness of mind for it?)

Just suppose we emerge to a stable community of survivors N, will your previous experience of the law be a help or a hindrance do you think? I know that 'common law' is a term used in your trade but that's all we'll have, common law. And I don't mean the common law in the law books, I mean the common law of the common man based upon that rarest of commodities, common sense. Ultimately it could simply break down to

"I agree entirely with your argument, but I've got the shotgun, so go forth and multiply", such a crude system and so unfair. Ours is so much fairer now isn't it, how does it go? "I've got more money than you, I can employ better lawyers than you and I'll continue to appeal long after you've gone bankrupt and are desperate to see an end to it". I think you'd better double the order for shotgun cartridges. I realise that the CPS has no financial constraints in this regard and occasionally come across prosecution cases for stealing a bag of crisps for example. Now, crisps aren't to be sniffed at, my local cafe charges £28,000/T for them and the salt would sting your nose. No doubt your office sits around debating 'what's in the public interest' or pushes for 'value for money' and other trite bollocks while paying out tens of thousands in lawyer's fees. I do agree wholeheartedly that it is in the public interest to pay lawyers exorbitant fees for what is essentially clerical work digging up case precedent from the times of King Alfred. Without these fees, the lawyers would be set free on the public at large: "I'm sure I can get £15k in fees for your £300 claim for a chipped fingernail" or variations on that theme. And if he really was that Great, why is the most common reference to him now attached to a fungus that attacks and kills ash trees while leaving small black bracket fungal bodies under the snappily entitled reference to King Alfred's cakes?

Don't get me wrong N, without you locking all the criminals up, we'd have to provide alarms and cameras and private security patrols just so we could sleep soundly behind our 5 lever insurance grade locks but only after shelling out for private insurance as well. I must remember to read my last council tax bill to see where all the money is allocated. I'm sure I missed the bit about police budgets.

R
XXX

Sent from my iPad

Re: Day 37 December 15th Thursday

Dearest N

I've sent this one through to your work email. Abigail was most upset, distraught even when I spoke to her earlier. She said you'd come home at 11.00 AM without a word of explanation in a very dishevelled state and gone straight to bed for six hours straight. She said that she couldn't get a word of sense out of you and decided you were drunk and left you to it. Even now you can't offer a word of explanation. Angry as she was, she still loves you, she said your haemorrhoids were really playing up. I think you need to tread carefully with Abigail for a bit, she'll only put up with so much.

The good thing with all of your little indiscretions is that they'll all fade into ancient history after the 20th. It's almost enough to make me take up shoplifting as a hobby, you know, just for the thrill of it. Nicking could help with my credit situation as well. How long does it take for a shoplifter to come to trial? A criminal records not going to mean much soon, is it? If I'm not dead, I'm sure I could live with that. Teehee. Thinking back, everything else begins to fade into irrelevance, I got 9 O levels and 4 A levels, fat lot there's going to do me now. I even passed some workplace health and safety modules way back when. I suppose I should be grateful for my education, they certainly taught me all I need to know to function in a post-nuclear world. It's just a shame they didn't manage it for the pre-nuclear one as well. Ah well, me didner ought too say to much did I, cos of Abigail being a teacher n all.

I suppose I can understand you getting drunk, we have lots to worry about and a little bit of me time never hurts, does it? I don't suppose you'll have too much chance later either.

I watched the last few minutes of BBC 2's Newsnight yesterday evening. Don't ask me why, I suppose I was bored. It featured an American and Brit arguing the meaning of Brexit and Trump. We had the usual leftie British view about the lurch to nationalism and by default fascism. The question raised by the programme was "Are we seeing a return to the 1930's" and by implication jackboots marching throughout Europe? The American's view was that the Trump vote was simply a reaction to the loss of American jobs as a result of globalisation and the hope of elements of protectionism to both stem the haemorrhaging of jobs abroad and the return of them to American shores. Hallelujah, I thought, at last a reasoned response to the question, as reasoned as the Leftist's remarks were predictable. Did you like the biblical term there N, there's no hope for me yet?

I slept on it, and then I thought about it, and then I thought about it some more and then I thought that the American's view was precisely that which is expected if you follow the 'party line'. You must forgive me N, it was late and I missed the two combatant's names but as ever they will represent some clever bods from opposing ends of the spectrum selected precisely because they are at opposite ends of the spectrum. That is not to say that the spectrum is a straight line, more a series of radial lines emanating from a central zone. That way you never run out of opposing views and you never need to realise an answer either. They will have to remain anonymous views because I don't care enough to watch it again on line. Who they were doesn't matter, they were both right and both wrong, the beauty of debate. And an illustration of its utter pointlessness.

Trump's party line is to achieve his election as president. He is president elect, party line achieved. Job done, herd recruited, herd now obsolete. Now Trump can enact his real ambitions having been democratically elected to his post. In the meantime, the election losers are now embarked on a recruitment drive to overturn the election result in four years' time. Perhaps Trump will now build his wall, impose his import duties, lock up all Muslims and ban their entry into America. Perhaps he won't, he'll simply suck up to his bosom pals and line his pockets. Perhaps he'll pick a fight with China and go to war. Perhaps he'll arrange for an arson attack on Capitol Hill and have some hapless Muslim confess to his crimes before dying in police custody. Perhaps he'll grant himself a state of emergency and override the normal rules of governance while simultaneously eradicating anyone foolish enough to oppose him. Your guess is as good as mine. The reality on the ground will not be known until it is history and what is it they say about history? History is written by the victors. But Obama is no longer the victor, he has had his time and will now be judged by all that follows and all that went before. Trump's day will come, unless, just maybe, there will be no days to come and his legacy rests absolute, beyond debate, beyond compare. But travel back to the heady heights of 1940 when to be German was to be king of the castle, conqueror of mainland Europe west of Russia. Hitler's herd, even the one's trained in orienteering, was content and happy even though they had been steered to a destination not of their making. Will Trump's herd be content to see Mexico struggle, China's economic boom stall and American's back in employment doing decade old jobs after decade old absences? That's a difficult one N, I need to think a moment. Halcyon days, until the Katanga hits the fan and China's new found rich are exposed to the peasantry who turn on their masters, until the Mexican government fails, unable to collect the taxes and reward the people, to be side-lined by the drug cartels who see no curtailment of their budget streams.

Wow, America first.

Where shall we measure the effect N? Do we measure the impact on jobs and earnings enjoyed by an upturning American economy or do we measure the unemployment in Mexico? Do we measure the slowdown in the Chinese economy or the reduction of prices in exports dumped into Europe? That's the thing about globalisation, it's global. Well I never. Poke something with a sharp stick here and the effect might well be felt somewhere else. But where will that else be? Will it be in Africa seeing its export of raw materials dropping in value and quantity? Will it be in South Wales where the steel industry collapses unable to compete on the world stage? Will it be measured in the increasing number of deaths of would be illegal immigrants perishing in the desert borderlands or simply despatched by their couriers eager to increase profitability for less effort? Would a collapse of the Chinese state ensure a future for elephants left holding their investment in ivory? Is there a pattern emerging here Neville, can you see it? I will call it business, as usual and not business as usual. I hope you can see the distinction N, it's subtle, but the difference is there if you look. But while I call it subtle, it's also profound. It does occur to me that what I am describing is a larger scale version of our own more local

Eurocratic hegemony that seeks to provide all things for all people and fails miserably at every juncture. Tell me again three reasons why we should stay in the EU. But if my memory serves me correct, you couldn't do it, you could only give me reasons why we shouldn't leave and that is not the same.

But what do we mean by the term 'business'? Is it the trading of materials or services or the noun for working? Those learned dictionaries refer to profit and non-profit organisations that seek to provide to customers. Customers that can be described as money rich punters in search of an advantage or destitute strugglers in search of a gift but still an advantage. Charities can provide emergency medical care in Syria or beds for the homeless. Non-charities can sell you a car or a bed for the night or a house, the list is endless. Can we define business on a simpler basis, as the route by which we gain advantage from our fellow man? We don't even need names, Peter and Paul are obsolete, all we need is me and not me. I am a parent and so are you N, I am sure you have gone through the "I'd kill to protect them stage" as indeed have I. "Been there, done that and bought the tee-shirt" ought to get the police's attention, do you think? But if we look at the 'generic' parent what can we find, drug addicts, food addicts, speeding addicts, war mongers, terrorists, smokers and others who all have one thing in common, the selfish gene. The gene that allows them to indulge in their own need before all others that constructs a ring-fence around their sensibilities. "Please don't smoke Daddy" just doesn't cut it. But I'll let you into a secret N, we all have it, the selfish gene, it is our default setting and has been since before we climbed the trees let alone descended from them. Mine is manifest in my bunker.

R
XXX

Sent from my iPad

Re: Day 36 December 16ᵗʰ Friday

Dearest N

Oh, Neville, Neville, Neville. You were supposed to buy some date rape drug, not use it. Didn't you get my mail about the Ketamine? Talk about taking one for the team. Still can't sit down properly I hear. N, respect, my hero. What have you told Abigail, I must have had a spiked drink? You'd better get yourself checked out old friend, I don't think we'll have too much in the way of antibiotics going forward. They used to call it the GU clinic for Genito-Urinary but I think they've changed the name again. Probably worked out that the great unwashed had worked out it meant VD clinic and needed to spare people's blushes. You honestly can't remember anything? I don't know whether that's a blessing or not? You might have enjoyed it, we'll never know.

One thing I know for sure N, if it doesn't quite work out and we end up as the last two people on earth … it ain't gonna happen.

N, thank you from the heart of my bottom, sorry, bottom of my heart, I keep getting that wrong don't I. But seriously, you've taken on such a burden and I thank you sincerely. I take it you won't be going by bike to see your dad on Sunday? Ok, ok, I don't want to strain our friendship.

R
XXX

Sent from my iPad

Re: Day 35 December 17th Saturday

Dearest N

That's half of our time gone N and I think we've made real progress with the preparations. I've started on the pre assembly of the 'bunk beds', or should that be 'bunker beds'? I've made a 'mould' the same profile as the tanks using the construction details from the manufacturer and while the space is tight it will be liveable. I have got the door organised for the old brick water tank and have already pumped the water out and built some block piers for the sub floor. It's all a bit rough but it doesn't need to look pretty. Jan never goes down there so I haven't had to answer any questions. When I get the timber floor delivered to the back gate she'll just assume it's for the 'birthday surprise' chicken shed. I really am that predictable, teehee. Both of the two bungalow treatment tanks are dry, clean and sealed ready for using and I've already packed a lot of our clothes in one. I have the air filters made and have fitted them to a spare bit of pipe. That's the advantage of the sewage tanks, they all use standard pipe fittings from the builder's merchants. As soon as we get the door for the brick water tank we can start trawling the supermarkets and begin stocking up. I have all the quantities worked out ready, but any mistakes and we can always add more until everything's full. I have collected more vacuum shrink wraps from the Amazon collect point so we can now start ordering your three's clothes. Be a bit more discrete this time Neville please. I can collect in the mornings while Jan's at the gym and have them packed and stowed before she's home. That's the beauty of a twelve acre garden, plenty of space and excuse to be busy. It's a good job I sold up and took early retirement really, I'd never have had the time to go to work as well. It looks like it's going to be a busy retirement, no sitting by the fire with my slippers on. The thing is though N, I've never felt so alive. I feel as though my whole life has been leading up to this adventure. So many of the injustices inflicted upon this planet are about to be neutralised and all it will take is one last monumental injustice. The ultimate betrayal of the human species, the culmination of our adaptation to life outside the trees. What would you call it Neville, genocide? But we are all complicit, we all accepted the Great Brain's and joined the bait ball. We all abdicated our individual responsibility and sold ourselves and the Earth for pathetic trinkets, for our egos. I will call it suicide, Neville, for it is as self-inflicted as the drug addict overdosing, the speeding motorway driver hurtling through the fog, the smoker dying of lung cancer. We have engineered our demise, just as we are engineering the demise of all around us and all without a first thought. And we have no off switch.

There's a cheery thought.

Night night N

R
XXX

Sent from my iPad

Re: **Day 34** December 18th Sunday

Dearest N

I am glad to hear that you can now sit without wincing. Abigail told me what a martyr you've been through it all, she really does love you, you know. I have been scanning through the online details of the 'Shooting Times and Country Magazine' and think we should try and get hold of some copies. While access to guns is highly restricted anyway we have the added worry of attracting attention from less well prepared survivors whenever we use your shotgun. I think the classified ads could yield snares and traps for catching rabbits and even squirrels. A builder friend of mine always used to say give me squirrel any day over any other game. On the one hand I think that rabbits and squirrels will quite rapidly lose their fear of humans this is likely to be counterbalanced by a need to hide from other predators. I know from my experiences in Spain that all the small game is always very timid. I never get to see squirrels over there like we do back home. What you do see though, is loads and loads of buzzards, hawks and the like and the brave squirrels are probably all dead squirrels. Of course the other problem will be in seeing them, they won't exactly be sitting out on mown lawns will they. We can also research fish traps and even duck traps for use on the lake if it survives. We can build a long tunnel that gradually narrows to a solid end at the lake exit point. You simply wait behind a screen until the ducks have entered and then you scare them into the dead end. Hey, if we bashed them on the head and put them in a large hessian bag we could call it a cull de sack, get it? Oh, never mind. I realise at this point Neville that the prospect of a rapid death may have some appeal, but it would be a shame to forgo your sacrifice for the team. Ok, ok, I won't mention it again, MY lips are sealed, sorry.

Have you given any thought as to how Abi and Edward are going to take it? It's not really something that we can prepare them for and we won't know what effect it may have until it happens. They'll have enough of a shock when the Ketamine wears off and they can't find the exit. I'm not even sure how Jan will react, all we can do is suck it and see I suppose. I think the first reaction will be that you and I are both raving lunatics and we'll have some anxious moments waiting for the first blasts. And then some more anxious moments waiting for the last. What's the worst that can happen, Trump's ego is sated with being leader of the most powerful nation on Earth and we emerge after 40 days to find that the communal sewerage is backed up all the way up the street, Edward has been expelled for missing a month off school, you and Abigail have been sacked and our wives try to get us both sectioned. Well, that's a risk I'm prepared to take. Think about it Neville, Trumpo is a billionaire, yet that's not enough, oh no, he needs to be President as well. Why settle for President of America when you can be President of the World. It seems perfectly logical to me. Putin is President of the world's largest country and still he wants more, the Crimea, Ukraine, where will his ego stop? But we all do it, who wants to settle for rolled oats when you can eat muesli? Who wants to holiday in Butlin's when you can holiday in Benidorm? Who wants to rule 27 countries in Europe when you can rule 28? Who wants to be an MP when you can be a minister? Even your priests get in on it, who wants to be Parish Priest when you can be Bishop? We are all motivated to exceed what we need.

R
XXX

Sent from my iPad

Re: Day 33 December 19th Monday

Dearest N

Neville, I thought you were going to be more discrete this time? Three weeks automatic suspension without pay for a second offence. What have you told Abi, you can't exactly run out of criminals to process can you? "It's just a bit slack at the moment so do have we any volunteers for a salary sacrifice for a couple of weeks" doesn't really work does it? Let me try and address your questions in some sort of order shall I N?

1) I know Abi has nerve damage in her hands from her carpal tunnel syndrome. It was me that insisted belatedly as it turns out, that she have the operation privately before the damage became permanent, remember. But I can't quite see your justification to your boss, what was it, ah, here we go "I'm going to buy some new underwear for my wife and need to know how easy it is to remove". A nice attempt N which might have been slightly more plausible if you were on Next's or M & S's website rather than the 'Teens Lingerie' section on the porn channel.

2) "Do I think you should appeal on the basis that you are still suffering from the effects of an illegal drug"? Let me think for a millisecond, NO. In fact I can see it positively harming your cause.

3) "How was I to know that they'd put a watch on my computer use"? How indeed N, how indeed?

4) Highly recommended, point taken Neville, but, and this is the important point, they are both judges and you aren't.

5) Ditto, but she is the Acting Chief Constable.

6) I have to say I think it's wholly unfair to try and lay the blame at my feet. Who's lives am I saving here?

Chin up N, this is a good thing, the woods coming tomorrow and you can help me assemble the beds and lay the floor. Don't worry about Abigail giving consent I will ask her for your help and, believe me, she'll thank me for getting you out from under her feet. Abi and I both know that you don't know which end of a hammer is the business end but that doesn't stop you from holding things in place while I drill and bolt does it? We need a plan of action, Jan's at the gym Monday, Tuesday and Thursday mornings. Abi's at the school three days one week and two the next. When they are both away we can stock up with food and water in the Pop 6 treatment plants, they are both ready and waiting, otherwise we can work on the 'chicken shed'. Oh, and try and order some clothes for collection from the local pickup point. We can both be a bit more covert with our behaviour at this time of year. They expect us to be sneaking out and hiding surprises away from them for the day. They just won't know which day that is.

I meant to ask, how will your suspension work around the Christmas holidays, no special court sessions on Boxing Day this year? Face it N, it's all win, win, win and you get to share in Abigail's school holidays.

Oh, by the way, you did ask the other day and I forgot to answer. BFF's. I thought you knew but of course you don't have much chance to watch daytime telly do you, well, didn't. There's an American crime series on when I eat my breakfast some days about BFF's. It features the murder of usually young girls by other young girls. But here's the twist, they were Best Friends Forever. They got the 'Forever' bit right anyway.

Coming back to an earlier point N, how is it, do you think, that I am blessed with carpentry and building skills when you are, well, not to put too fine a point on it, crap? We both went to school, we both grew up in big gardens, we both did woodwork and metalwork at the high school, we both had the same advantages in early life. We both got 'A' levels before you went on to Uni. Is it just possible that you were born useless? Sorry N, joking. What I meant to say was, is it possible that you developed into useless? Sorry, still joking. Seriously, you were born to push paper around and I wasn't, although that's not true either, because I've pushed my fair share of paper as well. At what age do you think that our potentials diverted or for that matter, were we born different? You have to ask the merits of treating all kids the same through the school curriculum don't you? Why can't the Great Brains accept that some kids are born to be bricklayers and some rocket scientists? By the way N, I'm not 'suggesting' that I'm better than you, I think the facts speak for themselves. (Still joking). We're just different that's all, part of the rich diversity of life. We can't all be bricklayers, we need architects as well. Mind, if architects also knew how to lay bricks that would be a definite advantage. Just a thought, how many great architects learnt their skills from common bricklayers? If we survive and live beyond the next few years to a new beginning, what will the new order be like? Will we make the same mistakes or will life itself be too precious to waste?

But it's alright Neville for the cavalry are hoving into sight, all it needs is 270 of the 538 US Electoral College members to vote against Trump and the world will be saved. Some Democratic electors have been trying to persuade their Republican counterparts to cast ballots against Trump and it all becomes a bad dream. We will have dodged a bullet, well an ICBM or rather our share of 15,000 of them and their kind. You see, there is a mechanism in place to protect us from egomaniacs. I could kiss my TV set and the BBC's Teletext for feeding me this hope.

Does this give us hope N, a stay of obliteration? Can 538 people override the will of the people and fail to endorse Trump? To think, all we need is the vision and courage of 270 collegiate members. But we all know they will honour the system above their conscience, will follow the pro forma coursing through their veins, actually, shouldn't that be arteries if it's coursing? Always assuming that they have an oxygen delivery system that stops off anywhere near a brain cell or two. Bless the BBC, give us hope and dash it simultaneously with the reality check of 'formality' which wouldn't, by any chance, be a rubber stamp to the Great Brain's, a deference to the Bait Ball. After all, failing to endorse Trump would generate a constitutional crisis which would play straight into Putin's hands. Ooh, it's so good, it's win, win, win for those damned Russians and all without a single bullet being used. I'm getting caught up in it all N, I can't differentiate between the lies anymore, which is the most plausible lie, I just can't tell. I gave up years ago looking for the truth, my quest would make Bilbo's look like a stroll in the park. There was an error in my opening statement N, what is the 'will of the people'? The only evidence we have of its existence are the crosses on the ballot paper. The lowest common denominator between literate people.

I'd nearly given up with the media, they are all getting in the end of year mould where holidays are paramount and they concentrate on the annual retrospective while the 'real' news drifts by. I suspect it's because most are away from their desks and these have been worked on over the year to bring out now to fill the column inches and airwaves with 'here's one we did earlier' and all without the use of sticky backed plastic. Then again, do they keep them on the shelf wrapped in Clingfilm to keep them from going off?

Just when you began to believe that we had a future it has been confirmed that Trump will be as the 45th President. Curious that they are numbered, does it confer any significance I wonder? Are they amazed that it got to 45? There won't be a 46th.

The evening news was looking at Internet news stories born outside of wedlock as opposed to the official true news born with married parents present. Half of Americans source their news from the Internet and false stories have been rife. The "pope endorsing Trump" was one such falsehood quoted. Another was Trump's apparent claim whereby he'd stated something along the lines of "If I was going to run for president, I'd run for the Republicans because they'd be stupid enough to accept me" which had been seen 1,000,000 as a news item while the 'correction' had been seen by 30,000. America is now served by two truths it appears. But the fact remains that Trump has run for the Republicans and he single-mindedly destroyed the rest of the field during his campaign. How strange that you begin your career as head of a party by destroying all of the other front runners to achieve your goal. Many Republicans have stated that Trump is unsuitable and have failed to endorse him. Is there a parallel here with Corbyn, reviled and worshipped in unequal measure? But in a sense he's only reversing the movement begun by Bliar who took the Labour Party to the centre ground. Why shouldn't a socialist hijack a centre left party and lurch left away from Bliar's, after all, what goes round, comes round. But the point about Bliar and Trump is very simple, the one thing the Great Brain's love above all is a winner and winning secures the respect until the inevitable failure. Like racehorses that secure victories, our political elite secure the prizes while the losers face a certain future at the dog food plant. Or should that be at the lasagne factory? Trump certainly made mincemeat of the rest of his field and yet, he had the least to lose. For him life would have just gone on, that's the thing about being a billionaire, nothing really matters, there's always another option. It has to beg the question, why be president?

But coming back to it, how many truths are there? How easily the media determines the veracity of its own production while denigrating the unofficial. Trump saw an opportunity to expand his ambitions into politics and he had the option as standing as Democrat, Republican or Independent. Billionaires have often stood as independents without success, he sized up the opposition and he made his claim. What was his value judgement? Given the option couldn't Bliar have hijacked the Conservative Party and moved it left towards the centre ground? He must have taken a value judgement as to where his greatest chance of success would lie. How cynical am I, Bliar went for where he could win, while you thought he followed his socialist principles? But he had no socialist principles, only a desire to win and knowing how to achieve it. Are all these leaders not followers with a head start? Bliar, Trump and all, have one thing in common, the instinct to spot weakness and the ability to exploit it.

Does the pope not endorse Trump? Trump democratically elected by the will of the people to become President. Who is the pope to deny his success and position? Or does the pope not believe in popularity contests and the principle of voting. Did all his beliefs disappear up a chimney somewhere in a stream of "*fumata bianca*", that's white smoke to you and me? Did the pope not seize an opportunity to state his case and win a fashion parade among his peers? He began his career from such humble beginnings and now enjoys a lifestyle resplendent in riches and adulation. A lifestyle that would require the resources of a billionaire to enjoy and the adulation worthy of a reality TV star. It's true Neville, I won't be going to heaven for making this comparison, but, hey, I can die with that thought. I know you're not catholic so I might get some agreement from you on this at least. CofE if my memory serves and that stirs another thought; Christians, Muslims, Hindu's, Buddhist's, Sikh's, Jews and others all have their beliefs and truths, can they all be right? But even if they were, they are all divided into different branches or sects of convenience. Quaker, Mormon, Protestant, Catholic, Methodist, High Church, Low Church, Jehovah Witness's to name a very few. How many truths is that? At least the media only give us two, well no, the media gives us one and untruths by definition. Can I define your choice of religion as of being akin to that old parlour game reminiscent of kid's birthday parties of a bygone age? Now, which game N, pass the parcel, kiss chase, Chinese whispers or how about that old favourite, pin the tail on the donkey, no peeking, mind. I don't know why physicists spend so much time trying to observe quantum mechanics when its effects are all around us if they would but look. Simples.

R
XXX

Sent from my iPad

Re: Day 32 December 20th Tuesday

Dearest N

I have to say that the beds flew up. I thought it would take longer but your help really came into its own. They are quite basic I know but we can utilise the time elsewhere. It will be a great shame to lose the use of all my electric power tools. We could perhaps consider sourcing some photoelectric panels and an inverter for after the event. We'll have to see what we can salvage, it's too late to source them through the grant system and too many jobsworths asking too many questions. It's nearly time to devote all of our attentions to our families over Christmas and the New Year. Funny thing is, this year we are actually devoting more time than ever before, they just don't know it yet. We've had half a day to talk yet I still find things to add. Good job we don't spend all our time talking otherwise we'd get nothing done.

I thought about what you said and have gone a slightly obtuse route but think I have the solution. I popped into Ashby Saddlery and had a chat with Virginia. As I thought a lot of the 'controlled' medicines are more readily available over the counter. I have used antiseptic gel pastes before, you just slap them on the wound and it hardens to form a waterproof, fly proof coating. Flea powder, not an obvious thought is also readily available and for that matter human worming treatments are available from the chemist. Hygiene and food security may be difficult to maintain and we should be prepared. Its early days but I have the makings of a first (and only) aid kit. If we emerge to nothing we'll have to make do otherwise we can scout around any remaining chemist shops which may still feature at the beginning.

I had thought about trawling the Internet trying to research blast radius, radiation levels and the like but because we have no way of knowing where precisely or imprecisely targets are going to be I decided not to bother. Let us take one day at a time N, if we survive the blasts we can shelter from the dust for just so long and then, we'll just have to deal with what we find. My plan is better than an ostrich's because our whole bodies will be underground. I remember back in Reagan's day where they proposed to site America's missiles in densely packed narrow belts on the basis that incoming missiles would be inaccurate given that previous blasts would interfere with those still in flight. I thought at the time that the idea was flawed because if their missiles couldn't function properly while landing then neither could yours taking off. Right or wrong, I think that these are not going to be precision instruments.

We have no way of knowing how many people will survive and where they are. We may emerge to a small community of survivors or none at all so we'll plan for the worst and hope for the best. In the best traditions of drama/documentaries we may be safer to keep our heads down protecting what we have. The law of the jungle is likely to rule and we need to be careful of our stocks and resources. Can you remember your job interviews where you would fight for life chances? We might be fighting for our lives instead. I know you think I'm too suspicious of my fellow humans, but we spend our whole lives competing with other people. You see it in kids competing for toys at pre-school toddler groups and you see it in the behaviour of adult motorists.

I bet you didn't know that Churchill wanted to carry on bombing the Soviets at the end of the Second World War. Papers released show he tried to persuade Truman to tackle the Soviet dominance by going nuclear. There was a small window of opportunity before their spies secured the secrets and they built their own bombs. It does occur to me that all that had to happen was the death of one man, Stalin, for history to have been entirely different. But of course, different doesn't have to mean better. Then we could start playing the 'if only' game, if only Hitler hadn't been an egomaniac, if only Churchill hadn't been an egomaniac, if only Chamberlain before him hadn't been an egomaniac? Can you begin to see a pattern forming N? They all had one thing in common N and that is the belief that they knew best. Place yourself in their shoes and ask yourself where the conviction was founded? If you want a simpler example just look at Trumpton, either one will do. What makes Hillary Clinton believe she's the best man to be President of the United States? On the one hand she's seen the other past and present candidates up close and can make a value judgement. On the other, you need a monstrous ego to believe that you are the best. I couldn't do it. I can see too many variables, too many rights and wrongs, too many doubts. None of which is an issue for Trump, or Clinton or Putin or Bashar Al Assad or Bliar or. ... Face it N, the whole concept of leadership is flawed because always the decisions are flavoured with "what's in it for me"? When submerged in your Pop 40 N, you have the control of your universe including the food rationing. You can decide whether to feed yourself over your loved ones. But outside the bunker, you could have the choice to feed your loved ones or the ones you don't love, strangers. Or will that be supporters who voted for you or the ones that didn't?

How perverse when you stop and think about it N, the whole election process is designed to polarise the electorate before the winner is expected to rule for all. When I was a kid at junior school our teacher would select two captains who would then take turns selecting football teams. Favourites would be snapped up quickly while the same 'useless' kids would always be left until the end for selection. The captains instantly assumed the role of 'dominant' ape while the selection process conferred status, or lack of it, on the rest of the 'team'. We have seen it post Brexit with May's appointments to cabinet offices. The media salivating over Boris for Foreign Secretary, Hammond for Chancellor and just as importantly, nothing for Osbourne. We can see it now with Trump's selection of Hugh, Hugh, Parsley McChew, etc. The smart ones look as earnestly at who has been left out as they do at those bought in. (That's not a typo, I didn't mean brought). The tell-tale warning signs for me are how many 'fierce critics' have suddenly declared that they had their fingers crossed while previously slagging Donald off and of course they can support their newfound status working for themselves in Trump's administration. Tell me again why we have elections? The junior school team selection process seems to be the model. Even the teacher would select the same small group of 'captains' to pick from.

R
XXX

Sent from my iPad

Re: Day 31 December 21st Wednesday

Dearest N

Thanks N, door fitted and the floor laid in the brick tank. We are all ready now for stocking up with provisions. I think we can now have that holiday over Christmas and concentrate on the rest later. We still have nearly three weeks after allowing for the break. Not too many mince pies remember. Actually, remembering is what we will spend so much time doing in the future, if we have one. We shall miss so many things, birthday and Christmas cards, gift wrapped presents, silly jumpers, eating to excess. We ought to celebrate going on into the future. Do we abandon the old traditions and invent some new ones? Sounds a bit of an oxymoron, new traditions, after all if they are new they are not traditions. But all the old traditions were new once and then they've been corrupted over time. No meat in your mince pie, I take it N? I wonder, when it all comes down to it, how many of our new inventions are simply reworked old inventions, rebranded and reworked for a newer audience? Take cars, they still talk about horsepower under the pedal and go back far enough and they were horseless carriages or ox carts or even dog carts no doubt. Variations on a theme but they all have one thing in common, each superseded its predecessor and consigned them to the also rans. I think that what we'll end up doing is trying desperately to reinvent the old traditions. Jan's dad started off his working life as an apprentice wheelwright. He used to turn up the spokes on a lathe and when he had too many he would then make ladders using the spokes as rungs. The blacksmith would expand the iron rings with heat before dropping the ring over the wheel and cooling rapidly to cramp everything together. He told me a tale once about an oversized wheel rim that had to be heated red hot for cutting before hammer welding it back together. The first cut was made and the rim placed on the anvil where the chisel was placed before the hammer blow. The red hot shard of off cut shot out the forge door only for it to be chased and swallowed by a duck. The duck stood for a second before collapsing dead on its side. Strange to think that this activity was common just 80 years ago. What would we give for this technology going on into the future I wonder? But if you stop and think, the technology continued hand in hand with desire, or did it? You'd think nothing of a set of car wheels (not the tyres) surviving hundreds of thousands of miles whereas how far would a metal rimmed cart wheel travel? But the thing was, the cart wheel didn't need to travel hundreds of thousands of miles and neither do we 'need' to do the same today. But it doesn't stop us, the lack of need, does it?

R
XXX

Sent from my iPad

Re: Day 30 December 22nd Thursday

Dearest N

Just been thinking about some of the things we take for granted, hot water on tap, clean clothes, fridge/freezers, even the good old maligned weather forecasts. We won't have the chance to compare one with another to see which is the most wrongerest. We won't even know what the temperature is, yet alone whether it's warm, hot or cold without them telling us. I read somewhere, I've forgotten the source and the exact figures, but it's around about 18 degrees Celsius. It is our optimum temperature, Brits anyway, because every degree above or below this figure sees an increase in the death rate. I filed it away in the really useful recesses of my mind and every now and again it surfaces to take exception to the weather forecaster's statements. "Yes, it will feel really pleasant tomorrow with highs of 28 C". "Perfect summer weather". And how about the really inane and regular banker for stupidity award that goes something akin to this, "it's been terrible, with six months' worth of rain falling in 6 hours, yes that's 0.01mm of rain in the Gobi desert, in six hours". It is part of the 'let's describe everything in readily visualised terms for simple people to understand" mind-set that substitutes for intelligence. Can you remember what six months of rain looks like N? This may be a rhetorical question for people who live in the Atacama Desert or even Antarctica where it's too cold to snow. How about "It's the length of three football pitches and the weight of 11 double decker buses". Sorry to be objectionable N, but I prefer cricket and I tend to weigh things in Tonnes. I used to get pissed off with David Attenborough describing "moths as the size of a small dove". I used to keep birds remember, was that a collared dove or a diamond dove? How could I tell, everyone nearly knew what a collared dove looked like whereas the Australian diamond dove, or what about the Indian zebra dove? We could come up with our own internationally agreed Standardised Units of measurement going forward N. We could describe the weather as 'fucking freezing', 'hot enough to make your balls sweat' or 'call that a nuclear winter, I've seen worse'. We ought to be able to calculate the weight of a tree on the basis of Diplodocus units which we will of course be much more likely to encounter than a big red two storey thingy. Oh bollocks, I bought an Oyster card when down in London watching the tennis and it's still got some money left on it. Hey, don't forget the 'chapel hat pegs chill' or could it be she was just pleased to see me?

Is it any wonder that we are incapable of thought when our minds are constantly assailed by a constant stream of abject bollocks, not to be confused with the right whale bollock weighing in at twenty barrow loads of apples (Pippin, Cox's Orange, I knew you'd ask) and mind numbing attempts at simplification? What is it they used to say, I've no idea if it was the truth or not, "A yard is the length of the distance from the Kings nose tip to fingertip"? Let's hope he wasn't picking it at the time or we'd all feel short-changed. "Ah, thank you Sire, so that's the length of 27 pine processionary moth caterpillars on route to their pupating site, I'll let the merchants know Sire". (*Thaumetopoea pityocampa*, see, I wasn't making it up).

It makes it all seem worthwhile doesn't it, all the effort to ascribe a unit of standardisation so that some braindead clerk can convert it into a non-standardised readily unidentifiable object we can all relate to provided we switch our brains off first. I have it, the braindead clerk wanted some company. Suffice it to say, if I was king, said clerk wouldn't be relating anything else to the size of his own testicles, unless of course he had a bloody good memory. Distance will be irrelevant as well N, I remember taking my kids ponies and a couple of horses to the mountains in the Cevennes region of France. I had my Shire horse back then and he was huge. I used to get the same reaction in Spain the year before as well, you would see every car three times. The first time they drove past, then they turned around to have another look before turning again so that they drove past again as they continued their journey. Anyway, I digress, the horse truck was parked next to a manure stockpile and the truck filled up with flies so we asked the hotel owner how far away the town was so we could get some fly spray. His reply went along the lines of "We don't talk distance, we talk time because the roads are so narrow and winding". But we may not even have time as a measurement N, once the last watch breaks or batteries fail. Can we get there and back before it gets dark will be the question?

Another thing that strikes me will be the absence of light pollution. Anyone with a telescope should be able to study the stars better than they have done for years (once the dust clears out of the atmosphere, anyway) only, there won't be much point will there? But, what was the point anyway? It is really, really important that we 'know' how the universe was formed and the forces and mechanisms involved. We can use this knowledge to build weapons of mass destruction, and then use them. Yes, that sounds like a plan to me. I could summarise the whole process as of taking the toy to pieces to see how it works only to find that we can't put it back together again.

The horse thing reminds me of something else. The first year when I took my horses to Spain I had to export them to Spain via France and then reimport them back into England. Before leaving England I had to have them all vetted to ensure that they were fit to travel. By vetted, I mean a proper qualified Veterinarian had to inspect them and sign papers. We also stopped off at what I will call a 'Customs Stable' on the hill above Dover for further vetting to check their health and welfare. For the return journey from Spain the proper qualified Veterinarian turned up at the hotel bar and signed the papers. It was only after he had signed the papers and his bill had been paid that he went to look. But the only reason he went to look was because the hotel manager had told him that I had a Shire horse. It was in this way that I ensured that we took no horse diseases into France and Spain. We may have brought some back though. It certainly made the whole process seem worthwhile.

Here's a cheery thought for you N. Just imagine what we can have to talk about after 40 days of imposed isolation. I don't imagine we'll have much chance to get bored. While bereft of my company there is a game you can play which won't use much oxygen. We often play it around Christmas within the family. It's a variation on Charades but with a twist. You still get to ask a series of questions as you filter your answer down. We call it 'Guess Who's Dead'? We normally try to concentrate on recent celebrity bucket kickers. On the one hand you won't be short of material or potential answers, but the skill will be in narrowing it down to the correct one.

Spotted this on the telly.

Donald Trump has called for the US to take action to "greatly strengthen and expand" it's nuclear arsenal "until such time as the world comes to its senses regarding nukes. This was Trump's response to Putin's call for Russia to boost its military nuclear potential. The US nonpartisan Arms Control Association suggests that they have 14,400 nuclear weapons between them.

Not only, but also:

Economist Peter Navarro, a fierce critic of China, is to be appointed as the head of a new national trade body the White House National Trade Council, and serve as director of trade and industrial policy.

Mr Navarro a Trump campaign adviser has written books titled The Coming China Wars and Death by China.

Mr Trump even found space to squeeze in billionaire investor Carl Icahn to become a special adviser on regulatory reform.

There we have it N, Trump's peace on Earth and goodwill to all men's Christmas message. We must redouble our efforts to secure our bunker future and nothing less than a complete 'root and branch' overall of our strategy will suffice. I propose that we adopt a fresh brainstorming approach to our predicament and implore you to ensure that 'all lessons will be learned" while we still have the chance. Nothing less than 110% of our capacity will provide for our post-bunker era. I usually say that the tripe in the butchers counter is 'offally' good but what I really mean here is the trite is offal. By my reckoning that's brought Trump and his supporters full circle and we are back to the alimentary canal and its waste products. Katanga has its uses, it supports its very own subculture of bacteria, fungi, moulds and insect life to name a few while nurturing the fecundity of the soil it contaminates. What subculture will Trump's Katanga nurture I wonder, it seems to be woefully short of insects even though must are visible to the naked eye. What it seems to have no shortage of is billionaires, that most underprivileged sector of society that needs every assistance that we can muster. Presumably some residue will remain to boost the fecundity of the supporting strata. I would suggest that time will tell, but time now is very limited and there will be precious few of us left to listen. How innocuously the dawn of the new age of a new world order is drip fed into the public realm. It's there for all to bear witness to, if only we were not so intent at hiding from danger behind our neighbour.

Notwithstanding this, consider Trump's quote "until such time as the world comes to its senses about nukes". I wonder who Trump thinks will be in charge, for 'they' ought to do something about it. Well worth becoming president for, to be in charge. I suppose I'd welcome Trump coming to his senses, I wonder where they are? Let's have a 'phone in with suggestions, but don't vote for your favourite location just yet, phone lines won't open until January the 21st 2017. Please ensure you have the bill payer's permission before calling, calls made before the 21st will not be counted but may still incur charges. Members of the new White House team, their families and affiliates and senior Republicans may not enter. A proportion of the profits raised will be donated to aid destitute billionaires as they adjust to playing second fiddle to Trump. Suggestions such as Boatie McBoat Arse or in his head will be disqualified from entry on the grounds of stupidity and charges may still be incurred.

R
XXX

Sent from my iPad

Re: Day 29 December 23rd Friday

Dearest N

Will this be the last Christmas for mankind? Will it become something cherished and retained into future generations or will it wither away, stripped of its excesses and beyond the scope of simple survival? I know it originated in Pagan times and was hijacked by Christians who failed in their earlier attempts to halt it. The Romans celebrated the rebirth of the sun on the 25th which corresponds neatly enough with the winter solstice, 'Dies Natali Solis Invictus', the 'birthday of the unconquered' (Sun rebirth) at the end of the Saturnalia. I think, provided we get to see it that our 'Dies Natali Invictus' will occur as the nuclear winter begins to clear and the sun truly returns to its former glory. How apt that we will seek to begin our rebirth alongside that of the sun. For while we may exist until that point on borrowed time, borrowed from the tinned and dried foods we have stored, true life will not begin until that day. On that day forward we will have a future. And before you tell me that the solstice is on the 21st of December, it doesn't always land on the 21st but can extend to the 23rd. Always assuming that the Earth retains its orbit and tilt from the sun we will be hard pressed to notice any lengthening of the day before the 25th. I don't suppose that our climate will magically transform on a given date but will creep up on us unawares until we realise that it is gradually improving. Where shall we place our stake in the ground to record its rebirth? We have been here before, not you and me but mankind way back in 1816. We shall perhaps endure 2017 as 'Two Thousand and Froze to Death' just 202 years after the eruption of Mount Tambora in Indonesia that cause three years of severe climate disruption, or should that be severe climate eruption. The 'Year without a Summer' in 1816 led to widespread famine as crops failed and was swiftly followed by disease epidemics compounding the issues. Truthfully I don't think we need worry too much about disease simply because I don't think there will be enough people at enough density to allow for rapid spread. Surviving cities could provide optimum breeding grounds though with the collapse of the supporting infrastructure. Without fresh water and sanitation and the constant input of food from the surrounding hinterland I think they could well be dangerous places to gravitate towards. Strange to think that cities that seem to offer the optimum environment for people could rapidly degenerate into anarchic disease ridden ghettos.

Sorry N, not exactly cheering anybody up here am I? I just thought I'd have another dig at your church, it's not hard and you are immensely patient with me, thankfully. How is it that Trump has been elected to President on the Republican bandstand when they represent such a high proportion of the bible bashers? A rhetorical question really, because, to believe in God lays you wide open to all sorts of alternative scams and lies that rely on the suspension of thought and logic. Oh, I almost forgot, I must tie a knot in something to remind me, I cannot countenance any time in the bunker and beyond without the singularly most important tool in my entire arsenal. For while you are content to turn to the power of prayer I have a practical alternative that really works. As luck would have it I stumbled across it in August when clearing the 2nd floor for decorating. Jan never throws anything away and while Sooty himself is getting a bit threadbare, his wand is still in perfect working order. Seriously though N, believing in deities leaves you wide open to believing in any other logic defying principles. There is an alternative, which I can best frame with a simple question, "Who in their right mind would vote for Trump/ton"? Whenever a small child had been brutally murdered I would often hear elderly relatives commenting along the lines of "Who in their right mind could harm a baby"? I never commented but would sit quietly accepting that they had answered their own question "Who in their right mind" with the answer that they were not, in fact, in their right mind. If belief in God requires the suspension of logical thought and reason then don't be surprised at what these obviously enlightened 'thinkers' can also subscribe to. I am not singling out God-squadder's here N, although they are such an easy target, stop and think and. Ah, but there's the rub, stop. And think. Ignore the herd, suspend the suspension of thought, think the unthinkable. But that's not right either is it, think the unthinkable? If you can think it, it cannot be unthinkable. Or does it mean countenance the act, having thought it? I may be tying you up in knots now N, but I feel a paradox coming on, for we celebrate the thinkers who thought (thinked?) the unthinkable. Where would Einstein or Newton be if they hadn't thought the unthinkable? In one case I could suggest that the splitting of the atom and the immense release of energy produced within the resultant chain reaction might not be on our agenda now, having refused to leave the 'In Tray' so to speak.

It strikes me Neville that all we ever needed for news was the BBC's Teletext pages. They are such a rich source of seemingly innocuous comments that culminate in such a portentous conclusion; Putin says Russia is 'stronger than any potential aggressor' because it has modernised its nuclear missiles and other forces and can 'beat any aggressor'. The US withdrawal in 2001 from the Anti-Ballistic Missile (ABM) Treaty had 'created the conditions for a new nuclear arms race".

On Trump's election victory, Mr Putin said "nobody believed he would win, apart from us". Mr Trump has strongly praised Mr Putin and I can't for the life of me think why.

Its official, Putin has a sense of humour, "nobody believed he would win, apart from us". I wonder why that would be, a bit like betting on the underdog when you know the race is fixed? Alternatively, it's a bit like rubbing the American's noses in it when they suspect it was rigged and it wasn't. Claiming credit for something you haven't done. Undermining the entire American election process with just 8 words. I wonder how Trump will prove his independence of Putin. But not for long, wonder, that is.

R
XXX

Sent from my iPad

Re: Day 28 Christmas Eve Saturday

Dearest N, Abigail and Edward

If you have chance please pop in for a convivial drink and mince pie. We would love to meet up. We are free from around 3.00 P M onwards.

R and J
XXX

Sent from my iPad

Re: Day 27 Christmas Day Sunday

Dearest N

Dies Natali Solis Invictus.

Merry Christmas to the N household from the P household.

Cheers

XXX

Sent from my iPad

Re: Day 26 Boxing Day Monday

Dearest N, A

Thank you so much for your delightful present, as ever, you are both so very thoughtful. My own personal copy of the bible. You really, really, really shouldn't have put yourselves to such trouble, really. I shall cherish this to the end of the Earth.

Imagine N, first Boxing Day at home in ages. Let someone else lock the criminals up for a change.

I wonder, do the magistrates share in the Christmas spirit? No I don't obviously, I know they all get pissed, what I meant was, are they more lenient than usual, or stricter because they'd sooner be somewhere else as well?

I still had time to dip into the Teletext pages and turned this up on cheetahs;

With an estimated 7,100 cheetahs left the species should be reclassified as endangered rather than vulnerable. They cover huge ranges outside protected areas and regularly come into conflict with humans.

It shouldn't be a problem soon if the human populations take a rapid tumble although I don't know how much Africa will be impacted by our immediate problem. I hope it won't take any direct hits sub-Saharan especially in Namibia but the nuclear winter must have an effect. Is there a contradiction here in the earlier statement? 'They cover ranges outside protected areas'. How does that work then Neville, you don't get wet if you stay indoors while it's raining? Having a roof above your head serves no purpose when you have to walk 30 miles to find food. How then would you define a 'protected area' for a cheetah? It seems to me that the area is neither protected or an area if it serves no purpose.

R
XXX

Sent from my IPad

Re: Little sister

So Robert,

Yes my dad, an only child married the elder of two sisters, I did and my son is going the same way? Is that a coincidence, a trend, an observation to be reduced to a mathematical model or ...

Neville

Sent from my IPhone.

Re: Little sister.

Dearest N

Sometimes I despair for your future. Did you go to school? This may come as a surprise to you, but, what part in the mate selection process do you think you engaged in? I will ignore the presumption in Edward's life choice as being somewhat premature. That said, there is indeed a pattern emerging. You will probably be aware of the mating habits of the praying mantis, well known for its habit of eating the male partner during copulation. Male partners that escape this fate fade away to a sorry death as they have served their purpose and are unable to mate again. Studies have also indicated that the extra protein boost taken by the female increases the number and viability of the eggs that are laid thus increasing the life chances of the males DNA. Your respective partner's choices can be best described as akin to their eating of the parents testes. That is to say that they have rendered your father impotent and sterile thus ensuring that your respective mates offspring inherit all of the grandparents and parents estate. There will be no sharing amongst siblings for them. It is a cunning deception nearly as old as the rules of inheritance beyond the eldest sibling inheriting all. I am sorry to say it N, but you have effectively married a cuckoo intent on securing all of the resource for her single offspring. I have a solution for you N, no need to thank me, it's the least a good friend could do for you. To thwart her premarital shenanigans you should frustrate her by disinheriting her and the fruit of your loins. It will be a sacrifice but I am prepared to accept your accumulated estate into my holdings. You must do it now to frustrate the taxman and inheritance tax under the seven year rule. You really owe it to yourself to expose her premeditated ambitions. I will send you my bank account details through under separate cover. In the meantime I have instructed solicitors to draw up the paperwork to provide an irrevocable contract that will she will be unable to challenge through the courts. Don't let her get away with it, protect your real future. Your family seems to have been predisposed to this scam over the generations, act now to bring this shameful history to a close.

Underneath that pleasant veneer of Abigail's lies a core of steel, realise that you've been taken for a fool and frustrate her, soon, preferably before my Christmas Visa bill becomes due.

Alternatively, your secret love was for the younger sister who was unattainable and you married Abigail so as to remain in familial contact with your true heart's desire.

Merry Christmas.

R
XXX

Sent from my iPad

Re: Little sister

Dear Robert

Ouch!

Sent from my IPhone

Re: Day 25 December 27th Tuesday

Dearest N

There are some good offers on in the sales on clothing, but you'd probably worked that out for yourself. Can you remember when the Primark warehouse at Magna Park burned down? There share price went up because all the stock was insured and they'd effectively had a bumper sales period. Speaks volumes really when their stock was worth more as ashes than it was on the shop floor. Well by my reckoning all the High Street chains are about to have a bumper sales period with nothing left, including the sales floor. Have you got the heart to tell them that the insurers won't be paying up?

Money and the pursuit of it is all about to end. It will cease to have value, to have currency. How does that work then N, money having no currency? What should we stow away as currency for the future N? Food, clothing, access to water, hunting grounds, steel knives and stainless pots and pans. I think the one thing we need above all else is knowledge. It strikes me that our modern history could be described as the accumulation of knowledge. It starts with what food to eat and where to find it. How to trap it, hunt it, tame it or grow it. When to sow and harvest and how to store it. How to breed it and protect it. Now our soon to be immediate problem is going to be, we don't know how to do these things. As we developed and become more and more learned we also became more and more specialised. Collectively we became more and more able while individually we became less and less able, a seeming paradox. The cleverer we get the less we know. We are about to enter a new age where our combined knowledge will fail to provide for the individual because only individuals will remain.

Did it ever work, the collective providing for the individual? Have I asked this question the right way round? Did the individuals provide for the collective? The collective is obviously comprised of individuals, the individuals have pooled their skills to form the collective. Seems fine in principle, but? Somewhere in here I'm looking for the herd; wildebeest in their tens of thousands trekking across the Savannah in search of food, water, shelter, protection, sex. It's a collective but there's no organisation, no leader, no Great Brain orchestrating the movement just individuals responding to the same desire and need in the way that only wildebeest do. But the herd is more than that, it relies on the subjugation of thought, the surrender of self, the loss of free will, the copying of neighbours. There is the issue, the copying of neighbours who are copying you. And if you are copying your neighbours who are copying their neighbours who are copying their neighbours the last rational thing you would want to do is give them a ballot paper and the ability to mark a cross. The clever people in Pennsylvania have gone one better than that, for the paper has been replaced with a touch screen and now, assuming your knuckles aren't too sore from dragging them on the floor, everyone can vote without the need to hold a pencil. Eighteen fucking months the herd had to weigh the arguments, debate the debates, search the soul, scan the conscience, deliberate the reasons. Eighteen fucking months the Great Brains had to preen and pose their candidacies, set their ideals, prove their validity. We have just 25 days left before the reset when we become truly the less than great unwashed. I have to take it for granted that we survive, because if we don't, we cease to have any relevance, we become extinct, including the breathing bit.

How then to plan the new utopia? To design the new herd?

When I was a kid my elder brother and I used to go ferreting for rabbits. My sister used to babysit for the local farmer and consent was given for us to try our hand on their land. It was always a winter pastime because any youngsters caught underground would be eaten before the ferret would quite literally hole up and go to sleep. We would scope out the warren and quietly lay purse nets over the entrances to catch the fleeing rabbits.

I'm going back to the late sixties and although myxomatosis had been around for a while rabbit behaviour hadn't caught up with it. As time progressed and rabbits died of disease underground the warrens became uninhabitable and rabbits began to live above ground. Even today, in spite of significant numbers of rabbits in my garden I don't have what you would describe as a warren. I wonder N, will we learn to alter our behaviour? Can we perform as well as rabbits?

Did you know that rabbits were once a highly sought after and expensive commodity? They ranked up there with carp and pigeon as a source of fresh meat in the winter. The name Iberia is thought to originate from Phoenician for 'Rabbit Coast' and our British rabbits struggled with our less than Mediterranean climate for centuries. They were carefully nurtured and cared for in warrens I suppose in a similar way to how we treat turkeys. (No holes in the ground though, for the turkeys). Remember Bernard Matthews who made his fortune bringing turkey to the masses all year round? Back in the day others did the same with rabbits, although I don't think the peasants had much of a look in. The thing is though, if you look at the history of the rabbit over the last 2,000 years it has got hardier and more robust whereas we have got softer and are wholly dependent on central heating and air conditioning that we just can't live without darling.

I was bored, it happens occasionally, I need some external stimulus to vibrate a brain cell and I watched some of the BBC's Weird Nature with Chris Packham. The BBC had caught up with the newspaper report from the summer. They decided to close the show with the activity of chimpanzees bashing rocks against trees that had recently been observed in Africa. The researchers that discovered the activity offered two suggestions, firstly that it was aggressive males proclaiming dominance and secondly that all chimpanzees within a group banged the trees to maintain and reinforce contact between the separated group members as a call to reassemble. Obviously if all chimpanzees were doing it, including baby carrying females, this discounted the male dominance theory. The rocks were often thrown while accompanied by the 'assembly call'. The BBC are clever in their presentation, by offering idea 1 and then discounting it with idea 2 they have laid the pattern for discounting idea 2 with the soon to be revealed idea 3. So then in their wisdom the final word on the subject was given to some theologian who prattled on about spiritual and electrical centres of attraction and began to talk about the evolutionary origins of belief in God.

If any evidence was lacking in the utter loss of sanity on Earth then this provided it. I am torn between persisting with the bunker and just dying along with the rest of the herd. Am I too late to launch my own religion to the Great God Turdus? Can I recruit Trump to my ranks to dissuade him from his course of action? Can I enlighten him in the ways of the Great God Parus? Can I achieve a stay of execution for the planet and mankind as I lead them away from the precipice in the clouds towards the noughts behind my bank balance? How fast can I bring my new gods to the population and secure my future as god's aviculturist on Earth? What am I to do N? Just when I thought all was lost, the BBC has offered me an alternative to letting Trump run his course. But we only have 24 days to save the Earth, how can I gather the exposure and launch the new paradigm in such a short space of time?

R
XXX

Sent from my iPad

Re: Day 24 December 28th Wednesday

Dearest N

Jan disappeared off to Kilworth House for afternoon tea with her friend Mary so I took the opportunity to load up some more clothes into the Pop 6 tank. We should be pleased with the progress to date, we really have made an impact. I suppose 'impact' is not exactly the term to use given where we are about to end up. We will hopefully be protected from the blinding light and blast but I wonder should we worry about the noise? I will get hold of some of the 'in the ear' ear plugs we used to use at the factory to be on the safe side. We will need all of our senses to survive if we are to have a chance. It does strike me that we may emerge to a very quiet world indeed. (Assuming our respective bunker sharers haven't deafened us with shouting), I tried to sue my Estate Agents once for property misrepresentation just after I moved in. The sellers agents described my property as 'quiet and tranquil' which was fine until the wind changed to the east and the constant drone of the motorway assailed our ears, even while inside. I made the mistake of taking advice from another agent who basically talked me out of it for fear of upsetting the apple cart. NB this is an apple cart and is not to be confused with a barrow full of apples. The conversion calculation will require a factor of 3.141 which the more astute of you will recognise as pie, or something similar. Pastry crust will be required to top and BOTTOM otherwise it is some sort of inverted tart which requires a different conversion factor of 1.5705 or half pie. Anyway, I digress, double glazing throughout and the new 'whisper tarmac' has made the house better which just increases the surprise when I walk outside.

That's sort of half of Christmas out of the way, just the New Year to see in. Talk about eat, I am just not used to three course meals plus multiple mince/cake/chocolate/sausage rolls servings in between. I nearly fear for my own ingress into my temple of Parus. They are invariably sized for blue tits as the desired species worthy of our assistance and consequently great tits are denied access. How's your diet coming on N, do I need to increase the physio on my shoulders? Isn't it strange? If you think about it most grannies are content to feed the tits with nuts and invariably dispense them in containers designed to dissuade bigger and uglier birds from partaking. The sacrificial offering providers are perfectly content to see blue, coal and great tits indulge in exchange for a flash of colour and a dose of acrobatics. Yet the same benevolent agents nail nest boxes up specifically to exclude the larger great tits from gaining access. This is blatant tit discrimination if you ask me. Where's 'disgusted of Titbridge Wells' when you need him? We could, no, should launch a campaign to end discrimination and allow all tits to have equal access for what is such an essential prerequisite for successful breeding. Anything less than full and free access without discrimination is titist and we should take a stand. Tit emancipation should be the call, but not when on your employer's computer N. What frustrates me greatly with the whole tit thing is the way that our less than benign institutions actively promote the existence of one species by ensuring the death and destruction of others. How dare the RSPB promote the feeding of our selected garden birds by denying food and habitat from other birds unseen in other fields and other continents? How dare they sell their ideas as of being helpful to the situation? I would remind you that RSPB stands for Royal Society for the PROTECTION of Birds. I can see a justification, it's akin to pest control. If all the ground nesting birds in a reserve were to have their eggs eaten by a badger (fucking *Mustelids* again) then, in the eyes of the world, the RSPB could not countenance the killing of the badger on the grounds that it is 'wildlife' and should be supported. Their solution is to erect a *Mustelid* proof fence (We need one of them in the Houses of Parliament) to ensure that the selected birds can survive. Said *Mustelid* now has two options open to it, starve to death or search elsewhere for alternative food. This food would include any ground nesting birds stupid enough to have read the "Keep Out Nature Reserve" sign and thought it meant them. It would also increase the pressure on the surrounding area whereby the badgers foraging range has just been condensed by the erection of a wire fence and the surrounding area is increasingly compromised. But, here's the thing, birds outside the reserve are not really the RSPB's concern. They cannot earn from them, whereas they can earn from the visitors to the official reserve through memberships and car parking fees and donations and the selling of blue tit boxes and wild bird seed to the lovers of birds. Of course, there is my preferred solution, which is to shoot the *Mustelids* before they can vote, sorry, eat the bird's eggs in the surrounding area. But they cannot conceive that the badgers should be denied the right to life, because that would be wrong. They can conceive that vast acreages of land can be taken into agriculture to produce vast amounts of bird seed so that we can preserve the birds that visit our garden feeders, but, only the pretty ones. If I was really cynical I could suggest that the RSPB has a vested interest in ensuring that rarer birds only breed on their reserves. There wouldn't be much point in going to Longleat to pay to see the lions if you could drive past them in the fields on the way there, would there? And there is the rub, because if birds weren't rare there wouldn't be any need for the RSPB and they would all be out of a job. But birds are rare, casualties of changing land use driven by agriculture and other human activity such as the growing of bird seed and the exclusion of badgers from their home ranges. Another thing to add to the list N, the end of benevolent arseholes. And it's all been done without a debate, no opium needed to arrive at this benevolent asinine unthought process. Actually I think I've spelt asinine wrong, isn't it arsenine?

There was this badger, see, wondering along quite happily minding its own business, right, when it comes across this fence, see, and when it stood on its hind legs, right, and peered over the top it thought "Wow, the grass is so much greener over there". It devised a plan, yeah, and worked out that it could dig underneath the fence in just one spot, see, and gain entry into this overstocked larder of food, see, and it indulged, my, it indulged and ate all the food it could find and it could find a lot see, because it was all concentrated in just one area because badgers had been excluded from there for such a long time. Now this badger was an educated sort and thought to himself, I'm worthy of my northern cousins moniker, known when he's not in some film or other stuffed full of Adamantium, to his friends anyway, as Glutton.

R
XXX

Sent from my iPad

Re: Day 23 December 29th Thursday

Dearest N

There was this peasant, see, wondering along quite happily minding its own business, right, when it comes across this fence, see, and when it stood up fully, right, and peered over the top it thought "Wow, the grass is so much greener over there". It devised a plan, yeah, and worked out that it could dig underneath the fence in just one spot, see, and gain entry into this overstocked larder of food, see, and it indulged, my, it indulged and ate all the food it could find and it could find a lot see, because it was all concentrated in just one area because peasants had been excluded from there for such a long time. Now this peasant was an educated sort and thought to himself, I'm worthy of my title of breadwinner for the family and when my family sees the bonus I'm in for when I sell this tiger pelt and bones all our 'Dies natali solis invicti' will have arrived together.

It has been said that Donald is respectful of Putin. It is one of the reasons that we have our immediate problem, well in 24 days immediate. If Trump yields an inch, Putin will take a Baltic state or three and World War Three kicks off without so much as a vote. The media has established the command and control structure of Russia and has determined that Putin is in the hand of the Russian oligarchs, the billionaires that hold the former state monopolies. That's the complex administration of the largest country on the planet sorted.

El Trumpo on the other hand faces none of these issues at home, he is simply filling his political stations with multi-millionaires and multiple billionaires. As hard as I try N I just can't see any parallels. Is Putin a closet billionaire? Now as luck would have it, a former Russian investment expert has claimed that he has a worth of $200 billion and has been stealing for years. Oh, and that also makes him the richest man in the world. Even 'The Sun' has picked up on it so it must be true.

What on God's planet would Trump see in Putin to respect? Equally, what control or sway over Putin would the other oligarchs hold? Of course Putin's wealth is similar to that of our own hereditary oligarch, HM QE2 in that neither of them can spend it. Just popping down to Windsor N, our gracious majesty is holding a car boot sale of family treasures. I fancy a punt at a Holbein or two doesn't really work does it? Now don't think I'm having a go at our Queen, N, strangely I have a deep felt respect for her and the entire process. You only have to consider the prospect of President Bliar to put her into perspective and who would have thought that Michael Foot's hobbit lookalike would be President of Eire? It will all be somewhat academic in the not too distant past, (we haven't got a not too distant future).

This whole process of accumulated wealth poses further questions N, for why would you jeopardise your wealth over a Baltic state or three? Where is the advantage? Of course oligarchs get to enjoy privilege, who wouldn't want to own a top flight football team, if only they were for sale, or have their pick of the world's most beautiful women/yacht/supercars/palaces/ wine cellars and the like to massage their otherwise impoverished egos? What possible motivation exists to increase your wealth from 200 to 220 billion whatever's? Because, and this is the important bit, even if Putin could spend it, what could he possibly spend it on that he doesn't already have 20 of anyway? I couldn't be a billionaire N, I just can't see the point of increasing your wealth beyond your unimaginable dreams. I would have long since given up and retired to life.

But they haven't, they still seem to be searching for something that has eluded them, is it love, is it recognition, is it simply the feeling of "I'm considerably richer than you"? I tease N, for the only thing left is ego. What purpose does the drive to succeed hold when you have succeeded, are they all addicts? I should try and convene the first meeting of BA, yes, that's right, Billionaire's Anonymous. "Hello, my name is Donald and I am a billionaire and I am considerably richer than you". "I harbour delusions of grandeur beyond my wildest dreams". "I am on the 2015 Forbes rich list of 1,826 billionaires and am not content to be in the top 0.0000002467% of the population, I want, no I need more". "Please help me, I have no control over my urges". "I want to be President of the most powerful nation on Earth". "I have such a good life, I don't need to do this, I don't need to be a President". That last one N, is paraphrasing one of

Trump's electioneering soundbites. Oh, I think you do, would be my reply. But will it make you happy, Donald, at best you only have eight years to be 'King of the Castle' and all you'd be left with is a library and the roars of the crowd fading into memory. One benefit is that you no longer have to fund your own security staff.

The thing about addicts N is that they have their own inbuilt suicide gene that renders them incapable of rational decision making. I will not bet/drink/shoot-up/smoke/masturbate/Facebook etc. A definition of addiction is that it is a 'medical condition characterised by compulsive engagement in rewarding stimuli while ignoring the later adverse consequences'. 'Addiction patterns and habits are typically characterised by immediate gratification coupled with delayed deleterious effects'.

That's all right then N, we can enjoy the short term gratification, it's just the delayed deleterious effects we need to worry about, or rather, not worry about, just attempt to live through. Whatever happened to those psychological profile tests they indulge in as part of some job interview processes? "Ah, Mr Trump, come on in and take a seat. We have analysed your profile and have determined that you are in the 0.01 percentile section of the graph bordering on the megalomaniacal/clinical insanity boundary. Congratulations Mr President Elect, in our view you are perfectly qualified".

Our species through design or accident has arrived at the perfect paradox whereby the very last people you would want to be leaders are invariably the first amongst the candidates. Democracy then is the expression of a biological control within the electorate. I will call it the Bait Ball gene, a variation of the suicide gene in that the end result is the same in spite of the apparent good intent.

When the button is pushed and the sirens wail out those among us with a brain cell to vibrate may be asking one simple question, "Who put them in charge? The answer is simple. You did. A thought does strike me N, a quarter of the electorate voted for El Trumpo but three quarters didn't. What we could do with is a different sort of ballot where the electorate votes against candidates. On the face of it this is nonsense but bear with me. Three quarters of the electorate failed to endorse Trumpton with Trump or Clinton only achieving a quarter of the support each. So the real winner was, none of the above. Have the fashion parade and let the candidates pimp their wares on the hustings but then vote against them until you arrive at the least disliked candidate. I know it's a non-starter, the voters would never arrive at a consensus and the same old candidates would float up to form the scum on the pool of talent. One of the things it would do is destroy the evident mandate of Trump to rule. It might even weed out the egomaniacs. Nah, bollocks would it.

R
XXX

Sent from my iPad

Re: Day 22 December 30th Friday

Dearest N

I wonder how we'll survive without media hyperbole? It's been at the back of mind for ages and I was reminded about it today. I'd just come out of the cafe in Lutterworth when I took a tumble. It's alright, I wasn't hurt and managed to walk back to the car. It was close at one stage N, I swayed at least 0.9 degrees from the vertical. Now I know what you would be thinking N, if you're Maths was any good, 0.9 degrees is only one percent from vertical. You can wake up to the headline "Pound tumbles against Dollar" and carry that thought around with you through the day only to discover later that it dropped by less than one percent. Equally the news can lounge around posted on Teletext or the Internet throughout the day or even days on the 'net. Of course, using my new found post retirement freedom I can check the indices during the day to see that the 'tumbling Pound' in fact recovered its earlier losses by 9.00 AM, thus invalidating all the previous headlines. You can imagine the furore if the football result was posted all day as England 0, Germany 1 when the last minute goal was disallowed for offside after the third umpire review. Our 'News' then is out of date before we even see it.

Those Brexit rear-guard snipers think nothing of colouring the entire day's attitude of the public by introducing carefully constructed untruths that can be exposed as such with very little effort, but as always the damage has already been done. The media then becomes an instrument of the Bait Ball. But that isn't quite correct is it? Because the media is part of the Bait Ball. How then to form an opinion that has any basis in fact? But fact doesn't exist either does it?

After the 20th there'll be no bait ball just stragglers. I've said before, but you've probably forgotten, apocalypse also means 'the revealing'. Well our own apocalypse will certainly be a revelation to all the survivors. That's what excites me so much N, the new world unorder. Bloody spellchecker keeps trying to correct my misspellings, it's not disorder, it's the removal of order, an unorder which is not the same thing.

You can imagine all the questions that will be asked, how, why, who let it, why couldn't, why wasn't, what was? All questions that could be asked today, all questions that are being asked today, all questions that are being answered today but all within the confines of the Bait Ball. Trumpton was elected because of the Bait Ball. Religions exist because of the Bait Ball. We kill strangers and not the ones we love because of the Bait Ball. We are driving our fellow passengers to extinction because of the Bait Ball. But for Bait Ball's to function the most essential requisite is that of population density, it simply doesn't function without sufficient numbers. But if less means the end of the Bait Ball, then more means the extension of the Bait Ball. To coin Marx's phrase about illusion and the condition that requires illusion, we have found our illusion and I have called it the Bait Ball. That is our real suicide gene, not the addiction gene, the driving too fast and too close to the vehicle in front gene, the let's go to war with a song on our lips gene, the real one is the Bait Ball gene. This is the one that will spell the end of mankind, the death of the species, our own personal extinction level event for, as we visit them upon our fellow travellers, we visit one upon ourselves. Have we reached the critical mass yet? Thresholds are many and varied, we have crossed it for the passenger pigeon, the great auk, the northern white rhino and accelerate our approach for tigers and elephants in our carefree world laced with illusion. Will our threshold be 8 or 10, will it be 13 billion souls on Earth? But these are rhetorical questions N, because we know it will be the 20th of January 2017 and we will be ready.

R
XXX

Sent from my iPad

Re: Day 21 December 31ˢᵗ Saturday

Dearest N

Just a short note to confirm that our bash starts around 7.30 tonight. I'll open the back gates up so you can all walk round, or drive and pick them up in the morning after everyone's sobered up. Good idea of yours to go for an 'End of the World' themed fancy dress party. It's got everybody thinking in the right frame of mind but for all the wrong reasons. Jan wouldn't let me wear a loin cloth, she's got no sense of occasion. Can't say anymore for spoiling the surprise, see you chaps later.

R
XXX

Sent from my iPad

Re: Day 20 January 1ˢᵗ 2017 Sunday

Dearest N

Happy New Year.

How was I to know that you were coming in a loin cloth? A little warning wouldn't have gone amiss. How you got that by Abigail I have no idea. Respect. Yes, I can see where you've lost weight, thanks.

You need to be careful with the drinking, N, thankfully they all thought you were in character. "You're all going to die" can get a bit concerning after a while. Whatever happened to "I lub you, I really lub you"?

To recap then for last night, 15 guests, 1 Robinson Crusoe, 1 Girl Friday, 10 Zombie apocalypse's, I'll put you down as Lord Greystoke and 1 Jane. How the fashions have changed, the end of the world equals zombie apocalypse. Oh, and just to remind you, I wouldn't want your drunkenness to get in the way of a good bit of embarrassment, you kept going on about Helen's zombie makeup and how brilliant it was, when she was the only one not in character. I don't know whether you should apologise or just leave it be. She's not exactly going to cut you out of her will is she? I keep thinking how pretty Ed's girlfriend is, it's such a shame there's no room and no hope, but there's only so much we can do. We have to be firm N, we have to be selfish, otherwise no one will survive. On the one hand it's nobody's fault, but on the other, it's everybody's. We should all share collective responsibility for failing to act but we should also share collective responsibility for doing what we do. Damned if you do and damned if you don't. Let's be selfish and make a decision to be selfish.

I've been dipping into the BBC text pages again, precious little going on during the holiday period. It makes me laugh watching the 'nearly's reading the news, the backroom understudies presenting the news to camera while the 'real stars' are at home enjoying Christmas. The only reason they do it is in the hope that they'll be noticed and brought to the dominance that their obsequiousness deserves. That's the thing about Teletext, it's both concise and informative. And yet it's also extremely short of detail. To get a fuller understanding of the subject matter more research is required. But we never bother with the further research and so we are left with a comprehensive mind-set of an image that we parade proudly on our CV's to any that will listen. Our knowledge is not unlike one of those pictures composed of smaller images that magically transform into a larger image. Each individual picture acts like a pixel in the larger image. We take the sum total of our knowledge, our prejudices, our instincts, our education, our interactions with our fellows travellers to arrive at a 24 million pixel image that sits comfortably as our mind program. An image in HD that we view through cloudy lenses. Or do we, for years we were content to view low definition screens until the newer technology launched and suddenly we have to be able to see the individual squares on a tennis court net. For years we were content to view the world through gossip and discourse with our neighbours, occasionally a passing stranger would inject excitement into the proceedings with exotic tales of sea monsters or butterflies as large as small doves. Until the technology beamed near instantaneous coverage of 'news' into our enlightened lives and suddenly we are expected to care about events a world away. Events spun and carefully crafted to fit the pro forma, the recipe of the day, the horizon of the Bait Ball. Where shall we glean our news after the 20th N? What horizon will we be watching? A former colleague, a Geordie told me about the Hartlepool hanging of a French spy during the Napoleonic wars. Cross-examined at the trial the locals were unable to translate the French to English and vice versa. They hung the 'spy' whose sole crime was to have been a monkey. The tale has endured for two centuries and may or may not be based on fact.

Hartlepool foils French invasion.

A French ship was seen floundering off the coast of Hartlepool and the only survivor was dragged ashore and arrested.

Local fishermen tried the French prisoner and having satisfied themselves as to his guilt hung the spy until dead.

The fishermen's spokesman declared "he refused to answer any questions and we concluded that his reticence was due to his underlying guilt".

BBC Teletext January 12th 1803

This is the world we live in. We anaesthetise ourselves with knowledge that has no meaning and serves no purpose. We quote and cite learned individuals who also participated in the grand scheme without ever questioning it. What question will we face on D Day plus 40? We have no way of knowing but they will all be relevant. Life will be an awfully big adventure.

It's seems strange to me really, although on reflection, perhaps not. The media has raised the spectre of nuclear Armageddon and the increasing tensions between East and West and yet it has failed to gain any traction in the herd's consciousness. Don't they know that we only have capacity for one threat at a time? Global warming holds centre stage and everything else is relegated to the status of a sideshow to be ignored by all but the diehard fans. But in its way, that's maybe a good thing, because if we were to concentrate on Armageddon we'd have no capacity for global warming or population control or extinction level events and the thousand and one other things that we don't have capacity for, so, in fact, no change. Is it because women are not in charge? Are we doomed to extinction by the dominant male's inability to multitask? Although that is not always a good thing, Confucius once said "woman who cooks carrots and pees [sic] in the same pot, dirty woman". Sorry about the translation from the original, they spelt peas wrong, probably a university education thing. This begs a wider question, is there a league table of pertinence? But how would this work? The media works within the confines of a self-reinforcing loop, news has to be interesting to generate revenue, revenue generates the media. The unpopular, the unpalatable, the same old, same old trite has had its day and costs in footfall and revenue generation. Except it hasn't, for the same old, same old trite bollocks works perfectly well for football managers, useless wankers sacked one week to be resurrected as experienced heavyweight saviours a month later. The memory of their pathetic failure expunged from the public record as fast as their clichés leap the moon. For some reason I keep thinking of football managers and really have to fight for control of my index finger that keeps trying to put an 'r' in the middle of moon, as in over the. Just think N, just how verbose I could have been if I'd learnt to type with more than one finger. You are getting the shortened version. You can thank me later.

R
XXX

Sent from my iPad

Re: Day 19 January 2ⁿᵈ Monday Bank holiday in lieu

Dearest N

It's such a shame really isn't it? Every time we have one of these communal shindigs I am reminded of how ours is such a nice community. The age range disappears and we all get along ish. I think you do need to apologise to Helen, I've heard one or two things if you get my drift and I'd hate to think that your car could be 'keyed' by an octogenarian. Feisty zombie or what? I know, you were only saying what we were all thinking, but you said it. Anyway, you won't be eating humble pie for long. Is that to be our future N, the living dead? When all around have disappeared and we are all that is left will we feel blessed or cursed? Cursed by the memories of all that has been lost or blessed by the new reality, a new life free of constraint and utter, utter, utter, abject bullshit. A life where success is measured by the fullness of the belly, the warmth of a blanket, the waterproofness of the roof above your head, the wonder of a lesson learned, an advantage gained, a life fulfilled. Bollocks to the mortgage, interest rates, pension drawdowns, taxable allowances, planning consents, FIFA, 'A levels', fucking jobsworths, double yellow lines and bus lanes. We will lose so much and gain much more if we apply ourselves to it N. The end of the Bait Ball. And it only took the end of Mankind to achieve it. I would consider that to be an evolutionary disadvantage N, an inbuilt mechanism that ensures our self-destruction. Is it all part of the Great Game that Mother Nature plays, where ultimately it's her bat, her ball and her rules? A failsafe to ensure that the means to end are inbuilt into our very fabric, an off switch, a kill code that defaults to end imbalance when the rules are being broken. Cor, don't I go on? But you know I do, and secretly you enjoy it, the stimulation, the oblique way of viewing life. Or, it goes in one ear and out the other. But I believe N, that given enough time I can break the pro forma of your mind and unleash thought processes that have lain dormant and subjugated for too long. There is another way. Mine is a lone voice whereas Trump has the trigger finger. Mine is a voice that will not be heard by 98.8% of the population whereas Trump's will not be heard by 98.8% of the population, but for a different reason. The end result will be the same, a product of our evolutionary disadvantage and one that we have earnt. But not deserved, because to deserve reflects a desire, an ambition, a plan achieved and not to stumble blindly into the abyss that awaits us.

BBC came up with this; Len McCluskey, head of the Unite union and one of Corbyn's closest allies, described the party's standings in the opinion polls as "awful". Jeremy could step down if things don't improve said Len. Both Corbyn and shadow chancellor John McDonnell were not "desperate to cling onto power for power's sake".

A Unite leadership rival accused Len of trying to be "Labour's puppet master" and of issuing a "public ultimatum".

How very, very strange. Perverse even. A recognition that Labour are doing terribly in the polls and a need to change tack. And this at a time when the party is being 'revolutionised' and being driven near violently left with threats of deselection. A recognition that the followers with a head start are leaving the bulk of the herd behind, lost and milling around in need of fresh followers to lead? What makes me laugh, not too much mind, my intercostal muscles are still sore, is the statement "desperate to cling on to power". For the one thing that JC does not have, nor never will have, is power.

King of the hill holds no sway when what you need to be is king of the mountains. To be fair, I can't see white with red spots being JC's colour, he's more a solid red, but the problem even then is the yellow of the general classification that wins the contest.

The other issue is that of the 'fortunes of the Labour party' as though they give the remotest shit about the Labour Party when their sole purpose in life is to cling onto the power that their office provides. Then, get this, the other candidate for Unite then issues a statement about "ultimatums" and "puppet master". Priceless, you work out your union role and ambitions to achieve it and then denounce your competitor for having achieved it. Why can't I write a work of fiction, I just don't know how to fire up my imagination to come up with these bollocks?

R
XXX

Sent from my iPad

Re: Day 18 January 3rd Tuesday

Dearest N

Why do I believe that the more we know, the less it helps us? They would have been a time when we didn't know how to smoke tobacco or manufacture crystal meth. We certainly didn't know how to destroy cities in mere seconds, although we knew how to destroy them in weeks or months. There would have been a time when we didn't understand the principle of global warming, let alone how to prevent it. There might come a time, if you follow my argument, when you might understand that we don't know how to prevent it only exploit it for our ends. There was a time when we disadvantaged our neighbours by stealing their choice grub (the wriggly kind) or forced them away from the best fruiting area of the tree, when we risked others' lives by driving them to the ambush prone edges to provide the buffer between the hunter and the hunted. If you were born weak or recessive then you suffered at the paws of the strong and dominant. Nothing has changed. The weak are still disadvantaged, the strong still dominant and we are still not polite about it, no please and thankyou's. How have we allowed the dominant 'silverback' to grab the reins of the world? How can an animal whose range was controlled by line of sight and strength of arm have risen to control billions while retaining these base instincts and primal urges to secure the best future for themselves? I asked you before N, how did Sepp Blatter take an inflated pigs bladder and a bunch of kids enjoying some exercise and turn it into the multibillion circus we know as the 'beautiful game'? How can modern America built on the desires and promises of immigrants and refugees fleeing persecution from Europe and abroad revert to the same standards that drove them to the Americas in the first place. The simple answer is, it's within our nature, we are climbers. We climb trees, metaphorical trees to replace the ones we used to swing through. We climb over the backs of others to reach the heights and having reached the slopes our energies are turned to maintain our position by preventing others from climbing.

Our immediate problem post-bunker will be that we do not know enough. That is only partly true, for we will also know too much, what was, what might be, if only we can achieve it. How to reconcile our difference between what we want and what we can achieve. If Magna Park and its huge reserves are lost to us then life will be immeasurably more difficult from the outset but only if we let our ambitions exceed our abilities. How shall WE control our ambitions within our abilities? We take each and every day as it comes N, enjoy the simple pleasure of being alive beyond survival and we should rejoice in our new found freedom. Why will we be in this mess, N, it's as simple as letting our ambitions exceed our abilities? But as ever I am talking obliquely, for it is Trump whose ambitions have exceeded his abilities and it is Trump that will push the button. But let me be obliquely oblique because it is we that will have let him. It is we that created the office, built the weapons, fostered the electoral process and surrendered our will to the Great Brain that will never be satisfied with all that one Earth can provide. "But we're not American" I hear you say, but theirs is a system borne of democracy, of compliance with the Great Brains, of pyramids built off the backs of the subjugated, an order of Man built by Man. Trump truly will provide a government of the people, by the people, for the people and they shall receive what they have allowed to pass for therein lies the kingdom, the power and the glory until the end of Man. I have a simple question for you, a route to a solution to our imminent destruction that proves the fault in our process. "Stop Trump, how"? There lies the problem N, for there is no method, no process, no mechanism for stopping him. I might as well ask how we can stop the sale of ivory into China. I could ask how we stop cocaine entering the bloodstream. I could ask how we stop the profligate waste of resource within the NHS or the Welfare State. I could ask how we stop highway engineers. I could ask you how we stop the RSPB from killing birds by 'saving' ours. But the real question, the one that only Trump has an answer to, is how do we stop? But Trump's solution is a lie. Trump's solution proves my point precisely, because we shall stop because he can't.

Having depressed you enough for the moment N, I scanned the text pages and found these items:

Ford Motors cancels $1.6 bn (£1.3 bn) plant it planned to build in Mexico and instead the car giant will spend $700m on expanding the plant at Flat Rock Michigan.

El Trumpo has criticised both Ford and its rival General Motors over production of models in Mexico and threatened them with import duties.

And:

One of the Labour supporting 'think tank' organisations has questioned Labour's ability to form a government. Andrew Harrup, the Fabian Society's general secretary, said there had been a "huge meltdown' of support in Scotland and that Labour is too weak to win a general election on its own. Andrew's study cited JC's unpopularity and muffled approach to Brexit. Corbyn's spokesman leapt to his defence by saying that he was an alternative to "failed" UK politics.

Both were on my beloved BBC Teletext, I'll really miss its simple information service and have to contend with real life instead.

Anyway, El Trumpo has struck, he's not even in office and yet Ford have turned turtle over their previously announced plans. All it took was the threat of a massive import tariff for Ford to come to their senses and SPEND $900,000,000 LESS on an existing home grown facility. "Gee, I wish my government had provided Ford with $5.9 billion of cheap loans in 2009 to overhaul its factories and bring out more fuel-efficient technology so that they could export all the jobs to Mexico". "I'm so glad my tax-dollars are not wasted on supporting Mexicans". Will Trump chalk this up as his second victory to follow his election success? Do you think the success will go to his head? Have we just seen the foundations poured for the wall along the southern border? Being a billionaire the sky is pretty much your limit, unless you are Elon Musk in which case just one planet is so passé when there's a red one nearby. Not wishing to get side-tracked, you never know, it could happen once, is America awakening to a new corporate order? America for American's.

Corbyn on the other hand seems to be languishing at the very end of the alimentary canal in the polls, pathetically clinging to any semblance of reality. If the inability to attract support could be deemed to be failure, a not unreasonable supposition I would suggest, then to what "failure" is his spokesman referring? We are not talking 'silent majority' here, oh no, it's more like a bound, gagged, encased in sound proofing very silent minority that he is championing. Jeremy, no one is listening, you are a non-politician, a verruca on the sole of politics, a waste of space, an anachronism on the political scene, a red double-decker thingy to measure tree heights with in just 57 days. I wonder, just a thought, would you forget to invite the leader of the Queen's official opposition to Whitehall's secure government bunker in the event of the three minute warning? Locked underground for 40 plus days listening to "I told you so" is enough to drive anyone to the ultimate sanction of taking another one's life. Except of course, the very fact that you are staring at the bloodshot eyes of Corbyn as you choke the life from his body within a sealed nuclear bunker is a bit of a clue as to the importance of 'ultimate sanctions', which by then would have become incredibly popular in terms of sanction, ultimate thereof.

Elon Musk seems to be intent on securing an alternative future for our species by establishing a foothold on Mars. A protection against super volcanoes, virulent disease and even nuclear Armageddon along with further technological developments yet to see the light of day. A defence against extinction is offered by Elon who is not content to be a billionaire with just one world as his plaything. And when it's built and manned with the great and good, quarantined from Earth by at least 54.6 million kilometres of empty void, will this make us safer or more exposed I wonder? But not for long. For then you can truly talk about an alternative future for our species. The good news is, Elon was born in South Africa and is ineligible to stand as President of the US.

R
XXX

Sent from my iPad

Re: Little sister

DEAREST N

Any further thoughts on disinheriting Abi and Edward? Only my visa bills due on the 16th and you know how I've always got your back.

R

Sent from my Samsung device.

Re: Little sister

Dear Robert

Mine too, for £7.5k

N

Sent from my IPhone

Re: Little sister

N

Yes, but that doesn't answer my question.

R

Sent from my Samsung device

Re: Little sister

Robert

Well I could manage a loan if that helps at nil interest for a good period?

N

Sent from my iPhone

Re: Little sister

N

I'll ring you.

R

Re: Day 17 January 4th Wednesday

Dearest N

Are we doing the right thing N, would it be better to bow to the inevitable and simply fade away? It's so easy to get wrapped up in the process of survival that we can end up losing sight of our objectives. I worry that we may suffer if we do nothing. A blinding flash followed by an instant of pain beyond comprehension seems like a welcome relief. But what if it we are out of range, far enough away to be blinded and burnt but not killed? Left to die a lingering death, to suffer. I believe the bunkers will protect us from this immediate fate and for that we need to be grateful. Time, then, is the next objective, to hide within our cocoons in the hope that conditions for life become more tenable.

We will be blessed as well N, for if we survive we will truly understand our objectives and our needs. For the first time ever.

I'm not ready to surrender my energy just yet, N and I would sooner die trying, to continue the adventure, to see what's over the horizon. The death of one world will lead to the birth of another and we can be part of it. I realise that this is nothing new, it's what we do, cross horizons, live. It's what we've always done, it's just the scale that's wrong. A scale that leaves nothing spare, an all pervading tsunami of destruction that scours our planet.

I've had a thought about the last days, N and I've booked Jan into Ragdale Hall for a two day spa visit. This means she's out of the way while I complete the final preparations for the Pop 20 so I won't need to use your toilet facilities, thanks, I'll pee in the bushes. This will leave me free to concentrate on the Pop 40 the following day. I haven't worked out yet how to keep the rest of the neighbours away from the unit while we alter it. "Just stocking it up with provisions for three to survive 40 days underground. Oh yes, white with no sugar please. Sorry, we'll move the cars off the drive when we've finished, should only be a couple of hours now and you'll be able to drive through". I could open my back gate up so they can drive through my garden which sorts the cars out but we need some thought as to how to keep them away. Maybe we could pump it out and clean it out during the day and then stock it up after dark. That makes sense, because they know we're sorting the 'blockage' out and need to pump and clean it down to solve the 'problem' once and for all. We could leave the pump in the road to seal the drive and that explains the diversion through my garden. We can rig the solar power 'back-up for the air pump', "bloody Environment Agency, keep changing the rules", so that we can see what we're doing inside the bunker. You'll have to pass the bed components through the hatch so I can bolt it all together and then we just have to stock it with provisions, fit the air filters, air pump and modify the 'toilet' pipe. I think we can lift the loose gravel and place the rainwater sheet collector for the toilet flush well before the event. I know Abigail spent some time weeding in the autumn and I could suggest the sheet as a weed suppression membrane, which would allay any suspicions and gain everyone's agreement. Then comes the bit I'm dreading, drugging our spouses and Edward so that we can get them underground. Needs must, I suppose, but it will be a real mental and physical challenge. After that everything will be plain sailing, providing Trump doesn't disappoint. I can't believe I just wrote that, Trump doesn't disappoint. If he doesn't destroy the world I'll be disappointed. It would be nice if he did disappoint but in the scale of things if it's not him it will be somebody else. If it's not somebody else it will be everybody else, 10, 11, 12 billion else's. We really don't have a solution.

Am I a reverse megalomaniac N, I don't want to make it bigger and better, I want to make it smaller and better? Put your knob thatch on N and ask yourself which is better, 7 billion people dying in a near instant or 12 billion people fighting and dying for resource in internecine warfare while the new equilibrium is established? Tough one that? If you don't have one then you have the other. The rock and the hard place. What a carefree path we wander. Of course, officially this question would never be addressed let alone answered. It's akin to the Liverpool Care Pathway whereby you were shuffled off this mortal coil by the denial of food and water. "Of course we haven't euthanized anyone, we've simply let nature take its course". (And helped it on its way). When push comes to shove N, our species will not hold back, we'll take no prisoners and simply engage in slow motion

Armageddon. Thinking about it, can we recruit Edward to strip the gravel back for the polythene membrane? A bit of pocket money won't go amiss for him and he'll be 'helping the community'. I can supervise to make sure we get the falls right. If he up for it tomorrow before he's back at college?

R
XXX

Sent from my iPad

Re: Day 16 January 5th Thursday

Dearest N

What is they say about fruit never falling far from the tree? Edward was a real help, nearly, once I'd stopped him piercing the membrane with the rake anyway. Education, education, education, we are so blessed. D Day plus 40 is when the real education begins N. Thinking about it we'll all be straying into your realm. There will be an infinite amount of 'trial' and error but you won't need your sheepskin rug for these life 'trials'. Actually thinking about it a bit more, the black cap might be more appropriate given the potential for death sentences if we get it wrong. I'm tempted to completely shun mushrooms, they have quite a potential for toxicity and even the experts can get it wrong, with fatal results. Hopefully our well water will be free of radiation and we can wash all food thoroughly before consumption. There is still so much to learn, water cress carries parasites from snails for example and while it's easy to gather it's harder to treat. I suppose we could boil everything before consumption. That will go down well, boiled salad. If nothing else, it will save on chewing. I think I'll get some stock of Milton sterilising fluid, it won't last forever but if it gives us a head start it can only help. It's pathetic really, kids get 15 years of schooling to prepare them for what? It certainly ain't living on a deserted island. It's nearly enough to drive me to watch all the Bear Gryll's video's from start to finish, especially the one where he takes the President of the US out in to the wilderness and leaves him, I wish. If you stop and think, all the life skills that we learn at school simply plug us into the matrix. No, not the matrix, more of a maze, where you have to learn the most convoluted route possible to solve a problem. "I'm hungry" turns into learn how to read and write and accept/give orders to others to dig a hole in the earth or build a tractor or count other people's beans when all you had to do was walk over to the nearest fruiting bush and eat some. But the funny thing is, and it isn't funny, the maze is so complicated and so involved that nobody ever works out how to traverse it while remembering the original question. The process is hijacked along the way to serve the process and nothing else. Now that begs another question N, what fruit and what tree? Our metaphorical tree is so far removed from being a tree it isn't a tree.

Edward will survive perfectly well in the world we are soon to abandon, he may go through life without getting his hands dirty, but he will get through it. The world we are soon to abandon is corrupt, it has lost any semblance of relevance or reason, we do what we do because it's what we do and this is how we do it. But imagine Edwards's life post bunker, no maze, no matrix, only real bushes with real fruit. "I'm hungry" translates into find food and eat it. I read years ago about the lords of the manor eating pigeon through the winter as a source of fresh meat. By feeding with grain they would breed through the winter and the dove cotes were a rich source of income in a world without meat preservation techniques. (Not strictly speaking true, creosote is from the Greek for 'flesh preserver' because they'd worked out millennia ago that wood smoke preserves meat and then of course there was salt, albeit in short supply). But while the lords had their dove cotes the peasants had their thatched hovels and ate the nesting sparrows instead. How do peasants find food now, why in the supermarkets of course, or the food bank and spend their wages or welfare. Whereas the lords of the manor still sit with all their grandeur obtaining wealth and resource from the echelons of peasantry supporting them. We all know that milk comes from milk bottles, (that reminds me, we need to cancel the milk after the 20th, we don't want to emerge to the smell of cheese everywhere) and that is all we seem or need to know, or did. I bet you view 'smoked salmon' differently now, now you know the flavour is creosote. Although, if wood contains creosote, why does wood go rotten, unless you paint it with creosote? I jest of course N, it's all a question of amount. If Magna Park survives, then all we have to do is descend on the Asdalavista bush and remove the crop of freshly fruited tins of peaches, strawberries, et al. We could go for prunes if the radiation therapy doesn't work for you Neville. It can be our 'Food Bank'.

Just a thought N, do we need a cover story for our absence? What happens if Trump is a bit dilatory with the end of the world? Say he's that incompetent that it takes him a whole week to destroy the world. We'll be underground arguing with our very immediate family (there's not much room) about why they can't find the exit, or why they can't remember entering, or why we are such mindless arseholes, while above us the neighbours could be mounting a search or worse still, inspecting the Pop 40 to make sure it's working properly. Not a problem for me, because I think I'll build a fence around my bunker to keep people out. One solution could be to deliberately spill effluent around the Pop 40, "Yeah, sorry, the pump sprang a leak" which ought to keep them away for a couple of weeks. That ought to be long enough because if Trump is that incompetent that he can't destroy the planet in two weeks there is probably hope for us to return to the surface. Although we personally might be a bit short of hope, given the reaction of everyone around us. "What, you mean you hijacked our effluent treatment plant because you knew we were all going to die and you didn't bother to warn us"? "I could have had sewage back flowing into my garden". "No wonder the bath took so long to drain, after you'd spent the Management Company's reserve fund on 'sorting' the problem out". At best we can persuade our fellow troglodytes that we were acting in their best interests. Or, if they accept the lie, at which point all we'll get is, "Two weeks holiday abroad, you don't look very brown" always assuming that the inlet pipe seals work properly. I still worry about drugging them, but I just don't think we can take the risk of reasoning with them. I'm overthinking again N, one of my major flaws. I'm just not dumb enough to be a Great Brain, I can see too many options to be able to take a decision. Everything we do revolves around robbing Peter to pay Paul and we have no answer to anything. Of course, if my name was Paul then the decisions would be very easy. Have I just cracked it, the essence of true leadership? Maybe I'm being too cynical? What actually happens is you commission a group of Great Brains to come up with the solution of robbing Peter before they present the findings to you so that you can then agree on the basis that it is the best possible solution. Unless your name is Peter. Not a problem, when your name is Paul. Sorted. Fucking typical, 16 days left and I finally worked it out. I could have been a Great Brain after all. Bollocks. I've wasted my life.

And yet?

R
XXX

Sent from my iPad

Re: Day 15 January 6th Friday

Dearest N

Seems like the start of the New Year, N, Edward and Abigail back at school, you back at work, Jan back at the gym. You'll have to tell me how your disciplinary review goes, this Tuesday coming isn't it? I can't believe they'll do much more than the suspension you've already served, although in the grand scale of things, nothing really matters, does it? I think you can be quite relaxed. I always used to hate this time of year, my order book reset to zero and I had to do the whole lot over again. I used to think about having two order books, one starting on the first of July and one on the first of January. At least then I would always have something in the order book. I used to console myself with 4 point moving averages at the finish, I plotted the average for the last four months on a graph to smooth out the peaks and troughs. My own personal lie that I understood was a lie and yet I persisted, no consoled myself with. Is that the drive to leave the autobiography I wonder? Write it down, colour it with rose tinted glasses, demonstrate how reasonable and considerate you were as you embarked upon your career in robbing Peter. Write the personal lies that you know are lies so as to console yourself with it. I'm sure you've come across guilt free criminals proclaiming their innocence while reviewing the DNA and glorious technicolour high definition video evidence arrayed before you and the court. Say it loud enough and long enough and some of it will stick or better still put it on record and write that biography. Scratch that rock with "I woz ere". Legacy. Do other Great Brains read these discourses, scanning for hints, scouring for examples of behaviour considered reasonable to be used as tools in their own arsenals? What are the limits, what can I get away with, will I be held accountable? What legacy will Trump leave beyond the ashes N? But Trump's legacy is already written for him, it was done in advance by the generations that went before him. In its simplest form Trump is only president elect because of Clinton. She shaped and fashioned the electorate as carefully and as craftily as Trump. She drove voters towards him as she endeavoured to attract them to her cause. Clinton failed because there was something that the electorate had seen before, that struck a discord that repelled them, that turned them off or turned them over. Half the people didn't vote, dissatisfied and disenfranchised by the whole process, by the previous failures. Perhaps, it's possible, that half the voters are Peter's whereas those that voted for Trump saw the possibility of changing their names to Paul's. I can feel a biological model coming on, the growing tip of a tree, the apical bud. This releases chemicals that inhibit the growth of side shoots and concentrates the resources to the growing tip racing for the light to form the classic Christmas tree shape that we are so familiar with. The side shoots become subsidiary and expendable and serve only to provide the resource to the tip. Under the American political model a choice is made, every 4-8 years to have an electoral race to determine which bud will become the apical leader. The new leader instantly supplants the previous one and puts them in the shade to wither and fail from lack of resource as the tree grows in a different direction which is always upwards. But the tree cannot function as an apical bud alone, it needs all the root and trunk and resource gathering facilities beneath it to give it life and vigour. A life and vigour it secures by denying life and vigour to all below it. But the tree is still there, subservient and supporting and without its presence and previous activity no apical bud survives either. Trump is no accident, Trump is the devil incarnate. Has that got your attention Neville? Sorry, did I say devil? I meant to say … If good and evil are at opposite ends of the spectrum that would make Clinton what, the angel Gabriel? I'm pulling your leg Neville, I know how you like a good splutter. Trump is the apical bud and his presence is determined entirely by the whole tree that went before it. We assume that the leader is in control of the tree whereas the tree is in control of the leader. Without the resource supporting the leader there is no tree and by definition no leader either. Who shall we blame for Trump then N, Clinton, or Obama or was it Bush? Is Trump simply Obama's legacy? But Bush, both of them, were also products of the tree before them. Was the tree planted by the Founding Fathers or did they simply reap that which was sown by the colonial rulers? Think about it long enough Neville and you will see that the tree is as old as modern humans themselves. Every individual supporting and providing, pushing the apical bud ever skywards in pursuit of, now, there's the rub N, pursuit of what? Let me rub salt in the wound N, for the modern human tree was nurtured by *Homo erectus* who borrowed it from *Homo habilis* who nicked it from somewhere else. Our tree supplanted that of *Neanderthal* and *Denisovan*. Who should scratch our legacy in the rock N, the apical bud or the tree? And to think that the time was, when all we had to worry about, was how to climb the tree to gain security, shelter and food. And that is all that

Trump has done, climb the tree. How many fucking towers does he need to build to gain a view? Can you remember the cereal joke about the cornflake that worked out (in the gym), determined to be the fittest and strongest he fought his way to the top of the box to ensure that he would be among the first to emerge. Can you remember the punchline N, I'll tell you tomorrow. (Serial joke). Less generously, but more importantly there was this sperm that worked out, swimming lengths, perfecting his technique absolutely determined to be the first to fertilise the egg and secure his future. Always at the front whenever the prostrate started to dribble he fought his way past lesser sperm to ensure his place in the lead. Shortly after, he was seen swimming frantically in the 'wrong' direction shouting "back, go back, it's a blow job". Well Trump has been at the apex, the top, so often and continues to seek out fresh heights that you have to wonder what it is he seeks in life that can justify the effort. Has he yet to spot an egg worthy of his ego? Is there an egg worthy of him? Now as luck would have it N, the University of California San Francisco has found that the life span of human sperm is as little as 42 days. By fortuitous coincidence nearly the same amount of time as we expect to be chez bunker, premature evacuations permitting, of course. How poetic N, we can erupt from beneath the ground to repopulate the Earth. Shame about the vasectomy, somehow I don't think my favourite expletive is appropriate, so, no bollocks.

Here's the thing. Trump, champion of the American worker, saviour of the Ford worker. Through his twitter account he is credited with the volte face by the Ford Motor Company. These jobs have not come into existence yet, but let us suppose that they had, in November 2016. Donald Trump, 700 jobs, brilliant, except? Except, in November 2016 the US economy added an additional 204,000 jobs to its workforce. Seven hundred jobs are not to be sniffed at and it is an achievement. But 700 jobs represents just 0.34% of November's. Hardly Trump the hero is it? Or, to put it another way, if your daily wage was £100 then Trump's actions are equivalent to a further 34p. Hardly cause for celebration, it can't even buy you a packet of crisps.

R
XXX

Sent from my iPad

Re: Day 14 January 7ᵗʰ Saturday

Dearest N

Anyway, having fought its way through to the top of the box, several times, (this is the abridged version) because it kept getting disturbed in transit, the cornflake sat waiting for the carton to be opened when this kid picked up the box and opened it upside down.

The legacy is the tree, how dare our Great Brain's seek out legacy and write their memoirs, although, why doesn't it surprise me. "Yes, well you see, I was in command when the battle was won, dangerously near the action I might add, you could hear the explosions if the wind was in the right direction. Of course I didn't wade through all the blood and guts, you have to have standards, what. And you can't get an appreciation of the battle near to, you need time and perspective to really understand my achievement".

Four years to leave your mark on the Earth, to scratch your presence, to become a note in history. Or should it be a life of breeding to leave your legacy, your DNA entwined with another's to persist forever in the bloodlines of our species? Is this not the biological ambition, the biological imperative that supersedes all others, the overriding urge to breed, to secure a future? Even in this we are corrupt, cheated by the biology for the constants are not the constantly diluted bloodlines but the mitochondrial DNA that passes only through the female line. Altered over the millennia by mutation only it could be argued that our single function is to provide a vehicle for mitochondria to continue to survive. I know that your biology is a little rusty N, a shame really given that your mother was a biology teacher. She taught me that chloroplasts contained chlorophyll that made plants green and made them capable of photosynthesis while mitochondria contained the means to release energy and to provide it for use throughout the cell. It was thought at the time that it was possible that chloroplasts and mitochondria could have existed as independent entities before incorporation into larger organisms. Thinking about it, your fruit fell some distance away from your mother's tree. But our nature is to secure resource, to steal energy from the sun while having no ability to produce it. We must consume what others have produced (no photosynthesis for you) by stealing and killing for it, it is the most natural thing in the world for us. These then are the ground rules for our species, 'The Prime Directive' is to steal and kill to secure life.

Now there's an idea N, can't we get those clever scientist type chappies to genetically modify us so that we can photosynthesise. Think of all the CO2 we'd absorb. There might be another reason beyond harvesting melanomas to lie in the sun. "Been abroad for two weeks on holiday, you don't look very green" ought to do it. Think of all the farmland we could dispense with. I wonder, what with all the mutation causing radiation we are about to be exposed to … should I store some aphidcide in the water tank N, to be on the safe side? We have a problem though N, for green things by and large don't tend to move very much. I should say under their own steam and not swept along by ocean or river current. Is there a lesson here N, to be truly sustainable we need to become sedentary and utilise only those resources that are at hand. At some time in our pre-pre-history a switch was thrown, an indicator that hurried us down one trouser leg of time to become consumers as opposed to the producers, those blessed with the means to fix energy from the sun. But we can't all consume, we need the producers to balance the equation. And that, in a nutshell is the one thing we have singularly failed to achieve, balance. Our lives today are out of balance with the lives we hope to live in the future and rely on our plundering of the past. But that is not all, for they are out of balance with today as well. Ours is a failing experiment. How will it end, will we fade away or shall we go out with a bang? A rhetorical question Neville that Trump has already answered.

Now wouldn't that be funny N, all the skinny young things lying on the beach to get an all over green tan would swell with carbohydrate and become fat. Everything in moderation I suppose. Another thought, don't go on a diet simply invite some caterpillars over for luncheon. You'd also have a heads up when people were about to die of natural causes, they'd turn yellow or orange or red or brown and you could have a party where they could attend as well. Have a pre-burial party, I'll call it an 'awake', the soon to be cadaver usually ends up paying for it through the estate so why shouldn't they get some pleasure from it as well? Just escort them to the bash while avoiding any strong winds. And as an added bonus, don't go for internment, head for the compost heap instead.

I wonder Neville, after the 20th will there be much call for 'gallows' humour? (Ok, you don't think there's much call for it now, misery guts). After Hiroshima people had just disappeared leaving only one trace, essentially a shadow on the ground or wall, a silhouette. I wonder if we'll see anything worthy of the adult's only section of the Pompeii exhibit. Will it raise a smile or generate only tears? Ours will be an uncertain future, but that's nothing to worry about really. Even without Trump ours is already an uncertain future, we just don't bother to worry about it. It's above our paygrade and after all, that's what we have Great Brains for isn't it, let them do all the ignoring for us.

Even without the home-made suns what do we ever leave behind, a memory, an idea, a notion? What will our legacy be do you think, Trump excepting, to future generations? Shall we be the caring, sharing, sustainable, conservation minded generation that presided over the greatest extinction level event since the asteroid that was heading north until it was deflected by the border wall and ended up near the Yucatan Peninsula instead? It won't matter, nothing ever does, it's simply business as usual. Or will our generation be remembered for constructing the wall, the latest, for I can't say the first, blow in the race for survival between the resource rich and military powerful and the also rans. The soon to be disenfranchised of life giving resource. Let's call them what they are N, losers, losers in the race for life. It is nothing personal, just biology.

I have stumbled across a potential solution to our apparent impasse at changing the way the herd is moving. Teletext brought the report of Sir Andrew Cook who has been a major Tory donor threatening to halt further donations if Theresa May's government takes us out of the single market. Apparently leaving the single market was 'chronic and dangerous' to the economy (and one of his four engineering factories that was almost entirely dependent on it). This might surprise you N, but Sir Andrew backed Remain. Can we organise a whip round to change Trump's mind, have we enough time?

Andrew has been an avid supporter of Remain and only became a 'Sir' in David Cameron's resignation honours list. According to Wikipedia, he has given £2.5m to the Conservative party and £300,000 to one of the 'In' campaigns. He generates his wealth from the manufacture of steel castings through his four factories with an estimated annual turnover of around £60m and employs around 600 people. All of which are significant achievements and deserved to be applauded. In the scale of the UK's annual turnover his achievements probably rank in percentage terms on a par with a single full stop on this page. Why then would anyone feel the need to take his threats seriously? Why then would anybody consider that the removal of party donations should hold any sway over the debate? If you can 'buy' the argument for £2.5m I am quite sure that we could organise a bidding war. Why did we even bother with a referendum? We should have just asked him. At least post Armageddon N, life will lose its corruption element. No, scratch that, we'll still puff out our chests to deter rivals, our wives will probably continue to paint their faces and adorn their bodies with bits of metal and Edward will learn how to project himself on any potential mates. I wonder, will we lay 'spoor' to mark our territory, markers to deter rivals from attempting to usurp us? In evolutionary terms, Sir Andrew seems to have mastered the bower bird technique of accumulating trinkets to adorn his stomping ground to attract attention way beyond the abilities of his base plumage. You are one man, who had one vote, yet you seek to dictate and dominate the procedure far, far beyond your qualifications. I begin to think you harbour aspirations to become a Great Brain.

There is a claim out there that a single elephants footprint can turn into a waterhole. Now this isn't some butterfly wing beat causing a hurricane chaos idea, its practical. In road terms it's akin to the formation of potholes. Every wheel passes through a water logged hole forces water into the surrounding strata and washes it away over time. What starts as a water filled crack develops into a small pothole that keeps growing until the repair is made. With unmetalled roads, hard-core, the process is very fast and potholes reappear rapidly even after the original hole has been refilled. The elephant's foot print can collect water which softens the surrounding soil making it more susceptible to removal by other passing animals. As the hole gets bigger it grows faster until eventually a full blown watering hole has appeared. There is no architect, there is no engineer, there is no leader. As a species we create self-perpetuating voids that start by accident and develop, slowly at first, rapidly later into vacuums.

I taught my Clara how to drive and for that matter my two son's before her. In truth, I couldn't actually teach her how to drive, the way they learn these days would have been measured as a failure in our day N. They keep it in fourth gear until coming to a halt whereas we learnt to always be in the correct gear on the approach to a junction. If you suddenly needed to take avoiding action 20 feet from the give way line you'd be stuffed trying to pull off in 4th at 5mph. What I used to do was offer them time and exposure to the roads and other users. I have a near encyclopaedic knowledge of local roads and would pick routes specifically to expose them to unusual and unexpected hazards. I would take my son's down a quiet country lane only for it to turn into the M1, M6, A14 interchange at Catthorpe, what a bastard I was. Of course it's all gone now, all flyover links and it only cost £200m plus to deprive me of the shock value to my son's. Of course I knew it was within their capabilities otherwise I would never have done it. Anyhow, Clara seemed to struggle with bends and I had to explain how they worked so that she could gauge the appropriate speed. I talked about horizons and how they change. On a straight flat empty motorway the horizon is as far as the eye can see. But as soon as other vehicles are involved the horizon has to change to accommodate their needs and the hazards they present. Equally, the faster you drive the further ahead your horizon needs to be. You can't drive at 70 mph while looking 20 feet in front of the bonnet. Similarly, you can't look 200 feet in front while trying to park in the supermarket car park. What I showed her was the way that the horizon alters as you approach a bend. For this purpose the horizon is vertical and it is the limit of vision around the bend. The horizon is either open or closed. As you enter a gentle bend the distance to the horizon is relatively large and constant and speed can be maintained. But as the bend gets more severe then the horizon is reduced and speed needs to be reduced. She soon learnt to differentiate between opening and closing horizons and could match her speed to suit. Job done. Big deal. But you know a bit more about me than you used to N, so you also know that more is to follow. If we examine that statement N, then your knowledge of me and how I think has opened up to you. In the past I presented a horizon of self to you, we were polite, we were friends, we were neighbours. When you first moved in to the community, all the other residents were 'tight bends' to you with limits on the horizons that they offered you. Our household has always been more of a gentle bend because of our cumulative history. With the looming crisis, the bend between us has disappeared. If we think back a few years, the real 'ice breaker' within the community was the need to resolve the sewer problem with an economical and equitable solution for all involved. The combination of a failing Victorian sewer system and the Environment Agency rule change forced us into cooperating. One horizon was being limited by the problem imposed upon us. We found a way. We overcame the obstacles. We increased our horizon again. But in the process, many of the community bends disappeared as well and to this day you hold regular management meetings, organise inspection rotas, and collect money for electricity and maintenance costs. But outside the practicalities, friendships have developed as the horizon limitations have been removed. Our species has enjoyed a history of crossing horizons, exploring, adapting and developing to the new experiences that horizon crossing produces. Trump is about to close our horizons down. In the very short term our horizon will be the plastic face of the bunker, just 1.4m wide.

If the history of modern man can be summarised as the crossing of horizons what about our more recent history. I would suggest that our horizon crossing has become inverted. I think of Edward having just passed his exams as he has progressed on towards his A levels prior to university. For Edward to progress he has to pass his exams and qualify to cross each of the horizons erected before him. He has to cross the threshold of entry. He has to achieve the approval of his peers. It becomes a closed shop, the membership of the club is controlled by the guilds or if you'd prefer the unions. Why do we accept the control, the subjugation? Silverback subjugation by post. For horizon read pro forma. It's time to stop talking about D Day plus 40 and to call it something else. The usual cliché is 'the first day of the rest of your life' and so it will be, but it's also horizon free day, welcome to the world day, we survived day, happy birthday, even *dies natali solis invicti*, assuming that the suns still visible. What shall we call it Neville, adventure day? What are your thoughts?

Because while Trump is about to close our horizons down, it is only the final act in centuries of the same. Trump is simply the ass with his finger on the button, he didn't invent the button nor any of the hierarchy that put him in that position. If an elephants footprint could form a watering hole what was the footprint that led to the nuclear arsenals? The first understanding of atoms and the physics of their structure, the realisation of the power contained within, the threat of an enemy developing the weapon before us, all are potentially valid starters. The Manhattan Project was the name of the programme to develop the first nuclear bombs during WW2 and it has oft been described as a race to beat the Nazis. But the same documentaries will inform you that it was an immense undertaking, the largest ever programme of works undertaken. How would war torn Germany have had the resources to achieve the same? But just as validly what was the footprint that led to Trump? We can consult all the history books we like but we will not find the answer. The scale and complexity of the root is beyond comprehension but it will not stop learned people trying. Was it the first footprints our ancestors left in the soil when they left the trees? But we cannot discount the life forms before we even climbed the trees. Is it inevitable that we will see the process through to its apocalyptic climax? I think I have the answer, N, I'll call it *dies natali*, day birth. How strange, 'survival of the fittest' should lead to *dies natali*. Have I stumbled across the great lie, the falsehood at the base of our species? Religion would have us believe that our superior brain and consciousness is gifted from God and with it comes dominion over the beasts of land and water, ours to control and exploit. The lie is simple, we use our superior brain and consciousness to hold dominion over our fellow species. Our footprint then, is the handful of gene mutations that led to the increased size of our brains, the same brains that have devised our end, the brains that fail to have an off switch, that fail to comprehend life outside the Bait Ball. If we get it wrong N, then *dies natali* might actually be *dies natali* dies, the death of birth days.

If we travelled back in time would we discover some unpalatable truths I wonder N? Knowing what we know now, would it not be reasonable to suggest that Sapiens is directly responsible for the extinction level events that overtook both Neanderthal and Denisovan. There is probably no proof, just a track history of exploiting the rest of the human species of whatever flavour. If the geneticists are correct then the genes for addiction are bred in from Neanderthal's. How ironic it would be if the 'suicide' gene was 'obtained' from Neanderthal perhaps as a defence mechanism against the 'new kids on the block'. It wasn't enough to save Neanderthal, it won't be enough to save Sapiens, for if it's not Trump, the mechanism for oblivion remains. Have I just voiced a great taboo, an acknowledgement of our genocidal tendencies? Shock, horror, or just business as usual.

We are so close to our end N, the end of all that went before, the climax of our intent, the final horizon to be crossed. It should come as no surprise, but it will, because the Bait Ball is about to be reduced in density to render it unworkable. For those of us that survive, the revelation will be forced upon us, knowledge buried in the herd will surface as we are finally exposed to the truth of our circumstance. Life will begin again, once more in pursuit of our own destruction as our technology advances as we subjugate the world around us. It has been reasoned that a 'near extinction level event' around 60,000 years ago forced our species to adapt or die. A bottleneck in our horizon that we overcame. Can we ever know what the event or solution truly was? I bet it wasn't the Environment Agency. Here we sit 60,000 years, call it 3,000 generations later, contemplating the immediate reduction in our horizon. How shall we adapt or die? Our current dilemma N is borne of Man. How does that work, when we are both the cause and solution? There is a form of pig found in SE Asia where it has protruding tusks growing out of its snout that curve back until eventually they can grow far enough to pierce the pigs brain cavity to cause death. (*Babirusas*) Ours is a dissimilar situation for it is our brain that effectively has grown large enough to pierce itself, but not on modified teeth, rather on weapons of our own design. But is that not the utter stupidity of our actions N, our brains offer both the cause and the solution if we would but exercise our thought processes beyond those of the herd?

R

XXX

Sent from my iPad

Re: Day 13 January 8th Sunday

Dearest N

Do you think we could ever overturn our biology N? Is it possible to deny our default setting fused within us by our DNA? Could we think our way out of the problem, always supposing we could recognise the problem? That would be a start I suppose, but a start is never enough and our nature would cut in to return us to the matrix. What we really need N, is a God, an all seeing, all powerful hell and high fury type that could bully and cajole us into submission and compliance. None of this airy-fairy love crap. "Repent and all will be forgiven" won't bring elephants back will it? Then again, there's always Plan B, Trump. It should be possible to herd ants, to steer them in a given direction. All it would take is the right chemical scent line laid down and they would follow it. Where is our scent line? The Great Brains don't have one, nor our religions (alternative culture Great Brains) nor our criminal gangs (alternative, alternative culture Great Brains) nor our scientists (force multipliers) nor our educators (force multipliers) and it is not within the wit of Man either. The herd doesn't have one (society), because for herd you should read Bait Ball and in spite of our desire to cross the horizon we are all blinded by our neighbours.

Over Christmas I watched part one of a BBC documentary about elephants featuring Gordon Buchanan. Actually I lied, I watched part one of a documentary about Gordon Buchanan featuring elephants. I could have written earlier but it took some time gnawing this particular bone to get to the marrow of the story. We are told that 80 elephants a day are being killed for their tusks and all to provide man with ornaments, trinkets made of ivory. Trinkets that serve only one purpose, the ego of man. They are being driven inexorably toward extinction unless we can find a way to save them. The alluded premise of the story was for Gordon to stand on foot within the herd of elephants while filming so that he could feel at one with the beasties. We were exposed to his early introduction and immersion in this semi-wild herd of previously rescued orphans and their wild bred offspring. Obligatory peril was introduced into the proceedings to establish the 'princess' element of this dangerous pastime with the over boisterousness of key individuals and the frequent appearance of passing bulls intent on making their presence known. With all of these things, the producers are looking for the 'money shot', the special eye-catching, or should that be eyebrow raising, breath holding picture that sucks in the audience and justifies the cost and salaries appended to the participants. So what was the shot, the money shot to justify the whole premise of the programme? Essentially it was of Gordon, eye to the viewfinder, surrounded on all sides by 'conditioned' elephants which was of course taken by lesser cameramen deemed unfit to spoil the shots of Gordon at work. Let me rewind a little to the opening statement about elephants dying for the ego of man. Which ego is this I wonder, the ego that sees elephants reduced to lumps of carved ivory upon the mantelpiece or the ego that demands that Gordon should risk life and limb to achieve shots of himself surrounded by elephants? Of course Gordon could have filmed elephants in Sri Lanka or India and been surrounded by them, habitualised, tame, working elephants and could even have edited the shots of their handlers out of the picture. Go back far enough and he could have had a ride around Regents Park Zoo without even the need for a passport. Go back even further and he could have filmed the battle scenes of 'Hannibal, The Movie' without the need for a makeup or special effects department while Hannibal sought to impose his ego over those of the Romans. Of course Gordon's ego is a good ego because no elephants had to die in the making of his picture. How then do we differentiate between the good and bad egos? Hitler's ego was bad because he waged war, while Churchill's ego was good because he refused to sue for peace. Gordon's ego is good if it encourages us to donate to elephant charities while it's bad if your tiger charity loses out to the rekindled interest in elephants. Gordon's attempt to curry favour for the demise of elephants and their elevation into the public's orbit of interest as ever is a double edged sword. For interest in elephants (live ones) can also extend to interest in elephants (dead ones) in the mind of the consumer. And in the minds of the consumer, both thought processes are valid. Arguments have raged about the presence of faux furs and their influence on the brain dead rich who insist on having the real thing, after all, they are already dead so you might as well save what you can. Some guy did a Congo Basin transect sponsored by National Geographic. Something that had never been done before. Something that was impossible. His aim was to document and measure these hitherto pristine habitats for the future, a future that he has single-handedly blighted by proving that it is now possible. I would look his name up on the Internet to give him the respect that he is due, but, I have no respect for him at all. Science as a force multiplier. Essentially he has single handedly given the keys to the jungle door to all and sundry.

R
XXX

Sent from my iPad

Re: Day 12 January 9th Monday

Dearest N

I will cross my fingers for you with your disciplinary, you never know it might impact on your future prospects. Then again, when Trump performs any smears on your character will be erased. Why does it matter N, is the principle of wasting time at the root? While watching teenage girls undress you were stealing time from your employers, the State, and dipping your hand into the pockets of taxpayers. I realise that this principle is sacrosanct to your bosses who religiously and conscientiously ensure that not a single drop of resource is wasted. There is not an ounce of spare within the organisation that employs you and your actions should be met with the abhorrence that they deserve. My view is that you should be chemically castrated at the very least. I wonder how many times you have sat quietly in court listening to abject bullshit from the defence or accused when you could have been more earnestly employed. I wonder, can you possibly measure the performance of your operation on any meaningful scale. Can we add up the sum total of all fines imposed, the community service hours worked or the number of days detained at Her Majesty's displeasure to arrive at a figure of attainment? Should that be edited to remove the amount of fines that have been unpaid, the community service hours not worked or the custodial sentences reduced due to overcrowding? Or is the measure to be one of deterrence, the number of crimes not committed as a consequence of the fear factor induced by your justice factory? Then again, is the true measure of your performance to be found in the peace of mind enjoyed by the population? Is this peace of mind to be measured before or after the supplementary elements have been considered? These supplementary elements will include private security patrols, house alarms, car alarms, CCTV systems both state and privately owned, house contents insurance, car insurance, licenced door staff, security fences and lighting to name some. Will it be measured in the number of released criminals who go on to reoffend and even kill I wonder? Should we factor in the cost of changing all the prison officers' uniforms to remove the royal crest and replace HMP with Noms, the National Offenders Management Service? I met my brother-in-law just before Christmas and he related a tale about his most recent visit to his local hospital for a regular blood-letting. His nurse had been promoted to Sister and he congratulated her on her achievement. "Actually I was promoted 18 months ago and have only just received my new uniform. You see this coloured braid on the sleeve edge? The Trust spent 18 months trying to decide what colour it should be" was her reply. It seems to me N, that whatever pleasure viewing pretty girls removing underwear gave you was a merest pinprick in the grand masturbatory scale of the government and its agencies that you so ably serve. Even the disciplinary will waste more time and resource many, many times over the time you spent indulging. But why did you do it in the first place N, did it give you pleasure? Why do you do anything N, is it for the pleasure? The pleasure of earning a crust, of owning a house, of marrying and providing a stable environment for Abigail and Edward. The utter pleasure of having me as a near neighbour. Is it the pleasure of seeing your life blood drip away pulse by pulse into the vacuum of the Justice Department in exchange for the pleasures that your monetary reward can provide? If we emerge unscathed on D Day plus 40 how will you measure pleasure then N, the sound of a bird singing, the breeze in your face, the laughter of your family or the very fact of being alive? Will D Day plus 40 be the first day of the rest of your life, a rebirth, a second coming (assuming you haven't been chemically castrated?). Will it be day one of the new order, an order without Bait Balls? Please realise that while my comments appear to be deeply personal, they are, it is not my intent to victimise you as an individual. Rather it is to give you a personal example that you can relate to. An example that can be multiplied up to incorporate our civilised world.

But back to pleasure; pleasure is a universal motivator, a driver that impels us towards ... what exactly? We laugh at the donkey chasing the carrot dangling tantalisingly close to its muzzle. We laugh at the hamster pedalling furiously within its wheel striving for a fresh horizon. I laugh at the poor idiots on bended knee pursuing a chaste life in return for an afterlife, the workers intent on providing a pension for their last hours on Earth, the halcyon days of freedom with all debts paid as they slip into the grave.

Very few of us are foolish enough to attempt to walk up a down escalator, so why don't we recognise our lifelong attempts at doing the same? Most of us spend our lives walking up the down escalator without ever realising it. If the purpose of work is to provide pleasure in another orbit away from the desk and papers and interminable boredom that most of our careers supply in huge order then why can't you find a short cut? We all do the calculation, we determine the exchange rate between hours worked and pleasure purchased at the start of our careers and then lose sight of the sum with distant horizons committed to and rarely reached. We append the 35 year mortgage in return for the roof over our head to the near 50 year work contract to achieve our retirement and the final pursuit of those of life's pleasures that we can still remember and can physically endure. The carrot has long since lost its appeal and yet we still trudge determinedly behind it. And through it all we plough our furrow in search of that pay rise, the betterment, the recognition of peers and the casualties we discard along the way content to discard 40% of our effort into the government's coffers for the Great Brains to preside over and waste with industrial efficiency. Strange isn't it, the only thing our government is efficient at is waste (the production of it).

Perhaps I have found the real alternative to the suicide gene, the Bait Ball gene, the addiction gene and should have called it the pleasure gene. It is pleasure that motivates and drives our actions above all others in search of reward that is in control of our entire enterprise. Is that to be our sole distinction between ourselves and the 'lesser beasts', the ability to subjugate our immediate demands in exchange for a pleasurable future? Why else would we devote lives to the creation of monuments to another's vanity unless to receive a reward of our own? What other species feels the need to create pyramids or stone circles or cathedrals or skyscrapers or to cross the horizon in search of a better future? There are examples of providing for a future; squirrels hiding nuts, pica's gathering hay, bears piling on the pounds to survive the winter and all is done without a thought, reacting to a hard wired compunction outside of cognitive control. Welcome to our control mechanism. You had no control over your shortcut to pleasure Neville and indeed your employers rely on that fact, for if you had the control you wouldn't be in need of employment and the whole pyramid would come crashing down. You are addicted to pleasure and all addicts seek out their next fix at every opportunity, it is the human condition. Your 'business's turnover' is in pleasure addicts who cannot control their compunctions to steal or fight or cheat or inject or snort any more that you can control your compunction to pay your mortgage or save for your retirement. Your knob-thatch distinguishes them from you and renders them available for punishment, punishment for being human. But for human read animal, for the distinction between squirrel's frantically burying nuts and saving for your pleasure interludes can only be made in scale. Your customers have crossed the line between earning and taking and will be punished for it (I wish), whereas your employers … Your employers take on a grand scale in return for …? An end to crime, the ability to spend your life without fear of assault, of being the victim, of being safe and secure. But they also take your life, recruited to their enterprise that solves nothing but secures their future as they deny you of yours.

Let's see you try and explain that to them tomorrow N, good luck with that one.

But I haven't finished with the pleasure gene, oh no, for while it motivates us towards a better future it also denies us of the one we have. Take this seed and sow it into prepared soil, protect it from weeds and drought and chase the crows away until it achieves its zenith and then reap and store it for your future needs. Agriculture, the promise of food tomorrow in return for effort today. Reconcile this with that nicotine fix for now in exchange for years off your life. The pleasure of an overfull belly in the pursuit of a premature death, the pleasure of your own personal motor transport in return for premature deaths from pollution. The pleasure of a pay rise while denying your providers of their taxes. Face it N, we're fucked.

R
XXX

Sent from my iPad

Re: Day 11 January 10th Tuesday

Dearest N

Nearly time to start the countdown N, to light the blue touch paper and retreat 2.5 m underground. I am almost afraid to ask you how your disciplinary went but you know it won't stop me. I think we are ready, everything stocked and waiting for the final installation, I just have to erect the fence around my bunker. We'll really need to hit the ground running for the final 48 hours or so. So anyway, if I've got this right, watching porn on a CPS IT system is gross misconduct and the burden of proof is less than that for a criminal court and a 'balance of probabilities' is good enough to send you on your merry way. It's a bloody good job you don't concern yourself with justice for a career isn't it, otherwise you could be well and truly stuffed by this lot. I must say that the case you proposed to me seemed more than adequate to give yourself a fighting chance, a stay of execution, for all the good that will do you in the court of Trump. The most overriding consideration in my mind is the utter unfairness of it all. The whole Justice Department pisses time, effort and taxes up the wall from one end of the day to the next without ever pausing for breath. I heard before Christmas, it must have been in the pre-Christmas silly season that a group of former ministers and MP's had called for a halving of the number of prisoners down to 45,000. The prisons are becoming too dangerous and "half of them go on to reoffend within 12 months of release" so prisons aren't working. Yes, you utter wankers, but none of them reoffend while locked up so at least we get a holiday from their activities. The prisons are getting too dangerous because they are full of the 'criminal element', well I never, and the solution is to release half of them which presumably makes society half as safe as well. Let's extrapolate the scheme a little further and go for full blown riots throughout the prison system so that we are left with no alternative other than to release them all. Problem sorted. Do you think the Ministry of Justice can survive without your intellect N? What a shame Australia has introduced visa requirements for entry. I have heard that parts of Syria and Iraq are welcoming British expats who have a penchant for ignoring our societies rules, could we put them in touch with each other?

Then I saw the text report about our Health Minister Jeremy Hunt casting doubt on four hour waiting targets at A & E. If your problems are less serious you may no longer be guaranteed to be seen within four hours. It could be the only way to protect the standard which the government was "committed to maintaining".

Well, well, well, well, WTF?

Has one of our Great Brains had a rush of honesty, or is it a brain tumour like John Travolta's character in 'Phenomenon'? Something pressing on his brain enhancing his cognitive abilities before killing him. On reflection, I think not, for underneath the report lies the lies about the four hour treatment time. No change then, at all, nothing to even consider other than the affirmation of the fiction that persists all the way from the humblest trainee nurse at the business end of an enema through to the health secretary via all the echelons of hospital and government management. For the question still remains; what four hour treatment time? It doesn't exist, it's a fiction or if I use my preferred nomenclature, it is an abject load of bollocks. At least he was only talking to the WI, oh, what's that, it was the House of Commons? In spite of the fact that we have an official opposition why wasn't his claim repudiated and rubbished for the abject lie it is? The only conclusion I can surmise is that the official opposition play the same game themselves. "If we pretend it isn't real for them, they'll pretend it isn't real when it's our turn to be in charge". Sorted. And no one died.

And then I went shopping for the week's groceries and stumbled over the Daily Mail's headline along the lines of 'A&E crisis, it's all our fault'. Apparently the wrong people are going to A&E and a third of them should be somewhere else instead. One of the other things at the forefront of the media's attention are the proposed changes to the 'freedom of the press'. But our press already have all the freedom in the world to miss the point, to promulgate the fiction, to support the Bait Ball, to attack the symptom and always, always miss the cause. What will salve the media's conscience N? All they demand is the release of more money to the NHS, more money to be swallowed up in the behemoth, to dissipate and evaporate into all the deserving pockets before it ever reaches the patient. Let us wave the magic wand N, I can get it out of the Pop 6 unit nearest the rear boundary, I know exactly where I packed it and it's near the surface. Let us double the NHS budget overnight and see what difference it makes, not overnight, that wouldn't be fair, let's give them five years to measure the difference. A shame we only have ten days left to find out after today, but it doesn't matter, because we already know what the answer will be. No change. Debate is the gift that keeps on giving, journalists need never run out of things to say or write and they want to keep it that way. It's how they make their living.

Now there's a thought Neville, I could write the newspaper for the 21st of January, you know, the day after the world ends. What shall the headline be, **"Armageddon, It's All Your Fault"**

Our reporters have been working undercover for years and have concluded that all the warnings cryptically inserted into our decade's long coverage gave ample warning of the ongoing conflagration. Our senior political reporter advises "The people have finally got what they have been asking for all these years. I've gone blue in the face trying to warn them. They just wouldn't listen". On a brighter note, our transport reporter advises that the Southern Rail dispute impasse appears to have been resolved. Latest reports suggest that all of the Southern Rail's region has been utterly obliterated. We spoke to regular commuter Fred Smith's cat on holiday at his niece's midlands boarding home during Fred's holiday who meowed something along the lines of "Mucking mypical, mget mhe munion's magreement mto muspend mhe mstrike maction mjust mwhen mhe mnetwork misappears". The interview was cut short by the need to visit the litter tray.

We must apologise to our surviving reader, but under the circumstances we feel sure that you will understand the small amount of print today.

R
XXX

Sent from my iPad

Re: Day 10 January 11th Wednesday

Dearest N

"Final written warning and the next transgression is out the door". Seems fair, I suppose, or rather it doesn't, fucking jobsworths. I bet they've never wasted a millisecond of time admiring a bit of office crumpet, male or female. Apparently studies have indicated that women eye up other women in a sexual fashion. While some men get condemned for scoring from 1 to 10 on the desirability level it turns out all women check out and rank other women. Trying to scope out their rivals for the dominant ape no doubt. At least you can look forward to a continuing career in the event that Trump dies before the 20th. I still think it's unfair that the fate of the world lies in the hands of one Great Brain until I remember that we all put him there. We must all carry an equal share of the blame N, we are all equally culpable. For that matter, why don't they condemn all the female workers for dressing attractively with their tight clothes and painted faces adorned with bits of metal? Many spend their lives 'on the stomp' for prospective mates which must distract and upset fellow workers in equal measure. I'd have gone for the biological defence myself and told them that I am only human and it's what we do, seek out pleasure in whatever form it manifests itself as. Let's see them condemn you for being born. But, we know the answer to that don't we, for they simply follow the pro forma, umbilically joined to the Bait Ball, bereft of sentient thought, immersed up to the neck in sand (head first). Gosh, I wish I was clever and worthy of management. Just a thought N, how do ostriches breathe when their heads are in the ground, osmosis through the skin, modified and extendable nostrils, SCUBA (Self-Contained Underground Breathing Apparatus)? Or do they come up for air really fast, faster than the human eye can see? We may find out if the air pumps fail. If we lost the desire for pleasure would we persist as a species? The pleasure of a full belly, a sated thirst, the act of sex, the feel of warmth and security, the pleasure of dominion over other people, the pleasure of grasping the clean end of the stick. It seems the most important factor in our upcoming odyssey will be the pursuit of pleasure and that must be our measure of attainment. How ironic, for it was the pursuit of pleasure that landed us in this upcoming predicament.

When it really comes down to it N, is the only reason we voted for Brexit or Trump because, in the 'balance of probabilities' and with 'the burden of proof is less than that for a criminal court' we voted for the scenario that generated the greatest amount of pleasure for those that could be bothered to have an opinion? Does that mean that poking the establishment in the eye with a sharp stick is a valid reason? It works for me.

R
XXX

Sent from my IPad

Re: Moseley

Dearest N

I'm surprised at you think I'm right wing.

Left leaning Fabian, right wing fascism are all simply labels for what the herd will accept. Any right wing party is instantly portrayed as fascist with the automatic spectre of gas chambers and forced repatriation. The Israelis learnt the value of ghettos and have their own, it's called Gaza. No gas chambers, little employment, little power, it's all controlled by Israel. The biggest murderer of the 20th century was Stalin, was he fascist? How about Pol Pot in Cambodia or the Ruanda tribal factions. As a percentage of the population, good old Henry the Eighth worked his way through more people that Stalin, was he fascist? We are back to the 'wipe clean' memory facility of *Homo sapiens* whereby this particular memory resists erasure but the cause of the memory has long since been forgotten. We react then to the 'ghost' of the problem and not the problem. Fascism is bad, I've said it, but it was borne of the herd, for they did not have to drink it when led to the well. We vilify Hitler but cannot vilify Germans because that would be untenable. We will vilify Trump but he didn't seize power, he was democratically elected by due process. So then the process is wrong. The process is borne of millennia of 'silverback' command and control corruption that has adapted from best food, shelter and mating rights to the control of nuclear arsenals and global territorial ambitions. Note, I didn't say evolved, this isn't a survival of the fittest question, it is the adoption of delusion that ultimately signals our downfall. Hitler's final solution is a mere pinprick in history that commands a presence way beyond its weight. We will cause the premature deaths of six million people a year without a first or second thought. It's in our shit food, the polluted air we breathe, the poisons we trade in drugs, alcohol and tobacco, the dangerous work practices our drive for cheap goods imposes on strangers half a world away. We justify it by ignoring it, as the Germans justified it by ignoring Hitler. It's called business as usual. And we are masters of it, without knowing what it is we do, so in fact are we masters of it or does it master us?

For in the final analysis, the only thing we care about is our extended family grouping around the dominant ape, the silverback and all other groups are rivals. But that is not to say that no dynamic exists within the extended family grouping for plots to usurp, to breed surreptitiously, to steal and hide advantage from the rest of the clan are built in to this societal model. In life, it is every ape for himself. So it is that our species sprints towards the precipice in the clouds, in spite of the presence of contour maps, a knowledge of the terrain. That's the thing about herds, the suspension of thought and supplication to the will of others. But when all the members do it, it seizes to be a herd and becomes a Bait Ball where we simply hide from danger behind our neighbour. The neighbour can die as long as I live is the sole compunction as every neighbour strives to endanger others so that they can live.

What distresses me is the collateral damage we wrest upon the face of the planet as we reduce it to a husk of its former glory. Our species has no appeal to me, they are like another locust within the swarm for they are simply rivals for resource, shields from predators, opportunities for gamete exchange. On D Day plus 40 we will hopefully emerge to a new world unorder, a world where the order has been removed, where life's chances are laid bare. Where the path from hunger to food is not corrupted by 15 years of education and career advancement and all the other extraneous bollocks that we so earnestly engage in, but is simply a walk away to the nearest fruiting bush. Have you ever wondered why lions don't go to university? Because they don't need to, any more than we need to, but that will never stop us, the lack of need will it? Our sole qualification as a species, our particular USP (Unique Selling Proposition) is our ability to corrupt for that is all we do.

By the way, I only type with one finger. Think how blessed you are, only getting the condensed version. Otherwise, I could really go on, and on, and on, and on, and on …

Are you suggesting that fascism is at the root of my political doctrine? In reality, my political doctrine is that politics doesn't work. The Great Brains, politicians, simply hijack the dominant ape gene to ensure their own brighter future at the expense of subordinates; that would be everybody else then. Our biology betrays our thought processes as completely as the male mantis's compunction to copulate. Given that the copulation continues even after the head has been consumed is it reasonable to assume that some part of the 'brain' exists in the mantis's testes? That could explain a lot. As our population density increased beyond the remit of the 'silverback' our species adapted to all forms of extraneous command and control mechanisms as we attempt to create a 'sense or purpose' to our activities. There is no sense or purpose beyond furthering the existence of our own threads of DNA into future generations. Even this great imperative is a lie given that at every procreation our DNA is halved through the sexual process. I'm surprised that the compunction to clone ourselves to secure a real future for 'self' has not risen to the fore. In reality, our human process could be analysed down to our purpose to act as a vehicle for our female line mitochondrial DNA which only changes through mutation. We are all mitochondrial clones from a handful of bloodlines. You will find it impossible to conjure any meaningful purpose for our sorry lives that can override the biological imperatives. All that is left is to 'enjoy life' for what it is, without the need to conform to societal rules, elaborately constructed from the corrupted imperatives that served their purpose while we were still swinging from the trees. The 'silverbacks' command and control structure was never intended to provide for millions and billions and yet it is precisely from this base that we have constructed such elaborate concoctions as religion and government. Our so called 'greatest achievements' are all illusions for a species that needs illusions to survive. So, given that we cannot survive without illusions, illusions are a good thing, aren't they? Moseley's illusions may not have been as radical as Hitler's but they were borne of the same thought processes, the same illusion and were designed to command and control the masses for the benefit of the 'leaders'. But, you will remember, we have no leaders, only followers with a head start. You can lead a horse to water, but you cannot make it drink. Biology on the other hand will implant the nervous control for thirst that will motivate and dictate the urge to find water and drink. That is where the real control lies, beyond the human mind-set which we corrupt with addiction. We can murder 6 million Jews because we have the biological imperative within us to achieve it. Trump can destroy the world for exactly the same reason. Seven point four billion people are destroying the world without compunction, simply by being. There is no higher purpose nor any control mechanism that we can invent that is beyond the corruption of our species.

That will have to do for now, I need to stock up the boiler.

Trust you enjoyed Willie Spokeshave, is he bringing out anything new do you know?

R
XXX

Sent from my IPad

Re: Day 9 January 12th Thursday

Dearest N

Thank you for your enlightenment with regard to the Crown Prosecution Service. I should have realised that the CPS would have its own set of targets. We can't possibly measure your performance in terms of criminals locked up or sentences or fines imposed. How very silly of me, beyond your personal satisfaction of a career well spent and the appreciation of your peers there is a more measurable scale. A scale that sits easily within the orbit of the Great Brain's, one invented by them that they are blinded by. And the beauty of this scale is the portability and longevity, one could even describe it as hereditary. What is required is a failsafe system devoid of thought processes that can assume a life of its own. It begins life as a tool, a device to control before assuming its autonomous role as an end to itself. I refer of course to that much loved central tenet, budget. For whatever the CPS is faced with can be determined by its ability to spend or save money. But budgets are intractable and beyond control for they become the control themselves. All they will condescend to accept is tweaking, 2% here, 3% there and then everyone is content. A measure of performance that is meaningless for its only purpose in life is to stupefy and satisfy bean counters in equal measure. The question that it answers is how many and how often the barrow loads of money are emptied, justice is unquantifiable, undefinable and unachievable. Because it cannot be measured, the CPS doesn't bother to even try but that doesn't prevent it from pinning its achievement badge to its chest. No doubt its budget has oft been modified to suit the prevailing needs of the current crop of Great Brain's but all are simply blind tweaks to a blind system that satisfies the equally blind ambition of the Great Brain's. Let me turn the question around for you Neville and ask you to design a true level of performance that can represent justice. An impossible task beyond the scope of mere mortals.

I have the answer to your fascist accusation. It is a label, attach a label, job done, the end of the thought process, suspension of any further mental process. Worried about immigration, racist, seek to limit executives' pay, socialist, like to hang around and get pleasure from young kids, teacher, challenge the profligate waste of the Welfare State, Conservative. Challenge the profligate waste of the Welfare State and do nothing about it, Conservative. Attach the label, take your salary cheque, job done. Quote your source or fail your exams. Worried about immigration, racist, says who, where is your source you idle gits? But what does label actually mean? It means take the short cut, submit to the herd, accept the pro forma of thought, fold back into the Bait Ball. It means that you have accepted the arguments that went before without challenging them, it means accepting them because everybody else has, it means subjugating your will to the others that have subjugated theirs as well. It means being a follower. And there is the rub, for we rely on our leaders, our leaders that are followers with a head start.

R
XXX

Sent from my IPad

Re: Your transfer rates for January

Dear Robert

At lunchtime in Waitrose I looked Edward in the eye having read FT from cover to cover. He asked me what and why I was looking him in the eye as I did. My reply was that I was thinking whether to risk my today for his tomorrow! I'm sure you have had similar but tenfold similar thoughts!

N

Sent from my iPhone

Re: Your transfer rates for January

Dearest N

Waitrose, you posh knob, I wish I could afford Waitrose. I have to confess I have been dragged in on occasion in search of some unpasteurised yak milk or fresh roc eggs but I don't feel comfortable in there, I just can't manage the look of smugness demanded of its patrons. I quite like the FT, it gives a certain ambience to the smallest room when carefully cut and folded before having a string threaded through one corner. I'm surprised at you Neville, reading an anti-Brexit paper.

The eye of the future, stood proudly but quizzically before you with the world at his toes if only he can complete on the inheritance bit without the need to pass university and 40 years of worthwhile employment. But you have already failed in your quest N, for you have brought this bundle into the world and are hormonally obliged to surrender what was once your future to Edward. In simple terms, Edward is your future, your legacy, your achievement to live on beyond your grave. Yes, you might be tempted to risk your tomorrows for his today's, but that is not the way the equation resolves itself. Age will defy you and see you dribbling in your cornflakes long before his stamina is extinguished. You are simply the cock blackbird surrendering all reason and effort into providing for the welfare of your clutch until they fledge the nest and abandon you, after some supplementary feeding, of course. But, Edward is not ready to fledge just yet and he will need you more than ever in the very near future. Edward will not be the sole product of your ambitions, for it's only through the transfer of his genes down through further generations that your legacy can serve a purpose and you will nurture and encourage him to surrender his own future to those essential appendages of a life well led, grandchildren. Content yourself with the knowledge that at the end of the day you can give them back. Less seriously, I hope you have not been entertaining thoughts of ratting out of our sworn agreement to protect your inheritance from the previously aforementioned issue of issue, if you get my girded drift? Searching for financial advice in the pink one is simply asking for trouble. The merest whiff, an essence of an idea will see it dashed on the rock of ruin as swiftly as you can spell recommendation, for the secret of success is precisely that, a secret.

El follicly challenged one, Trumpo, sold around 6,000 'university courses' to asinine arseholes who would learn the 'secret' of his property dealing success. The secret of his success is that it was secret, for the instant it becomes public knowledge it loses all advantage. That 6,000 people would shell out mega bucks says it all really. But that begs a larger question, for while I deride these asinine arseholes for attempting to buy their futures through a tin pot university, what does it say about the near 50% of the British school age population that is expected to shell out £27,000 in fees alone to learn the secrets of …?

I know the answer N, the answer is, the secret of making universities richer. They do it by selling a dream, a promise of intelligence that is satisfied by surrendering all to the straitjacket of the pro forma. But there are only so many winners N, and they are the universities and all that partake of their ill-gotten wealth.

The vice-chancellors of Southampton earn £697k each at the top of the list while number ten comes in at £342k for Liverpool.

In years gone by my dad would interview potential workers for the factory. It was heavy dirty work back in the sixties before the machinery crept in. He would ask if they were married and had kids. If they said yes to both he would offer them a job. His logic was very simple, they needed to provide food for the table, no ifs, no buts. These are questions the PC brigade have banned from the interview process a long while ago. Somewhere between then and now university education has launched itself to the fore. Why? It's a simple enough question. If I took the view that the need for this higher level of education was as the result of a conspiracy, who is behind it? You might be thinking that I spend all my time describing conspiracy theories, but, I would disabuse you of that thought. That's the thing about the herd, there is no conspiracy, it doesn't need one to function, it is at once a super organism and at the same time the product of its lowest common denominator.

Will this do for now?

D
XXX

Sent from my IPad

Re: Day 8 January 13th Friday (lucky for some)

Dearest N

I know you commented on how fast I type my thoughts to you and I have already confessed my typing skills are limited to one finger. I must add that I rely heavily on the predictive text volunteered by my IPad. In fact, barely a third of my thoughts are actually my own, the machine has done the rest. I am nearly redundant, replicated and subjugated by machines trained in the pro forma's of Man. But while I make this confession to you N, I feel a mitigation coming on. I've been getting terrible headaches with flashing 'zebra'ing' in my vision. My optician advises that they are mitigation headaches or something similar. Can you remember at school being taught about the invention of new words? The very idea seemed spectacular back then to our pubescent minds so heavily engrained in the education process, being measured for the tailored straitjacket of our future lives. The quoted example was Charles Dickens and Mrs Malaprop who impressed her learned friends with similar sounding words, illegitimate for illiterate, for example. Some clever dicks coined the term 'malapropism' for such an event. For 45 years I've substituted malaproposition and never been challenged. For years at work I used to say nest box instead of 'n'es pas' (isn't it) and never once was I challenged. (We had a Scottish engineer who used to say "disney ken" which stuck rigidly in my mind, especially when I took my kids to Disneyland Paris, he said "doesn't know".)

Seems to me if you say anything with enough conviction it will be accepted. Do you think El Trumpo has worked this out as well? Nowadays of course, a veritable tsunami of new terms enter the orbit of our minds sired by the great progenitor of change, the Internet and its associated apps. I know you have a favourite word for 2016, N, one you hold close to your heart. Selected as the 'word of the year' for its prominence but soon to be utterly irrelevant, Brexit. Utterly irrelevant for us N, to be replaced with UDI which will hold no relevance either, population 5.

But what if it was population 80,000? And what if you were God? Could we build an Eden Project in our Independent Nation State? Enclosed behind a radiation screen, sealed from the outside world and utterly isolated and utterly self-sufficient. Everything has to be recycled and balanced perfectly with supply and demand. There simply is no alternative to the balance. Too many people will exceed the oxygen production, too much food consumed exceeds the food produced, too much water used outstrips supply. How would we police such a state N, there can be no exceptions, no bending of the rules, no special dispensation or 'get out of jail free' cards. Such an absolute regime demands an absolute ruler, one with the power of life and death. A God. Diet would be strictly controlled, no excess calories for you old friend, but this would be tempered with advantage, no excess salt or sugar, only human balanced food for human bodies and no poisons included in the 'special offers'. No making babies without consent, it would have to be strictly one out before one in. Jan always refers to the 'hatches, matches and dispatches' notices in the local paper, that's births, marriages and deaths to you. "Ooh look, number 76,196 has just died, that moves our application for birth permission up to number 1,184 in the queue". But that cannot be, for number 76,196 was a rocket scientist and we need to match the genetic profile of the replacement to this criteria. Ours would be the long game N, the only way to secure a future for the species. Dissent cannot exist for the actions of a few can jeopardise the very existence of the colony. We can match the very best of science to provide the very best for our chosen few. The perfect diet and perfect environment, free of pollutants together with strictly rationed exercise regimes could see the end of premature deaths and push our average life expectancies beyond 100. Whom shall we select for our Eden Project, how to conduct the interview process, where to advertise our, quite literally, God given opportunity. To start we must eliminate the undesirables, the believers in God, for ours can broker no competition for authority. We must engage in the very cutting edge of science to weed out the geniuses from the also rans. We must profile the DNA of all applicants and assess their mental health and attitudes to authority. We must monitor and police the inhabitants with covert observation to ensure that each performs precisely to target and utilises only the resources due to them. I suggest we implant a probe into each and every body to monitor oxygen, food and water use to ensure that optimum levels are not exceeded. Persistent offenders must be shown their way to the air lock and expelled but only after we have sucked all air out of the lock.

And when we have achieved our Eden on Earth N, we can move to extend our premises. When the all-clear sounds for radiation we can send out emissaries into the wider world to infect and poison those that have survived without bowing to our absolute doctrine. The slate must be cleaned, with all that went before expunged from the knowledge of our newly trained perfect humans. Discipline is the key to the survival of mankind, discipline to match need with supply. I extol this idea to you N for, it is the only way that our species can have a future.

While in the confessional mood, I must admit that this vision is not of my making, for it is within the stated orbit of one, Elon Musk, who plans to build his Eden on Mars. For not content with being a billionaire, he intends to be a God as well. There goes my vacancy application form into the shredder, ah well, I'll console myself with my bunker and Trump's pre-emptive strike.

Or, try this for an idea N, we do absolutely nothing, we breed, we utilise water, ground and energy without constraint, pushing all that went before us into oblivion until the only thing left to push into oblivion is people. I tried to get a patent on the first idea, but you've probably guessed, Elon can beat me to it. So I tried to get a patent on the second idea, but you've probably guessed it, ten millennia of civilisation claimed prior art.

If we survive N, I'll go for a patent on converting packaged sewerage treatment plants into nuclear bunkers instead. I think I'll probably get this one, but there won't be much market for them for several thousand years at least. Bollocks, another get rich quick scheme up the swannie. At least I can say I tried N, I know, I am very trying.

Could I write a book about Elon's scheme, I could call it Marsraker? I'll need a subterfuge, a plot to expose the scheme for what it is, a spy working for the good guys do you think? God, am I fucking brilliant or what? Booker prize here I come. Hang on, why not write it for a newspaper first to have a crack for a Pulitzer? I can always go for the book second. I must remember to keep the film rights back.

But while I say that only a third of my thoughts are my own, the machine has done the rest, I comfort myself that a third of the thoughts have been my own and not those of the pro forma that shepherds our Bait Ball. In that, I have a distinct advantage over most.

Not forgetting of course that Eden has already been built on Earth, it's normally referred to as the presidential bunker. Trump has passed the interview selection stage and his and his immediate families concerns have been met. With a rain of missiles falling worldwide it is absolutely imperative that the greatest leader on Earth is safely ensconced below ground to maintain his grip on the rains, sorry reins. Surrounded by the other great and the good and ably supported with security personnel to ensure his continuing rule, Trump has sorted his re-election out four years early. (But not that great, the others, that is).

I have lauded Trump for his actions of seemingly changing Ford Motor Company's mind. A Ford executive was giving a soundbite to camera announcing the spending of $700 million to extend an existing factory and to create 700 jobs. The maths is fairly simple and it only takes a second to see that each job costs $1 million to achieve. I am reminded of Bombardier, a Canadian train manufacturer based in the U.K. Bemoaning the loss of UK government train replacement contracts being awarded to Siemens, a German firm. Time after time the TV cameras wandered around Bombardier's shop floor. What struck me was the extensive use of crane beams suspended across the linear manufacturing sheds all supported off the building frame. Crane beam after crane beam was decorated with the company name of Demag, that well known German crane manufacturer. I've even bought one myself from Demag, in 2008. So if my primitive mind can do the calculation, it is wrong for the taxpayers to fund the purchase of German trains but right for Bombardier to purchase German cranes. The point I am trying to make here is the victory of Trump in securing 700 jobs while we ignore the $700 million dollar spend. I don't know the answer here, but humour me, the financial investment per job must involve the development of robotised production lines. Where will these be sourced from, China, Japan perhaps? The reason I ask you to humour me is the simple fact that the Ford executive missed a golden opportunity to announce the securement of 700 Ford jobs plus the additional jobs of their supply partners and the securement of those other jobs in the American robotics and production line manufacturers. Or, to put it another way, if every one of the Ford workers earns $40,000 a year it would still take 25 years to equalise the investment potentially spent abroad. At a master Twitter stroke, Trump has become the nation's job saviour without any of us understanding the scale of his achievement. But I still have questions, for the Ford announcement still holds a black hole in the deliberation. They planned to spend another $900 million on the Mexican plant, where has that gone? Is the plan to make the components there and have them shipped to the US for incorporation into 'Made in America' emblazoned Ford cars? It's beyond this mere mortal to work it out, but it doesn't matter, because nobody else is trying to work it out either. My father was approached once to do some voluntary engineering work in India, to establish a manufacturing plant for the production of concrete products to generate employment and stimulate the economy. He declined and chief among his decision making process was the fact that we made extensive use of machinery that negated the need for extensive amounts of labour. If the object was to replace British $100 a day labourers with machinery where was the incentive to replace Indian $1 a day labourers. Yet labour rates are cheap in Mexico, hence the desire to invest in manufacturing plants south of the border. So why the need to spend an additional $900 million? More importantly, why has Ford publicly capitulated to Trump's tweet and publicly established him as champion of the working classes?

Now, while Trump has twittered his way into the hearts and minds of the American worker he has simultaneously twittered his way into the hearts and minds of once hopeful and now to be ex-Mexican workers. Their minds and hearts are probably hardened to all things Ford and all things American and their purchasing decisions on all things imported may well change. Time will tell. Or would, if we had any time left. I suppose, it could even happen, that some of these disgruntled hopefuls might decide to smuggle themselves north to partake of the American Dream.

R
XXX

Sent from my IPad

Re: Day 7 January 14th Saturday

Dearest N

I've been thumbing through my Observers book of Coups again in relation to Trump. I was thinking about his press conference discussing the alleged security briefing of the media by the US intelligence authorities. CNN were quite persistent in asking for a question; "You don't get to ask a question" said Trump. Later, I heard learned commentators stating that Trump would soon replace the heads of the intelligence agencies with "those loyal to him". CNN's 'crime' was to have extensively reported the allegations about Trump having been compromised by the Russian spy network. Personally N, I can't see what all the fuss is about, billionaire Trump already has a gold door on his apartment in New York, it's worth more than Nigel Farage's house remember, why shouldn't he share a gold shower with a prostitute? Have we just witnessed a bloodless version of 'the night of the long knives' where Hitler removed his vocal opposition? I nearly said 'at one stroke' but you'd only need one knife for that. Trump doesn't tolerate dissent and now the journalists realise that if they want to be included in any discussion they have to submit to Trump's version of events. I keep hearing about checks and balances, it's offered as a 'comfort blanket', something to cuddle up with as you suck your thumb, something designed to keep the bogeyman at bay. The OBOC's section on securing all the government departments to your cause is quite explicit on this need. "Sterilise any dissent from the intelligence agencies and ensure that they work for you, or do not work at all. Free and independent intelligence agencies are to be avoided at all costs". In a similar vein it continues in another section about the media, "Sterilise and emasculate the 'free press' to ensure that they either support you or do not function. NB this is not as difficult as it seems, they already conform to daily briefings where the 'official' news for the day is disseminated to all. They already accept that to ignore the briefings is 'bad for their health' and readily comply".

Hitler did so much for the German people and not all of it was bad. He brought employment back to the masses with his works programmes and gave them a sense of purpose and pride in being German, something denied to them for a decade and a half by the treaty imposed on them by the victorious allies. It didn't help you if you were Jewish, disabled, socialist, unionised or a plethora of other 'undesirable' qualities and indeed was often injurious to your health, wealth and happiness. I can't see any parallels here with Trump, he just wants to marginalise Mexican's, Muslims and, if the commentators are to be believed, everybody else that doesn't qualify for Klu Klux Klan membership. He'll buy his friendship and support by strong-arming business leaders into providing employment and a sense of pride and purpose back to the disenfranchised white Christians. Hitler's problem was one of debt, he spent what he didn't have and eventually had only one choice open to him, go to war and plunder resources or, or nothing, he only had one choice remember N. I smell an oxymoron N, one choice is not in fact a choice. Trump has embarked upon his journey, his trip to the very apex of the greatest pyramid on Earth, to stand astride the acme of our planet. The problem that I foresee is not unlike that of my Wellingtonia tree. I went years ago, before Clara was born to Powys Castle to look at the tallest tree in England and Wales. It was a Douglas fir which, if my memory serves was around 182 feet high nearly 30 years ago. I couldn't find it. Now how can that be N, most tall trees struggle to exceed 100 feet so spotting the other 82 feet should have been easy. I had to ask. When I bought my house in 1994 we had the 'second highest tree in Leicestershire', a Wellingtonia that stood 30 feet above its neighbours. Powys Castle is perched on the top of a hill and the gardens are terraced down the small valley side to the 'wilderness' garden at the valley bottom around the stream (By wilderness, I think they meant "we can't be bothered to do that bit"). The Douglas fir was growing from the base of the valley and stood at a similar height to the trees growing on the top edge of the valley. The 'extra' 82 feet were below the other trees and not above them. My particular giant was struck by lightning in 1995 and pruned by 30 feet. Trump is soon to stand above the world, exposed and glorifying in his new found ego sating role as the greatest man on Earth. There is an old wives saying that "lighting never strikes the same place twice" which we know of course is wrong. Anything exposed at height is vulnerable to lightning strike and multiple strikes occur to our tall buildings encased within lightning conductors for that very reason. Trump is about to become the greatest lightning attractant. Metaphorically speaking, the checks and balances that commentators are fond of quoting are the equivalent of lightning conductors, they earth the apex, they ground it. They serve to join the apex to the base. But that's the thing about billionaires, they are removed from the base, it is below even their peripheral vision and below their comprehension. It's akin to "ran out of smoked salmon? Well eat the caviar instead". Some of the senate committees have been grilling Trump's proposed appointee's for pivotal roles in his administration, they have given some of them a hard time and then have basically rolled over and invited them to 'tickle their tummies'. "Absolute power corrupts absolutely" is the quote, but it's not the one I am looking for, for that suggests something greater than the reality. We don't need a Napoleon or Stalin or Nero, all we need is a herd, a Bait Ball where every individual hides for protection behind its neighbours and then, if we were but able to see it, we would understand what absolute corruption looks like. Absolute corruption looks like a Bait Ball. Welcome to planet Human.

R
XXX

Sent from my IPad

Re: Day 6 January 15th Sunday

Dearest N

I had the rest of the family round for Sunday dinner. One last get together before they depart for Namibia on Tuesday. My heavy heart was tempered with the knowledge, or should that be hope that they will be out of harm's way for the 20th. Perhaps I should have gone with them, but deep down we all resist change. I fancy a go at survival in my own backyard, so to speak. People have often asked why I never travelled further afield in search of flowers and beasties to photograph. Tropical species might as well come from Venus, much better to build on my local knowledge as I expanded out into Europe. I wanted to travel from north to south through the seasons photographing all I could find of interest. I would start within the Arctic Circle and finish at the Mediterranean and at the end of it would have compiled a working knowledge of related species. You never know, if Trump fails to perform, it might be an option for my retirement yet. As we get closer and closer to the 'happening' I am torn between ploughing on regardless and ignoring the threat or enacting the master plan. I am really dreading the drugging bit but not nearly as much as the waking up bit. We'll be in for major upset from our loved ones until the first impacts and then even more upset. It certainly won't be the easy option. It's a bit late now, but we should have incorporated some padding to the inside of the bunkers. At least we'd have some experience of 'padded cells' if we emerge to an unchanged world. I think your best defence will be to blame me N, I'll shoulder all the blame, you could even tell them I drugged you as well. This email trail ought to be enough to save your career with the CPS (but not this page, make sure you delete it). At least nobody can sack me and in that I am my own man. Everything seems so mundane, it's just business as usual. We'll be doing the weekly shop on Monday, watching the telly, cleaning the house on Tuesday, drugging the family and encasing them underground behind concrete walls on Friday. We still have to lie our way through the Pop 40 preparation as we keep the neighbours at bay. It really is enormous, this undertaking. It is so very, very difficult forging our own path away from the herd. I can see the imperative to conform and even knowing what I know, it is nigh on impossible to make that break. Let us trust to our friendship for the next few days N and help each other through them. If we emerge unscathed on D Day plus 40 we could take it in turns at being silverback. (Mating rights exempted).

R
XXX

Sent from my IPad

Re: Day 5 January 16th Monday

Just finished the security fence around my bunker, high tensile chain-link with 2.7m high crank top posts and the whole thing surrounded with 5 rings of razor wire. The only way in is through a solid steel door fitted with a guaranteed mechanically crop proof seven lever padlock. I've sealed the keys in my house safe to be extra secure until I need them.

You'll just have to risk it with the Pop 40, can't risk alerting the neighbours.

I've also installed the solar panels for my ventilation system and they seem to work just fine. The fans work at full power and there is enough left over to power the battery charger. I've had a secondary thought about it as well N, and have the idea in place to construct a manually operated 'bellows' arrangement as a supplement. We could physically pump fresh air into the bunkers if the solar panels are compromised by dust at either high or low levels. I have two old rubber diaphragms from redundant pressure vessels. They come from the pressure switch reservoirs off the bore-hole water pumping system. Anyhow, they are 30 and 40 litres in capacity and I can rig up a jubilee clip seal onto one of the bunkers inlet pipes and a valve system. Each tug on the diaphragm will draw in 30-40 litres at a time. It's always nice to have a backup for the backup. If the worst comes to the worst we'll just have to take it in turns to pump around the clock. Day and night will be all the same underground so it's just a question of getting used to it. I think I can fettle up a treadle system so that they can be operated by foot.

I've disassembled all the beds and lounge/diner set ups and carefully numbered all the adjoining components. I think they can be erected in a little over an hour for each with my power tools. I have some spanner socket drivers for my electric screwdriver. It should take around two/three hours to pump each tank out, yours is slightly bigger than mine, and then an hour to pressure wash and sanitise. We can pump the contents off to the old superseded sewer, it worked well enough for 100 years before the Environment Agency stuck their noses in it. It will be months before they notice anything, if ever. It was well worth spending £72 grand updating the old system for their petty rule change, not, especially as they haven't enforced it for any of the neighbouring farms who still discharge untreated into the ground. What was it the MP's said, "You can't expect to criminalise all these people for failing to comply"? Instead of which they effectively 'fined' us £72,000 because we complied. Bastards, one rule for the law observers and no rules for the law ignorers, no change there, then? What really gets my goat is the fact that we've already paid for the wankers to come up with the rules and enforce them only for them to fail to enforce their own rules. What purpose does it serve?

I've had a thought about the 'drugging' bit as well, technically this could be construed as kidnapping so I am anxious to delete any reference to drugs from the email trail as well. I would hate to emerge from my underground bunk bed after 40 days of self-imposed rule to find myself facing 14 years of similar but in someone else's bunk, if that makes sense. Do you think I could plead insanity? Sorry, make that 'temporary insanity' while the balance of my mind was disturbed by political events on the other side of the Atlantic. (I don't want to swap a prison bed for a hospital bed). What would the charges be for misappropriating the neighbourhoods sewer treatment facility be N, albeit only temporarily? Not my problem, as I own my Pop 20. We'd better hope that they all die and are unable to press charges. There, you see, if everybody else dies we are in the clear. It's enough to make you keep your fingers crossed in anticipation of the 'right' result. Actually, that could work, a quarter of the American voters obviously suffered from temporary insanity otherwise we wouldn't be worrying about Trump now, would we? It's a bit like the end of Lock, Stock and Two Smoking Barrels, where everybody's died which leaves them in the clear.

I must admit that I have one major worry about this whole adventure. Once Trump strikes and unleashes Armageddon and we survive, what the hell am I going to have to rant about? No central government, no local government, no NHS, no education establishments, no laws, even no more "No ball games allowed" signs. What's the point of hiving off football pitched patches of grassed of 'public open space' if you can't play games on it. "Oh, it's for public amenity". Dipshits, if you can't do anything with it why not space each house out further apart with a bigger garden and provide an amenity that actually means something.

Then again, I wouldn't need to rant, I'd have no reason to.

Something else to add to the list.

Just a thought N, you know how I like to think differently, bollocks to a 'Bucket List', I've got a 'Bunker List'.

R
XXX

Sent from my iPad

Re: Day 4 January 17th Tuesday

Dearest N

Just had a visit from a fucking jobsworth. I was so angry I didn't even bother to see where he was from. Apparently, "you can't store gas bottles on site without them being in a secure compound". Well whoopdefuckingdo. Fortunately, I say fortunately, I introduced him to my new secure compound complete with razor wire and steel door. I resisted the temptation to lock him in it. "It's more than my jobs worth to turn a blind eye to improperly stored gas containers". "Sorry", said I "we only completed it yesterday and thought we'd let the concrete post footings go hard before we filled it".

Where oh where do they get these brainless morons from? I thought they'd abandoned frontal lobotomy's years ago, obviously not. But it begs the question N, what is their job worth? What have they ever brought to the table, developed or achieved beyond the mantra of "It's in my rule book"? But they are just the apex, the pinnacle of stupidity manifest in their brainless actions, for they are the Bait Ball incarnate. Unseeing, unthinking, following and cajoling waverers into the fold where their sole purpose is to waver.

Apart from that N, I think we're ready to go.

R
XXX

Sent from my IPad

Dearest N

I've stopped spitting feathers. Can I change my mind? I think I'm going to change my plea to sanity. I'm the only sane person on Earth, it's everyone else that's insane. And if that doesn't prove my innocence then nothing will. It's called a double, double bluff. If I claim insanity that proves that I have realised my 'mistake' and need to be sane to do that. Whereas if I claim sanity that means I am still delusional and therefore innocent of all my actions. But I know I'll still get stuffed, because you cannot challenge the system. How can you point out the need for illusions to a society that only functions because of illusions? I'd have much better success if I simply proved that God existed; that would be easy. Can I start with the great God Turdus or Parus, at least I have a head start with them? Oh, why couldn't I have been born American, I could have stood as a presidential candidate and it could have been my finger on the button. I'll have to chalk up my life as an abject failure, wasted. If only I could have my time again. I could waste that one as well.

I've been watching the television news recently and there is one overriding consideration that is appended to every item of government. Every comment, every initiative is countermanded with the simple mantra of "It's wonderful, but without extra funding they are just wishful promises that cannot be realised". On '*dies natali*' money ceases to have a function, the wheels will have fallen off the cart and the horse will have bolted. The world will continue to turn on its axis, fingers crossed, and life for some will continue, fingers and toes crossed. If we could break into the local bank's vaults we'd have a steady supply of dry tinder for the starting of fires and precious little else. But we'd be the richest people in the world N, because we'd still be alive. And on that day Neville, God will have died, for on that day the source of all our worship will be seen for what it is worth. Nothing. *Librae solidi denarii* to give God its Latin name. God has died. I see a parallel here with an area within your orbit N, but whereas the son of your God died so that we can live I've gone for the director's cut version. That's the one where God dies so that we can live. And elephants. And tigers. And polar bears. And …

Into this new world how long will it be before God is reinvented? The creation of illusion, the recreation of the herd? What will be the trigger? If we understood the trigger we might understand our present predicament, but, then again.

R
XXX

Sent from my iPad

Re: Day 3 January 18th Wednesday

Dearest N

I had some email contact from Windhoek Kutako International Airport in Namibia. They have all arrived safely and are enroute into the bush. It's probably the last contact I'll ever have with them but at least they are safe, hopefully. I wonder, does it count as fledging the nest when the nest is taken away? I've done what I can and that's all I can do. I am delightfully saddened if that makes any sense at all? When all is said and done, this break is inevitable, death is waiting for us all after all. It's just a premature break. What have we missed N, what action, what path could we have taken, which stone did we leave unturned in searching for an alternative to the inevitable? Trump has a mandate, fairly won through due process, the due process of millennia of civilisation foisted upon us by the Great Brains, the herd followers with a head start. If we knew, if we all knew what Trump intends to do could we all have made a difference? It's a rhetorical question Neville, for we know, we entrust the president to control of the nuclear arsenal and in so doing condone the Russians to do the same. We are all complicit. We have all abrogated our responsibilities, all surrendered our wills to the herd and all deserve the result. If these emails are ever discovered and examined then the focus will no doubt be on the nuclear Armageddon. It's the usual trick of the human mind, it can only handle one threat at a time, for every other threat is wiped clean by the most 'pressing' one. ('Pressing' the button, get it?) Still time for a pun after all. Death of the planet through the trillion cuts of billions of people will not feature. We're killing strangers so we don't kill the ones that we love will evaporate into the vacuum between our ears, the gap between sentience and herd. Our failure, our epitaph, how shall it be written N? I have in mind a circular inscription without a start or end, "clever enough to know how to destroy the world stupid enough to do it". Stop and think for a considered moment Neville, look for the source of our dilemma, shall we blame the Manhattan Project? We crossed a threshold N, the beginning of the process, a process that began when we stopped living off the land and started the land living for us. For without agriculture we are limited by our activities, controlled by our environment, limited by the resource to hand, limited by what we can carry in the hand. To feast in times of glut and to starve in times of shortage. To be in natural balance. To have a future. Two steps forward, two steps back keeps us away from the precipice in the clouds.

Sorry to be a bit deep N, it's the email from Namibia I guess.

R
XXX

Sent from my IPad

Re: Day 2 January 19th Thursday

Where does celebrity figure in the grand scheme of things, I ask myself? But only after I've worked the answer out. Celebrity is a herd leader, a suspension of the thought process while you subjugate your mental activity to comply with your neighbours. Remember the one, this is where you bow to the intellect of others as they in turn bow to the intellect of others who are bowing, I think you get the picture. Celebrity is a named example of the Bait Ball. But in itself celebrity is recruited as a means to sell. Watch my film, buy my book, eat my recipes, smell like me, dress like me and in the process reward me with monetary advantage as I lead the way. But where do you lead? Celebrities lead you to their improving bank balance and nowhere else. We have progressed to the sales and marketing of illusion, it had to happen eventually. We use illusion to sell aspiration and desire so why not just sell illusion on its own? It saves in all the research and development costs of bringing a material product to market and it either succeeds or fails in quick order. But that is not to say that research and development doesn't take place. Sometimes the laboratory is exposed to the public glare and the research and development is conducted by the public themselves. So it is that less than humble television personalities can strut their stuff on the 'Strictly' dance floor and launch themselves and their careers into lucrative contracts. BGT appears to serve the same purpose but here the prize is secondary to the process and the process providers who are the real winners. It matters not that Britain's borders extend to the Far East or Russia because it is all grist to the illusion mill.

Nobody else has made the comparison N, so I think I'll get in first. Are we witnessing our own 'Arab Spring'? Britain has voted for Brexit. The US has voted for Trump. Italy has said no to its Prime Minister. Austria has elected a former Green Party leader to be president. True the right wing candidate lost but Green Party isn't exactly mainstream is it? The polls are predicting upheaval in Holland and the French are unsure as to where their voters will take them. What are we all reacting against, what is driving the electorate?

What of Nicola Sturgeon north of the border? Her ministrations have fallen on deaf ears in Brussels and evaporated to mere vapour. That is not to say that they had any substance before. Nicola then is peddling in illusion, demanding the sound bite, insuring her celebrity is manifest across the Scottish media and securing her position as 'Sturnamo', magician impossible. Pursuing and generating her own cult of presence as ruthlessly as ever Katie Price or Boris Johnson do. The Great Brains are the Great Illusionists deftly deflecting reality while fashioning their own version of it. And the herd sits enthralled, mesmerised and stupefied in equal measure while simultaneously anaesthetised and oblivious to the process. The process of the Bait Ball.

Is celebrity the conclusion to consumerism, the ultimate trade in nothing to complete the circle? We started with nothing to trade but wealth to trade with. We have finished with trade in nothing and wealth to exchange for it. Where does the future of Mankind lie within this vortex? Where does the future of everything else lie without this vortex? How bankrupt is it possible to be? Sturnamo, magician impossible doesn't even use a wand.

Trump has the answer N, for he has everything and more, money, celebrity and power and for him, now, the only way is down. That is why we need to be fearful N, for normal boundaries do not exist to a man like that.

R
XXX

Sent from my IPad

Re: Day 1

Bastards, bastards, utter bastards. The shits really hit the fan. Three fucking payments, just three fucking payments i've missed. bastards have foreclosed on my mortgage and turfed me out on the street.

I suppose the warning signs were there. HP seized the Porsche Cayenne yesterday. i know, what Cayenne? i just thought, you know, if the house survived it would be nice to have something comfortable for offroad driving or would that be no road driving?

They arrived at 6.00 .am, apparently standard practice, more chance of you being at home first thing.

The Banks high court baliffs gave me ten minutes to grab what I could carry while they changed all the locks and have given me two weeks to arrange for my goods to be removed. To be honest most of its already gone, baliff after bailiff scheduled it all. All i needed was just a few days and they'd have been in heaven. even Lutterworth tool hire bailed out with the sump pump delivery after they'd spoken to the baliffs. we are all quite literally in the shit unless you can hire one? at least they couldnt get anywhere near the bunkers. i just need to remember where i have put the keys.

I cant believe they acted so fast. Bailiff said it's one of the fastest actions they've ever seen. All the claims were stacking up and they fast tracked for wanton recklessness. The police have served a warrant on me to appear at the police station over potential fraud, they think it was that bad. Want to hear something funny, they only want me to have a psychiatric assessment prior to attending the summons. stupid bastards have set the date after the 20th, theyll soon find out who's in need of psychiatric assessment when they are all dead.

Shit shit shit shit shit what am I going to tell Jan?

Sent from my Samsung device

Re: Day 1

Dear Robert

I cannot face the future without your guiding hand at my side. There is no way I could engineer a future for us as you have so elaborately done. I wouldn't have a clue, you know how impractical I am. We've talked it through and decided to see in the new era by getting blind drunk with Dad at Abigail's parents' house in Aldershot. Edward's gone to his girlfriends. Thank you for giving us hope D, it was almost fun. When it comes down to it we are all decided and are resigned to our future whatever that holds. Perhaps we'll meet on the other side, I will seek out the areas without the 'jobsworths'.

N
XXX

Sent from my iPhone

Day Zero

"I Donald John Trump, do solemnly swear that I will faithfully execute the Office of President of the United States, and will to the best of my ability, preserve, protect and defend the Constitution of the United States, so help me God".

Trump will give a speech, summarised here as "Blah, blah, blah, blah, blah, blah" ... followed twenty minutes or so later by "blah".

Then for the most important part of the day, the traditional Congressional luncheon.

Donald Trump President, sworn in with all the keys to state. What a day it's been.

"Hello son, guys, guys, give me some space will'ya. I want to spend some time with my son".

"It's finally happened son, I'm President, leader of the free world, the most powerful man on Earth". "Here, I knew you were going to ask, let me show you this, I've got the nuclear codes here. You bring this thing up to your eye cos it checks your retina and put your thumb here for identification. Then you punch in these numbers here, I've used your birth date as the key code, see, then you press enter and that's it".

"No, don't worry, it's not live yet, it's still on test"

"Oh, here's Ron, he's head of nuclear security, just giving my son the lowdown. This thing is still on test isn't it"?

"Oh shit, pass me the phone will you?

"Hello, press office, no, let me dial again"

Hello, housekeeping, oh crap, I don't know what numbers where yet. Can you tell me how to get medical aid?

"Hello, that's better, yes Trump here. I need first aid in the Oval Office. What? Oh, it's Ron, he just went as white as a sheet and collapsed. I think he's having a heart attack".

"Bloody typical that, first day in the job and somebody dying in the White House. Well, it ain't gonna happen to me, get your paddle thingies up here and save his goddamn life"

"Sorry son, better leave them to get on with it, let's go and watch a DVD shall we".

"Let's watch Independence Day again, I know we've seen it before, but I like the way that the President leads the fight back to save the world. Call it a vain indulgence, I bags being Eagle 1".

"We'll have to slum it in the White House cinema now son, tell you what, go on ahead while I get this infernal wailing sound sorted out. Be right with you".

21.17 hours EST, 02.17 hours local time GMT

History is silent

One Day to Save the Earth

The European Environmental Agency has declared that 467,000 people are estimated to die prematurely in Europe every year from air pollution. Europe is bigger than the EU that had an estimated population of 510 million in January 2016. The premature deaths estimate for the EU is over 430,000 for 2013, the last year that figures are available for.

What we are saying within these figures is that as a by-product of our daily activities we are prepared to sentence 467,000 people every year to an early death in Europe alone. (1,280 a day. ISIS is doomed to fail with its terrorist acts, they need to drive diseasel cars and heat their houses to have a real impact). Europe will not be alone in this cull for Asia and the America's have similar issues. We have no figures for how early this death may be, it could knock 20 days off each life or 20 years, we cannot determine it from the information I have provided. The EU is very enlightened, if that is the term to use, as it is a precondition of membership that capital punishment is banned within its member states. Yet a significant proportion of these Europe wide premature deaths will occur within its borders. Deaths, which on the face of it, are considered acceptable.

Worldwide over 5 trillion cigarettes will be consumed this year (https://www.worldometers.com quoting WHO statistics). The most recent studies suggest that on average each cigarette deletes 11 minutes of life for every one of these 'life's little pleasures'. On average every smoker will reduce their life expectancy by ten years. The WHO estimates that 16 billion cigarettes will be smoked **today**. Let's do the maths. 16 billion multiplied by 11 minutes equals 176 billion minutes of premature death. This number is too big to contemplate so let us divide it by 60 minutes and 24 hours and 365 days of the year to arrive at the daily reduction in life expectancy expressed in years as a direct consequence of all the cigarettes smoked today. This sum yields a figure of 335,000 years of life, **today**. (Or should that be 335,000 years of death?) But what constitutes a premature death, dying a week before you would have done or should we look for a more substantial figure? If we considered that smoking is a worldwide phenomenon and took a figure of 60 years as a worldwide average lifespan then a truly meaningful premature death could be considered to be 20 years. The smarter ones among you will have already realised that this is twice the usual impact of smoking but, hey, I have a point to make. If we now take today's figure of 335,000 years and multiply it by 365 for the year and then divide by 20 then this figure equates to the number of premature deaths inflicted on the world's population by the simple act of smoking this year. We arrive at a meaningful figure of 6,100,000 premature deaths per year. Remember that these are lives shortened by a third although if you would rather, 12,200,000 lives shortened by 10 years. By a remarkable coincidence my earlier figure equates to the 6 million or so lives prematurely shortened by the Nazi regime under Hitler's 'final solution'. The Holocaust holds a special place in the psyche of the modern population and especially among the Jews. If you were to deny that the Holocaust existed then you can be prosecuted for such a statement in 14 European nations. Yet every single year our governments around the world ignore the premature culling of lives that equate to a war full of deaths in just one year. If you took an arbitrary figure of six years the Holocaust killed one million every year whereas smoking can achieve that in just two months.

But these deaths are invisible, airbrushed from our consciousness, stripped of any meaning because there is no murderous intent to kill otherwise innocent individuals singled out for their religion, race, sexual or political orientation or trades union membership. Yet we know that smoking kills and we make profit from it. So tell me please what the intent of the tobacco industry and the governments that effectively sponsor it, is?

Worldwide $360 billion dollars will be spent on illegal drugs (https://www. worldometers.com quoting a UN report from 2010).

Obesity, excess sugar, fat, hydrogenated vegetable oils, carcinogenic processed meat, tobacco, alcohol, illegal drugs, air pollution, noise pollution, murder, armed conflict, counterfeit medicines, starvation and readily treatable diseases are scything their way through the human population. In one way or another, whether active or passive we accept the causes of these actions/products.

We are all going to die. It is a consequence of life. Life is precious, inviolable, sacrosanct and is jealously guarded.

And yet we accept all of these 'natural wastage' elements, indeed, a significant proportion actually volunteer for it.

Humans have invented terms such as compassion and care, invested in Commissions and Non-Governmental Organisations and half-heartedly addressed these plagues on our houses. Cures invariably involve the spending of money, money generated by the very actions that sponsor death. Cures invariably treat the symptom and not the cause, electric cars reduce NOX but their increased weight means they release more minute tyre and brake particles. Whereas, if we simply didn't travel? We seal our houses to save on energy and trap the chemicals that we insert into our essential lives, air fresheners, deodorant, cleaning chemicals ... We design Eco-houses and shun straw ones?

Even religions have attempted to introduce love, compassion and care over the centuries although often by inflicting tremendous damage to their newly enlightened flocks who found God and measles in unequal measure.

There is no mechanism for protecting our species from what is essentially our mortal enemy, other humans, who, by simply going about their daily business, kill other people. The meat, alcohol, tobacco, diseasel, illegal drug, processed food manufacturers all factor/merchant in death as an acceptable consequence of their actions.

Human life is not precious, inviolable nor sacrosanct, it is a tradable commodity built into every supermarket, car showroom, brewery, drug deal, indeed virtually everything we do, is done at the expense of others. Humans are expendable.

Against this backdrop what hope does the rest of our expendable world have? Tigers, rhinos, elephants, whales, leopards, polar bears are all being shoved inexorably beyond the edge to disappear while we piffle about with peanut holders for our precious tits that adorn our back gardens. And we are ignorant of the deaths we cause to other species in pursuit of 'our good deed for the day'. And while I name these 'poster boy' species for their profile, a myriad of other anonymous species evaporate into nothing as you read.

Even our 'health professionals' barter their wages against the pot of life giving resource and who would deny their reward as they deny others of theirs? Don't even start with the so called management.

The term used is premature, an early death, a death caused by external factors where life would have continued.

Just imagine that a decision was taken, all the people of a given region agreed to tread lightly on the land and live wholly within their and their ecosystems means. They decided to adopt a Stone Age technological philosophy and work ethic. They survive for generations, no thousands of years unhindered and secure within their niche. Imagine what would happen when a neighbouring region with all of its technological advantages and burgeoning population put its head over the fence and thought "Wow, look at how green that grass is". But you don't need to imagine for it is carved into our history books if you would but notice. The indigenous peoples of Africa, the Americas, Asia and Australia have all felt the heel of technologically advanced boots across their lands and throats. We call it progress. They probably didn't have a word for it, just tears. Or was it the Romans carving their way through Iron Age Europe? We cannot put the genie back in its bottle. China is currently carving its way through the Earth's regions in pursuit of iron and copper and zinc and ivory and tiger's unspare parts and customers without a shot of conquest being fired, just please and thank you. But it is too late to imagine, for our enlightened region cannot protect itself from the pollution that spills into its air and water, the life that crosses oceans in ships ballasts to be dumped into alien ecosystems ... All fences around nature reserves are permeable and temporary and ultimately fail to provide a solution.

There are two ways to save the planet:

1) Control the population and learn how to return to the Stone Age and tread lightly on the Earth and its fellow passengers. I will call it a multilateral declaration for a future.
2) Press the button; nuclear Armageddon and be reduced to the Stone Age. I will call it a unilateral declaration for a future.

Billions will die, but they are just premature deaths and we have no issues with that. It's just business as usual. There will probably be no dinners.

It will not be easy, but the Earth may live. It is probably the Earth's only hope.

Debate is the opium of the masses. Action is what is required. No mechanism exists. No action can occur.

Press the button.

Prove me wrong.

Please.

Lightning Source UK Ltd.
Milton Keynes UK
UKOW03f0032270517
302109UK00002B/79/P